Treasured Grace

Books by Tracie Peterson

www.traciepeterson.com

HEART OF THE FRONTIER
Treasured Grace

SAPPHIRE BRIDES
A Treasure Concealed
A Beauty Refined • A Love Transformed

BRIDES OF SEATTLE
Steadfast Heart
Refining Fire • Love Everlasting

LONE STAR BRIDES
A Sensible Arrangement
A Moment in Time • A Matter of Heart
Lone Star Brides (3 in 1)

LAND OF SHINING WATER
The Icecutter's Daughter
The Quarryman's Bride • The Miner's Lady

LAND OF THE LONE STAR
Chasing the Sun
Touching the Sky • Taming the Wind

BRIDAL VEIL ISLAND*
To Have and To Hold
To Love and Cherish • To Honor and Trust

STRIKING A MATCH
Embers of Love
Hearts Aglow • Hope Rekindled

SONG OF ALASKA
Dawn's Prelude
Morning's Refrain • Twilight's Serenade

ALASKAN QUEST
Summer of the Midnight Sun
Under the Northern Lights
Whispers of Winter
Alaskan Quest (3 in 1)

BRIDES OF GALLATIN COUNTY
A Promise to Believe In
A Love to Last Forever • A
Dream to Call My Own

THE BROADMOOR LEGACY*
A Daughter's Inheritance
An Unexpected Love • A Surrendered Heart

BELLS OF LOWELL*
Daughter of the Loom
A Fragile Design • These Tangled Threads

LIGHTS OF LOWELL*
A Tapestry of Hope
A Love Woven True
The Pattern of Her Heart

DESERT ROSES
Shadows of the Canyon
Across the Years • Beneath a Harvest Sky

HEIRS OF MONTANA
Land of My Heart • The Coming Storm
To Dream Anew • The Hope Within

LADIES OF LIBERTY
A Lady of High Regard
A Lady of Hidden Intent
A Lady of Secret Devotion

RIBBONS OF STEEL**
Distant Dreams • A Hope Beyond
A Promise for Tomorrow

RIBBONS WEST**
Westward the Dream
Separate Roads • Ties That Bind

WESTWARD CHRONICLES
A Shelter of Hope
Hidden in a Whisper • A Veiled Reflection

YUKON QUEST
Treasures of the North
Ashes and Ice • Rivers of Gold

*In the Shadow of Denali****
*All Things Hidden****
*Beyond the Silence****
House of Secrets
A Slender Thread
What She Left for Me
Where My Heart Belongs

*with Judith Miller **with Judith Pella ***with Kimberley Woodhouse

Treasured Grace

TRACIE PETERSON

BETHANYHOUSE
a division of Baker Publishing Group
Minneapolis, Minnesota

Published by Bethany House Publishers
11400 Hampshire Avenue South
Bloomington, Minnesota 55438

Bethany House Publishers is a division of
Baker Publishing Group, Grand Rapids, Michigan

Printed in the United States of America

ISBN 9780764213403

Scripture quotations are from the King James Version of the Bible.

This is a work of historical reconstruction; the appearances of certain historical figures are therefore inevitable. All other characters, however, are products of the author's imagination, and any resemblance to actual persons, living or dead, is coincidental.

Cover design by LOOK Design Studio

Cover photography by Aimee Christenson

Dedicated to . . .

The rangers of the U.S. National Park Service at the Whitman Mission. In particular, to Roger Amerman and Stephanie Martin, who faithfully answered my questions and directed me to all sorts of wonderful resource materials. Thank you for your patience in answering my many questions. My job is made so much easier because of knowledgeable people like you.

Note to Reader

The Whitman Mission massacre is a well-known piece of history that forever changed the western frontier. Certain liberties were taken with that history to include fictional characters; however, a great amount of time and research went into keeping the history as accurate as possible. As I researched the various first-person accounts, it was obvious that each person remembered something a little different from the others. The knowledgeable reader may find discrepancies, but great care was given to share the factual account.

In my research I also found that there were often multiple spellings for the names of various mission people, as well as the Native Americans involved. For the purposes of continuity, I sought advice from historians and chose one spelling. The same is true for the Nez Perce words that have been sprinkled throughout the story. I hope you enjoy.

Tracie

Chapter 1

OREGON TRAIL
LATE OCTOBER 1847

So what do you plan to do now that he's dead?"

Grace Flanagan Martindale thought of the trailside grave where her husband, the Right Reverend T.S. Martindale, had been buried. The simple burial site, not even two hundred yards away, was nothing like the pompous, pretentious man it held. There wasn't even a proper marker, and that alone would no doubt have the man turning in fits of outrage.

"I don't know." Grace looked at the woman who had become her friend on their travels west. "I honestly don't." She shrugged. "But then I wasn't at all sure what I was going to do when we reached Oregon City either."

Eletta Browning grew thoughtful. At twenty-five years old, the petite, sandy-haired woman had been a wealth of information regarding the trail. She and her husband had read countless letters and articles created for missionaries regarding Oregon Country.

"We're supposed to make the Whitman Mission by Friday," Eletta finally said. "As I understand it, Dr. Whitman and his wife often take in travelers from the wagon trains. At least for the winter. You could probably stay with them."

"Yes, the wagon master mentioned it."

"We've become friends through correspondence, so Isaac will no doubt put in a good word for you and your sisters."

Grace cast a glance outside the tent opening. Her sisters were speaking to their friends in hushed whispers. Their brother-in-law hadn't been the only one buried that day, and the spirit of the camp remained sober at the nearness of death. However, Grace knew her sisters were relieved that the Right Reverend had passed on to his glory. No doubt he was even now instructing God as to how heaven should be run.

"I suppose it might be wise to stay if the Whitmans will have us." Grace considered the few choices available to her. "I know the girls are exhausted. Mercy, especially. She's nothing but skin and bones, and she was already so small for her age."

"It's been a hard trip. We've all had our share of problems. I might have lost my dear Isaac to cholera had it not been for you." Eletta choked on the words and then regained control of her emotions. "Mr. Browning and I are most grateful for your healing skills. There's nothing we wouldn't do for you and your sisters."

Grace smiled. She had been trained in the healing arts since she was a young girl. Like her mother and grandmother before her, healing seemed to come naturally to Grace—unlike her sisters, Hope and Mercy, who had no end of confusion when it came to gathering wild plants and roots to make medicines.

"I'd like to think I could offer my skills in whatever community I make my home, but since Dr. Whitman is a certified doctor, he might find my abilities primitive." She sighed. "If I could just locate Uncle Edward, I know I would feel better.

We sent him a letter early last spring before coming west. I'm hopeful he received it, but we heard nothing from him before leaving. Of course, I didn't really expect to. It takes months and sometimes years to get letters back and forth. The men headed west with the letters might even have been killed on the trail."

"Most of the wagon train will go on to Oregon City, Grace. I'm sure someone would take a message to him. Mr. Grierson, perhaps? Then your uncle might come for you and the girls before the winter is over."

"Maybe." Her uncle had written Mama a year ago, begging her to join him in Oregon City. He told her it would be a wonderful new start and she might even find love again. Grace knew her widowed mother would never love another man. She had been completely devoted to Sean Flanagan. And even though he was a hard-fighting, stubborn Irishman, Nancy Flanagan loved him with a passion that Grace could only envy.

A shadow crossed the opening of the tent, and Nigel Grierson called to her. "Mrs. Martindale, I wonder if we might speak."

She knew what he wanted. Eletta knew it too. Grace bit her lower lip and then exited the tent. She didn't bother to acknowledge his offered hand to help her. Straightening, she relaxed her jaw and waited for him to say something.

The tall, blond man gave her a sad smile. "Thank you for agreeing to speak to me in your time of mourning."

Grace nodded. "What can I do for you, Mr. Grierson?" She glanced over to where her sisters had been only moments before. Apparently when they saw Grierson, they had hightailed it out of there.

"Well . . . you know that . . . my Abigail died two weeks ago."

"Yes." Grace had no desire to make this any easier on him, but neither did she want to waste her time. She knew what he was going to say and decided to say it first. "So now that my husband is dead, you believe we should join our fortunes together and marry."

He looked sheepish and glanced away. "Yes. You see, Mrs. Martindale, I know from our long months on the trail that you are an industrious woman, just as my Abigail was. She and I admired you very much for your patience and skills, not only with people but the livestock as well. I believe we have a great deal in common. I hope to start a dairy farm eventually, and you have a small flock of sheep. It seems together we could make a proper go of it." He cleared his throat and seemed to struggle for what he wanted to say next. "And . . . well . . . while I don't like to speak ill of the dead, we both know that your deceased husband was hardly cut out for such a life. On more than one occasion I know he spoke with great disdain regarding his sheep."

"Yes. However, the sheep were never his to consider. They belong to me."

"But when a woman marries, her property belongs to her husband."

"Be that as it may, my husband hardly has need of sheep now, and what meager possessions we held are mine." She could see that her tone had made clear her irritation. She turned to go, but Nigel took hold of her arm in a bold move.

"Please, Mrs. Martindale . . . Grace." He spoke her name with great hesitation.

Grace fixed him with a look that caused his immediate release of her arm. "I cannot marry you, Mr. Grierson. I have no desire to give myself over to another loveless marriage. Good day."

She walked toward the wagon the Right Reverend had purchased shortly before their trip west. Purchased with money from the sale of her parents' house. It was loaded to the hilt—mostly with his prized possessions of theological texts and clothes. He had also demanded to bring several pieces of furniture, including an ornate pulpit and a large feather tick upon which he could sleep at night. He was one of the few travelers who insisted on sleeping in the protective covering of his wagon. Every night when they set up camp, Grace and her sisters had been required to empty the wagon of several crates in order to make room for the Right Reverend to sleep. It was ludicrous, given all of the other work required, but Grace went along with his demands despite knowing her husband was the talk of the train.

Now all of that belonged to her. At least Grace presumed it did, as the Right Reverend had no family. She looked into the back of the packed wagon. There had barely been enough room for Grace and her sisters to add a few trunks. Not that they'd had much to take with them. When Mama had died, Grace knew she would have to sell their small farm in order to survive. She had tried time and again since her father's death to convince her mother to put the property up for sale, but her mother had refused. She and Grace's father had purchased the Missouri farm when they'd first come west. They owned it free and clear, and it was the only thing of import to Mama. It didn't seem to matter that it was in need of constant repair or that the taxes increased every year. Selling the property had given Grace the money they needed to go west and to buy her sheep.

"Grace." The whispered voice was that of her seventeen-year-old sister Hope. "Did you get rid of him?" She peered from around the far side of the wagon.

"Yes." Grace rolled her eyes. "He is without a conscience, to be sure. Who ever heard of approaching a widow on the day of her husband's burial?"

Hope joined Grace at the rear of the wagon. "Conscience isn't important on the frontier. I've had a dozen proposals since we started this trip."

Glancing at her sister's womanly figure, Grace could see why the men had been attracted to her. Hope was by far the prettiest of the three Flanagan girls. She always had been, even though they all looked very similar with their dark brown hair. Each sister, however, had a variation on their mother's and father's eyes. Grace had green eyes like her father, and Hope's eyes were blue just as Mama's had been. Mercy, the youngest, combined the two for an unusual turquoise shade.

But Hope was the beauty of the family. The interest of young men had been on the increase since she'd turned sixteen, and as a flirt, Hope enjoyed the part she played. To Hope, the world was filled with admirers, and she was only too happy to be the focus of their attention.

"Mrs. Martindale?" The questioning voice was that of Mr. Holt, the wagon master, who was walking toward their wagon.

Grace offered him a smile. "What can I do for you?"

"I thought I'd make a suggestion, if you don't mind." He pointed to the back of the wagon. "Your oxen have suffered a great deal from that load. If you aren't attached to that heavy furniture, I'd suggest getting rid of it."

Grace nodded. "I think that's a marvelous idea. The pulpit alone weighs more than Hope and Mercy combined. I believe that would make a perfect marker for the Right Reverend's grave. Then there's that heavy walnut table. That can easily be discarded."

Holt smiled. "I'll get a couple of fellas to help, and we'll unload it."

"Thank you. I believe my sister and I will check on our flock."

Holt tipped his hat and left while Grace moved toward the area where her sheep were grazing.

"Smelly animals," Hope said, turning up her nose.

"You may be grateful for those smelly animals one day when we have a flock big enough to prosper us."

"I wondered where you went," twelve-year-old Mercy said, coming to join them. "I heard Mr. Holt say he and some other fellas are going to unload our wagon."

"Yes, we're lightening the load." Grace noted her youngest sister's long brown braids. Styling her hair that way made her look younger still. "You can ride tomorrow, if you like. I know you're tired."

"Mr. Holt said we needed to make up for lost time tomorrow. He wants to start as soon as there's any light at all and keep going until it's dark."

"I hate traveling," Hope said, blowing out a heavy sigh. "Everything is always dirty, and my shoes are completely worn out."

"Well, I managed to take the Right Reverend's boots off of him before we wrapped him in the burial sheet." Grace glanced around and lowered her voice even more. "I think they're just a wee bit big for you, Hope, although he didn't have feet anywhere near as large as most men. They should suffice. And you may ride the Right Reverend's horse. He's a very gentle mount with the right person handling the reins." The Right Reverend had never been able to sit the horse without some sort of trouble, but Grace and her sisters had learned to ride as children. Da had been a masterful horseman and saw to it that his daughters knew their way around horseflesh as well.

Hope wrinkled her nose but didn't refuse either gift. Grace knew she would wear the boots and ride the gelding and be grateful, because the road was much rockier than it had been coming across the prairies.

"I know it's not very nice," Mercy said, looking at the ground, "but I'm glad he's dead. He was mean, and I didn't like the way he treated you. Or us." She looked up at Grace. "Do you suppose God will be mad at me for saying that?"

"You're just telling the truth," Hope said. "I'm glad he's gone too. He was so bossy. I figure he thought he owned the three of us; he treated us like slaves."

"I can't lie and say that I'm not just as glad to be rid of him myself," Grace admitted. "But now we're back to trying to figure out how to take care of ourselves in the future. Most all of our money was tied up in this trip west."

"Won't Uncle Edward take care of us?" Mercy asked.

"We have to be able to find him first." Grace shook her head. "There's no telling if he's even still alive."

Hope frowned. "Then what are we going to do?"

"I've been giving that some thought. The train is splitting, with most of the wagons going on to Oregon City. Those with sick or who need a rest are heading for the Whitman Mission. Dr. and Mrs. Whitman are used to taking in folks from the wagon train and often let them stay for the winter. I figure we can help out with the chores."

Hope's expression took on a look of protest, but before she could open her mouth, Grace continued.

"Mercy can attend their little school. We'll send a letter to Uncle Edward with the wagon train folks who are going on to Oregon City."

"Why not just go on to Oregon City with them?" Hope asked. "Seems to me we've come this far, we might as well go the rest of the way."

"I thought about that, but honestly I don't think we have it in us. We're all three tired, and our oxen are nearly done in, thanks to the Right Reverend's overburdening them. Not only that, but the sick also need my help."

Hope shrugged. "I wish we'd just go on with the others to Oregon City. But I haven't had much say in this trip."

Grace turned to face the setting sun, ignoring Hope's comment. "Looks like we'd better get back. Mrs. Browning has invited us to share supper with them tonight, so we don't have to worry about fixing anything. However, I still need to boil some water for tomorrow's drinking water."

"That's so silly. Mr. Holt said he has never seen nothing like boiling water to drink unless it had coffee added to it," Mercy said. "He told me it was just a lot of extra work."

"Well, consider this," Grace said, motioning for her sisters to follow her back to their tent. "The Right Reverend didn't drink the boiled water or take vinegar daily as we do, and he died of cholera. The other folks who died from cholera also didn't boil their water. Our granny always said that boiling water was the best way to keep from getting sick."

"She also said boiling it made the water too hot for the fairies to touch and taint," Hope added. "Granny said a lot of things that were mostly superstitious Irish nonsense. You said so yourself."

"It's true that she had her superstitions, but along with the ridiculous claims, Granny had great wisdom." Grace could still hear her swear that she owed her eighty-some years of life to boiled water and vinegar. Both of which Grace's mother had sworn by and which Grace held just as valuable. If only those things could have sustained her mother from a broken heart.

"Come on, I need you to fetch water while I get the fire going." She heard her sisters mutter as they collected the buckets, but they offered no further protest, to her relief.

Grace had begun to put together fuel for the fire when the voice of a woman sounded behind her. "I want to thank you, Mrs. Martindale, for all you did for my Jimmy. He's feelin' a lot better. Even ate tonight."

Grace straightened and smiled. "I'm so glad, Mrs. Piedmont. Just keep doing what I told you, and he should be fine."

The middle-aged woman nodded. "I'm worried about my

Anna-Beth. She's feelin' a mite poorly, and I wondered if you could take a look at her?"

The wagon train was without a doctor, and Grace had been kept busy stitching up wounds, tending rashes, and overseeing the epidemics of cholera, dysentery, and the ague. It was good to be of use to people, and Grace knew that healing was her true calling in life.

"Of course," she told Mrs. Piedmont. "Let me get my fire going and the water on, and I'll be right over."

Hope grinned at the young man who'd just stolen a kiss. "Robbie Taylor, you are the most forward boy I've ever made the acquaintance of."

The sandy-headed boy gave her a lopsided smile. "I'm not a boy, Miss Hope. I'm a man full grown. Why else would I be sparkin' you?"

"Why, indeed," she murmured, batting her eyelashes.

Her coyness only served to encourage him to risk another kiss. This time, however, Hope pushed him away.

"I'm not easily had, Mr. Taylor. If you mean to court me properly, then you'll have to speak to my sister. However, you should know that at least five other fellas have gone ahead of you to ask for my hand."

Robbie's smile faded. "But, Miss Hope, you know I love you. I'm gonna get one of those big tracts of land and farm it. We'll put up a house, and you can plant a garden."

Hope wrinkled her nose. "I don't like planting and harvesting gardens. It makes my hands get all dirty and rough. This horrible journey has already been so hard on my hands, and I wear my gloves almost all the time." She sighed and raised her hands as if to offer proof.

Robbie took hold of her hands and drew them to his lips. "It don't matter what your hands look like. You're still the prettiest girl west of the Mississippi."

"Just west of the Mississippi?" She pulled her hands away and shook her head. "Honestly, Robbie Taylor, I don't know why I put up with your sweet talk. Now leave me be. I need to fetch water. I can't have Mercy doing it all by herself."

"Well, at least let me do that for you," he said, giving her such a lovesick expression that Hope couldn't help but giggle.

"Very well. The bucket is over yonder." She pointed, and without offering further comment, Robbie crossed to the wagon and took up the bucket. He headed for the river, leaving Hope to smile to herself.

It was always easy once they were stopped for the day to get one of the boys to do her bidding. She liked the way they all clamored for her attention. God had given her a pretty face and a fine figure to attract a good husband. It was surely up to her to use them to her advantage.

Grace made her way to the Piedmonts' wagon, passing several of the other families along the way. Most were gathered around their own shared fires and offered her condolences as she passed.

If they knew how little I'm grieving, they'd think me heartless. Of course, if they knew that my marriage was only arranged so that the Right Reverend T.S. Martindale could be placed on the mission field and that our marriage was never consummated, they might better understand.

She had been only too willing to refrain from sharing a marriage bed with the Right Reverend. He had declared that in answering God's call he needed neither wife nor children. However, the mission board had insisted that it was not good for man to be alone and they required their ministers to be married. Only then did the Right Reverend agree to be wed, and when Grace was able to present herself—and the money from the sale of her mother's farm—he thought her the perfect woman. However, he had no intention of becoming a true husband or father. He made that clear to Grace on their first night alone, much to her gladness. To be a widowed virgin might make others raise a brow in confusion, but to Grace it was a blessing for which she thanked God.

"She's over here, Mrs. Martindale," Mrs. Piedmont called from the back of the family's wagon. "She's been coughing and sniffling for quite a while, but I was so busy with Jimmy that I didn't give it much thought. I figured it was just a cold, but now she's chilling and her face is flushed. She says she hurts all over."

Grace made her way to where the seven-year-old lay curled in a ball, shivering. "Mrs. Piedmont, we'll need a lantern. Would you please bring one so that I can examine her better?"

"Of course." The woman scurried away and quickly returned with the needed light.

"Hold it close so I can give her a good examination," Grace instructed while carefully moving the child's head from side to side. "I heard you aren't feeling very good, Anna-Beth."

Grace could feel that the girl's fever was high. Her face was flushed, and from the sound of her cough her lungs were very congested. Closer inspection of the child's face gave Grace a start. Without bothering to check her throat or eyes, Grace unbuttoned the child's nightgown. The rash she found on the girl's chest made her diagnosis certain. Another epidemic was sure to follow.

"It's measles," Grace said, turning to the girl's mother.

Mrs. Piedmont's expression changed from worry to horror. "No. Not measles."

Grace buttoned the child's nightgown, then patted her on the head. "You rest a minute, Anna-Beth. I need to make you some medicine and talk to your mama about how to make you feel better." She led Mrs. Piedmont from the wagon.

"I never thought it might be measles. What are we gonna do?"

"Well, first off, we need to quarantine your wagon and your other children. They've both been exposed, but it's possible they won't take the measles." Grace knew, however, that the chances were slim to none. Once measles made its way into the camp, it would be hard to force its exit until everyone who'd never had the disease managed to catch it.

Mrs. Piedmont drew her fist to her mouth as if to prevent herself from crying out. She was near to tears.

"I've dealt with measles a hundred times before this," Grace said. "Try not to worry. My remedies are good to help. Now, I presume you and Mr. Piedmont have had the measles." The woman nodded. Grace smiled. "Good. Then you won't be at risk in tending Anna-Beth. What about the other children?"

Mrs. Piedmont lowered her hand. "Jimmy's had it."

"He probably won't take it again. The baby most likely won't take it because you're nursing her." Grace paused a moment to think. "You're good friends with the Culverts, aren't you?"

Mrs. Piedmont nodded. "Came west together. We've been friends since we were children."

"Good. I'll check with Mrs. Culvert, but I believe her children have all had the measles. If so, Jimmy and the baby can stay with them while you care for Anna-Beth."

After instructing Mrs. Piedmont to get some water boiling, Grace went about her duties, checking first with the Culverts and then retrieving some herbs and vinegar from her stores. Once she had completed instructing Mrs. Piedmont, Grace knew she'd have to inform Mr. Holt. Thankfully, the Piedmonts were already positioned at the back of the train with the other sick folks. It was most likely too late to hope that the disease wouldn't spread, but they would do whatever they could to try to hold it at bay.

Only one thought continued to trouble Grace. Mercy had watched over Anna-Beth and the Piedmonts' baby during Jimmy's sickest hours in order to free up Mrs. Piedmont to care for him.

"And she's never had the measles," Grace murmured to herself.

Alexander Armistead scratched his chin and focused on the cards in his hands. He had nothing better than a pair of sevens, and given the confidence with which his old friend was raising the stakes, Alex felt it was best to fold.

"I give up. You're just too good for me tonight." He threw the cards down.

Gabriel Larquette laughed and lowered his cards to reveal he had nothing better than a pair of threes. "You give up too easy, my friend." He collected the cards and the pot.

"Well, I'll be. You always do have all the luck." Alex leaned closer to their small fire and checked the roasting rabbit. "This is ready. Where'd Sam get off to?"

"Went to see about those last three traps. He'll be here soon enough." Gabriel put the cards in his leather knapsack.

"Gabe, do you ever regret your life out here in the wilderness?" Alex asked, giving the rabbit another turn.

"Why do you ask?"

"You said you've been doing this for nearly forty years, and I just wondered if you ever wish you'd done something else."

The older man shrugged. "Can't say I would have wanted to do anything else. You remember how I lived in Montreal?"

Alex nodded. "You said you hated the city."

"I did and I do." Gabe shook his head. "Can't breathe in

the city. My pa felt the same way, but my mother was a proper French woman who enjoyed her pretty dishes and silk clothes. She died when I was twelve, and after that I left school to trap full-time with my father. I've never regretted anything at all, except her death . . . and others'."

"Death has a way of making you regret a great deal." Alex felt the old melancholy settling on him.

"Seems to me we've had this conversation before," Gabe said with a shrug. "I've told you over and over how you can be rid of your regrets and sorrows."

Alex had heard it a million times. "By trusting in God? Seems my folks told me the same, but they're still dead . . . and it's all my fault."

Chapter 2

The Whitman Mission was a welcomed sight after their long months on the trail. At a distance in the east were the Blue Mountains, which had taken the travelers' last bits of strength to traverse. To the west were rolling hills and the immense Columbia River, although the latter couldn't be seen from the mission.

The layout of the Whitmans' mission was simple but effective. The Whitmans lived in a T-shaped mission house. This two-story building also housed the school, storage rooms, and several bedrooms. Beyond the house there was a blacksmith's shop, and beyond that another large house.

With the weather mild, some of the newly arrived chose to pitch their tents as they had on the road west. Others who weren't ill were content to rug up under their wagons. Dr. Whitman had instructed them where to park their wagons beyond the main mission grounds. They set up camp there just as they had on the trail, but instead of a large number of wagons, they were now down to just ten. Only eight families still recovering from cholera and dysentery had taken the mission route and separated from the main wagon train, including Nigel Grierson. Nigel had come along to act as leader to the small band and to be close to Grace. Or so she figured. And then there were the Piedmonts, who were dealing with measles. Nevertheless, the Whitmans welcomed the travelers and offered a hot meal and the doctor's skills.

The visitors were given instructions on the mission rules and events. Dr. Whitman explained in detail about the many Indians in evidence.

"The Cayuse village is just beyond the mill pond, as I'm certain you saw," he told those who'd gathered on the mission grounds. "Nez Perce and Walla Wallas also frequent our area. They are quite peaceful, but do not under any circumstances go to the Cayuse village. It is just a small gathering compared to one some eight miles to the east, but the Cayuse are especially hostile lately, and I advise you to avoid them."

Grace and her sisters stood nearby, listening to Dr. Whitman as he continued to offer his insight and rules. Despite her exhaustion from their last two days of what seemed to be endless travel, Grace found a sense of peace just in knowing she would remain here for a time. Isaac Browning had already spoken on their behalf with the Whitmans and received approval for Grace and her sisters to stay for the winter.

Once Whitman concluded his instructions and the people were dismissed to return to their wagons, Grace found Mr. Browning eager to introduce her. With Hope and Mercy at her side, Grace followed Browning and allowed him to make the introductions. Mrs. Whitman seemed a very proper lady with her hair neatly pinned and her dress crisply pressed. She offered a welcoming smile and a look of compassion. Grace thought her pretty and very well spoken. Dr. Whitman, on the other hand, appeared stern and fatherly with his beard, hooked nose, and piercing eyes.

"We are glad to lend you aid in your time of need, Mrs. Martindale," the doctor said. "And we are heartily sorry for your loss. I wish I could have been along on the trip to lend aid to the sick. You and your sisters will be welcome to take refuge with the others in the emigrant house." He pointed across the field toward the house that lay beyond the blacksmith. "I'll have one of my boys show you where to put your sheep and oxen."

"We are always happy to have extra hands to bear the burden of work," Narcissa Whitman added. "And of course your youngest sister will attend school with the other children."

"Thank you." Grace sensed it was best to say little.

After a bit more instruction on meals and the like, Grace found herself and her sisters dismissed to the care of Harriet Kimball, who lived with her husband and children in the house across the field.

"I'll show you around," Mrs. Kimball said, looking directly at Grace. "It's always nice to talk to someone new. I heard the doctor refer to you as Mrs. Martindale."

Grace nodded as they made their way across the mission grounds. The air was cool but not overly cold. "I'm widowed. My husband died a few days ago."

Mrs. Kimball stopped and patted Grace's arm. "I am so sorry. Do you have children?"

"No. We were just married before coming west. I'm here with my sisters."

"I have five children. We had seven." She dropped her gaze to the ground. "I lost two on the long road here. The Lord giveth and the Lord taketh away."

Grace nodded and cast a glance at Hope and Mercy, who seemed enthralled with their new surroundings—especially the Indians camped at a distance across the pond.

"There were a great many deaths on our journey here." Grace

quickly added, "We didn't have a doctor amongst the travelers, so I did what I could."

"Are you a midwife?"

"Among other things. I am a healer. I was taught by my mother just as she was taught by her mother. The tradition goes back for generations. Frankly, I find those skills surpass most school-trained physicians."

"Well, it's probably best you don't tell Dr. Whitman your thoughts. He doesn't appreciate his ways being called into question."

Grace nodded. "Thank you for letting me know. I apologize if I've offended."

Harriet shook her head. "Not at all. Here in the wilderness it doesn't bode well to take offense—at least not for long. We need one another out here." They stopped in front of the house, and Harriet Kimball opened the door. "This is the emigrant house. The Sager children call it 'the Mansion' when they visit from the mission house."

"Who are the Sager children?" Grace asked.

"Orphans adopted by the Whitmans. Their folks died on the trail here some years ago." Harriet motioned for Grace to follow as she stepped inside the house.

"There are six rooms here on the first floor and then an upper floor with beds. The Saunders family has two rooms here on the first level, and our family and the Halls have one room each. Mrs. Hays and her son stay with the Halls. Upstairs the people vary depending on travelers, but usually we have about thirty people sleeping in the house altogether."

"Thirty?" Hope declared in disbelief. "How in the world can you quarter thirty people in this small house?"

Mrs. Kimball seemed surprised by her outburst. She shrugged. "It is a tight fit, but we mostly use it just for sleeping. During the day the children attend school, and the men work with Dr. Whitman at the gristmill or blacksmith shop. There's always plenty to do."

"And the women?" Grace asked. "What sort of duties might we have?"

Mrs. Kimball shrugged. "Why, the same sort of work women do everywhere. Cooking, cleaning, sewing, preserving the food. We make our own candles and soap. We have no one to depend on but ourselves. The nearest fort—that of the Hudson's Bay Company—is Fort Nez Perce. It's over thirty miles away, however, and supplies are expensive."

"Hope and I will do what we can to help. Won't we, Hope?" Grace cast a look at her sister, who appeared bored with the entire conversation. Grace nudged her.

Hope rolled her eyes heavenward. "Of course."

Mercy giggled but covered it with a cough.

Mrs. Kimball returned her gaze to the room. "You and your sisters can sleep in here on the floor. I'm sorry there aren't enough beds, but it's warm and out of the weather."

"We're used to sleeping on the ground, so it really isn't a problem." Grace glanced around the simple room. "I'm just grateful that we've been allowed to stay."

Once they were alone, Hope edged closer to Grace. "Do we have to stay here? Why can't we move on with the others when they're well?"

"Because we have nothing waiting for us in Oregon City." Grace fixed both of her siblings with a stern look. "I don't like this any more than you do, but we have no choice. What money we have left won't be enough to see us through the winter. The Whitmans will allow us to stay here and earn our keep. That way we can save what funds we have."

"You were really smart to hide our money from the Right Reverend," Hope said in a hushed tone. "I didn't like him at all, but when he took all of our things and sold most of them, I hated him."

"Well, it's in the past, and hate isn't productive. Besides, there simply wasn't enough space in the wagon to take much with us." Grace tried not to remember how upset she too had been. "Anyway, we need to stay here for the winter. It's safe, and we will have plenty to eat and a roof over our heads. Come spring, the message we sent with the others heading to Oregon City should have reached Uncle Edward, and he'll advise us what to do next."

"What if he doesn't want us?" Mercy asked, her blue-green eyes wide.

Grace shrugged. "We will deal with that when it comes—if it comes to that. Right now we need to do what we can to be helpful and obey the rules Dr. Whitman laid out for us."

The next week was chaotic. Measles began to strike people at the mission as well as the Indian village. Dr. Whitman figured that given the incubation period required for the illness to manifest, one of the other wagon trains must have exposed the mission. Nevertheless, it seemed the disease was spreading like wildfire. There were so many sick that Grace was constantly busy.

Mrs. Piedmont was particularly fussy and wouldn't allow anyone but Grace to advise her on her sick daughter. Because of Mrs. Piedmont's confidence in Grace, some of the other women came to her as well. Grace was careful to avoid administering herbs and tonics in case word got back to the doctor. Instead she encouraged the women to utilize the healing properties of vinegar and mentioned various herbs that she had found helpful. She also insisted they boil their drinking water.

When Mercy showed the telltale signs of measles, Grace did

what she could to make her sister comfortable and instructed Hope as to how she could help. Hope had mostly been busy washing clothes, and she was grateful for the break.

"My hands have never been so chapped," Hope said, holding them up for inspection. "They used to be so soft and pretty."

"Rub some of the rose hips salve on them. They'll feel better almost immediately. As for Mercy, make sure to get fluids into her at least once an hour, and keep moving her from side to side. Don't let her sleep on her back unless you prop her up. Bathe her with the tepid vinegar solution in this jar." Grace handed the concoction to Hope, then cast one more glance at the sleeping Mercy. "There's a bundle of mending beside her pallet. Make yourself useful and do what you can to repair some of those things, but don't leave her. She's very ill."

Hope plopped down on the floor and pushed back her waves of dark brown hair. "I won't go anywhere. I'll see that she has constant care." She sighed and picked up a shirt from the pile of mending. "I suppose I shall be quite accomplished at sewing by the time we leave this place. That and washing clothes seem to be my lot in life. I don't know why we ever came west. St. Louis was a wonderful city. I'm sure you could have found a perfectly good place for us there."

"There's no sense in talking about it. We aren't going back anytime soon." Grace could see Hope's expression grow gloomy. "At least you have a roof over your head, and you've already had the measles, so you won't have to contend with that misery." Grace waited for Hope to offer further complaint, and when she didn't, it made Grace smile. "I'm glad you understand. I'm going to go check on the sheep and then stop in at the mission house."

"If you see that handsome Johnny Sager tell him I said hello," Hope said, looking a bit flushed. "I had a very pleasant time talking to him the other day while I was fetching water. He helped me carry the buckets back."

Grace gazed heavenward. The last thing she needed was her sister falling in love. "Just remember to give Mercy water every hour."

The sheep were settled in a pen not far from the main mission grounds where Dr. Whitman had instructed the travelers to park their wagons, and they seemed unconcerned about their surroundings. Grace knew Nigel was looking after them, but the distance from the mission made her uncomfortable. With the Indians a constant presence, she feared they might steal her animals.

It was funny that her original plans in coming west had been tied to ministering to the Indians. The Right Reverend had been firmly fixed on the idea of bringing salvation to the savages, while Grace just wanted to get to her uncle. Frankly, she was afraid of the Indians, and she knew Hope and Mercy felt the same. A part of her heart told her that the fear was simply of the unknown. But stories from her father's and grandfather's years of fighting in various Indian wars had left her with an uneasy feeling.

As Grace started back for the mission house, she was surprised to see her friend Eletta approaching. She was accompanied by a young man Grace knew to be Francis, or Frank, Sager.

"Eletta, I was hoping to come and see you." The Brownings had been given a place in the mission house, as Dr. Whitman wanted to discuss the new mission they were to set up some seventy-five miles to the north-northeast.

"I stopped at the emigrant house, and Hope told me you'd come to check on the sheep. Young Frank offered to show me the way."

"You shouldn't come out here by yourself, Mrs. Martindale," the boy interjected. "Dr. Whitman doesn't like the women to be out here alone."

Grace glanced around, then smiled at the fifteen-year-old.

"I suppose there are all sorts of hidden dangers." She felt perfectly capable of taking care of herself, but there was no sense in arguing with him. "I'm grateful to you for the warning."

Frank nodded. "If you're ready to go back, I'll walk with you."

"That would be very kind." Grace took hold of Eletta's arm as Frank led the way. "How are Mr. Browning and Dr. Whitman getting along?"

"Quite well, although Isaac has said nothing to him about having Cherokee blood. The doctor tends to look down on folks of mixed race, but Isaac believes it will better open the door for him to minister to the Indians if they know his grandmother was one of them."

"I don't know about that. I'm afraid I've had few dealings with Indians, but the Right Reverend thought them savage children."

"Well, we shall see soon enough. That's why I came to find you," Eletta continued. "Isaac says we're leaving in the morning." Grace's face must have betrayed her surprise, because Eletta stopped. "I know. I wish we could stay, but Isaac thinks we should press on and establish our mission because that's what God has brought us here to do."

"His heart is definitely in the right place." Grace noted that Frank hadn't seen them stop, so she urged Eletta to continue toward the house. "We should keep up with our protector."

Eletta nodded and resumed their walk. "Isaac believes, as do I, that we are in God's hands and the Indians need to hear the Gospel." She gave a sigh. "I hope you and your sisters will come to visit us one day. I shall miss our friendship."

"Perhaps we might write letters, although I know that delivery will be at the mercy of men trekking back and forth across Oregon Country. Still, it would be good to at least hear how things are going."

"Isaac has introduced me to a couple of the Nez Perce Indians. They are friendly and Christian. Both have been baptized and taken Christian names." Eletta said this as though it would put to rest any of Grace's concerns. "They helped build us a cabin and will show us the way."

"I hope it won't be a difficult journey," Grace said, hoping to sound encouraging. "I heard there are regular runners between the missions. Perhaps in time I could accompany one of them and come to see you."

At this Eletta's face lit up. "Oh, I would cherish that. Isaac said that once we are fully established, he wants you and your sisters to feel free to join us. I know you hope to locate your uncle, but just in case that doesn't happen—you have a home with us."

They reached the mission house, and Frank left them without another word. Grace took the opportunity to give her friend a hug. "I shall miss you so."

Tears formed in Eletta's eyes. "As shall I. I don't know what I would have done on the journey here without your friendship and healing gift."

The sound of raised voices brought the women's attentions to the front of the house, where Dr. Whitman was dealing with one of the Indians. The native man was clearly upset and motioned several times to the village.

"There is death and sickness," the Indian said.

From where she stood, Grace couldn't see too many details, but the Indian's scowling face was enough to make her stay put.

"I will come and tend to your people," Whitman promised. "As I always have."

"You must come now," the Cayuse man insisted.

"I cannot leave just yet. I have sick to attend to here. I will come as soon as possible."

The man shook his head and stormed off. Dr. Whitman remained only a moment before heading back toward the kitchen door.

"That's the closest I've been to a Cayuse." Grace gave a shudder. "I'm not sure I care to be any closer. I've heard that among all the tribes, the Cayuse are the most aggressive."

"I've heard that as well," Eletta replied. "I'm grateful we'll be working with the Nez Perce. Although I've also heard the two groups are close. Apparently there has been a lot of inter-tribal marrying."

"Mrs. Martindale! Mrs. Martindale! I cut my finger," Jimmy Piedmont called, running toward Grace. He held up his right hand. "Can you fix it?" The children on the wagon train had been used to approaching Grace for help.

She smiled at him, then looked to her friend. "I'd best see what I can do. I'll come inside once I determine the damage done."

Eletta nodded and left Grace to her doctoring.

"So, Jimmy, how did this happen?" Grace examined the boy's finger. The cut was deeper than she'd expected.

"I cut it on the axe."

"The axe? How?" Grace reached into her pocket and produced a small bottle of vinegar.

"Well, John Jacob dared me to touch the edge and I did." He grimaced as Grace poured vinegar to cleanse the wound. "It was sharper than I thought. Yeow! That smarts."

"I hope you learned your lesson. Blades are not for touching." She recorked the bottle and slipped it back in her pocket, then pulled out a small roll of cloth. Using this, she bound the boy's wound and had just tied the cloth when a man demanded to know what she was doing.

Grace looked up to find Dr. Whitman approaching. "I'm treating his cut."

"You are not a doctor. Such matters are best left to me." He stopped and looked down at the boy. "What happened?"

Jimmy looked terrified and backed away. "I touched the axe. I'm real sorry. I didn't mean to do wrong."

"Go inside, young man, and I will come and tend you." Jimmy hurried toward the house while Dr. Whitman turned on Grace. "You are not to interfere in such matters."

"It was a simple cut. I cleaned it with vinegar and wrapped it. Surely you cannot find fault with that. After all, it is only what any mother might have done. I don't suppose you forbid them from tending to their own children's needs."

He fixed her with a hard gaze. "You are not his mother."

"No, but he was used to seeing me care for people on the journey here. I am a healer and midwife."

"Obedience and conformity to rules is critical to our welfare here. I am the physician, and I will see to the needs of the people."

"I'm not generally given to arguments, Dr. Whitman. Especially when I am so indebted. However, I have trained all my life as a healer. My mother taught me as her mother taught her. I know a great deal, and I don't appreciate you reprimanding me when you know so very little about me. I might be of use to you."

The doctor was clearly surprised by her remarks. For a moment he sized her up. "I am formally trained as a physician, and I alone will be responsible for the welfare of my people and of the Indians nearby. I am well known for my skills and called upon to travel many miles to tend to the ill and wounded. You, Mrs. Martindale, would do well to learn your place."

"I know my place." Grace put her hands on her hips. "I am good at what I do. I believe it is a gifting from God and can hardly believe a minister of the Word would suggest such a gifting was invalid simply because it didn't come with a certificate. A minister ought not to be so proud that he can't accept folks for who they are and what they're capable of doing."

Without waiting for his reply, Grace turned on her heel and left. Muttering to herself, she rounded the corner of the house and plowed headlong into a tall, dark-haired stranger.

"I'm so sorry," she said, trying to right herself.

He took hold of her shoulders to steady her. "It's not a problem. I'd have suffered worse to hear someone stand up to Whitman that way. He can be rather arrogant." His dark eyes seemed to see right through her. "I'm Alex. Alexander Armistead."

Grace nodded and pulled away from his touch. "I'm—"

"Mrs. Martindale," he finished with a broad grin and added, "the healer."

Chapter 3

Alex couldn't help but like the Martindale woman. She was feisty and confident, much like his sister, Adelina. At least Adelina had been that way ten years ago when Alex last saw her. He frowned, pushing the memory aside to focus on the pretty young woman in front of him.

"I truly didn't mean to eavesdrop, Mrs. Martindale. I couldn't help myself though. When I heard you standing up to Whitman, I was shocked. Few men will even stand their ground with him. You're what my trapper friend Gabe would call 'up to beaver.' It means you can hold your own."

"Well, that's true enough. Experience has been a dear teacher."

"But a fool will learn at no other." Alex smiled. "My mother used to say that."

"Exactly. I've learned plenty over the years, and he had no right to chastise me. He has no idea of what I can do," Mrs. Martindale replied, not wavering from meeting his gaze. She cocked her head slightly to the right. "How is it that you know my name?"

"Like I said, I overheard."

She nodded. "I'd prefer it if you would call me Grace. My husband is dead. He succumbed to cholera last week."

He nodded, not sure what to make of that simple statement. She sounded so matter-of-fact, not at all grieved. Uncertain what else to say, he replied, "Then you should call me Alex."

"What is it you do here, Alex?" she asked, seeming to size him up.

"I'm a free trapper. Been hunting and trapping this part of the world for nearly ten years."

"So you don't live at the mission?"

He shook his head. "I trap with a couple of other men. We just turned in our furs at the fort and are making plans to hunker down for the winter. I usually stop by the mission when we're in the area. Whitman is cordial enough to let me share his table when I do. He really is a decent sort."

The wind stirred, and she pulled her shawl closer.

Alex motioned to the house. "Perhaps you'd feel better inside."

"No. He's in there, no doubt. I need a little more time to regain my composure. I'm sure to have to apologize later. After all, we are here because of Dr. Whitman's kindness."

Alex thought her such a strange young woman. She was willing to stand up for herself yet considered keeping the peace of utmost importance due to her host's generosity.

"So have you come west to start a new life—a great adventure?"

Grace shook her head. "Not really. I'm not the adventurous type. Not like you."

Alex chuckled and crossed his buckskin-clad arms. "I don't know about that. We're both adventurous, or we wouldn't be here in the wilds of Oregon Country."

She nodded and seemed to consider his words. "I suppose

you could say that. Although our reasons for being here are probably different."

"And why did you come here?"

She looked past him toward the river. "I suppose it's common enough knowledge. I was put together with the Right Reverend Martindale to come west and preach the Gospel to the savage Indian."

"Put together?"

She sighed. "Yes. I needed to come west with my sisters, and the Right Reverend needed a wife. Otherwise the mission board wouldn't send him west."

Alex could hardly believe that such a beautiful young woman hadn't already been snatched up by some eager bachelor from her youth. Still, she didn't appear to be a woman given to lying.

"So you wed a complete stranger in order to come to Oregon Country. Why was it so important that you come here?"

Grace's green eyes widened in what appeared to be fear—even horror. She quickly pressed herself between the wall of the house and Alex's frame and took hold of his arm. Alex turned around to find his good friend Sam Two Moons approaching. Like Alex he was clad in buckskin, but his long black hair flowed around his shoulders and down his back like a mantle. Alex had to admit he looked pretty fierce.

Alex turned back to Grace as she clung to his arm. He gave a laugh and called over his shoulder, "Sam, you're scaring the lady." Sam stopped mid-step, and Grace straightened to peer around Alex. "Grace, this is Sam Two Moons. He and I trap together along with Gabe. I assure you he's perfectly harmless . . . unless you are a wild animal with a salable fur."

She bit her lip and let go of Alex's arm. Sam offered her a smile and gave her a nod. "But he's . . . an Indian."

Alex laughed. "Is he? I hadn't noticed."

Sam chuckled as Grace's face reddened.

She straightened but let Alex remain between them. "How do . . . you do?"

Alex and Sam looked at each other and broke into laughter. "I assure you, Grace, Sam is completely safe. I know Whitman warned you against the Indians, but Sam's almost white."

"Hardly," Sam countered. "I wouldn't want to be white. Too much trouble."

Grace seemed to accept that the threat was minimal. She stepped away from Alex and squared her shoulders. "Are you Cayuse?"

"Nez Perce," Sam replied.

"You speak English very well. Did Alex teach you?"

"No. I attended a Catholic mission school when I was younger. I can read and write as well."

"He can also speak French and Chinook Jargon," Alex said, anticipating her question. "It's a sort of trade language among the tribes."

"I see." Wisps of her brown hair blew across her face as the wind picked up. Without appearing to care, Grace continued. "What about Cayuse? Do you speak their language?"

"We share our language," Sam replied. "They have a separate language, but many of the Cayuse have forgotten it. Much of their language has been blended into Nez Perce as our people have intermarried."

"And are you married?" Grace asked, seeming genuinely interested.

"I am." Sam didn't seem in the least annoyed by her questions. "I have two children and one that will come soon. And you?"

"No. I have no children. I was married—after a fashion. My husband is dead, however."

"How can a person be married after a fashion?" Sam asked and looked to Alex for interpretation.

"It's not important," Grace assured him. "I'm here with my two younger sisters."

"Why did you come west?" Sam asked.

"That's a long story. Our mother died, and we had no other family but an uncle who moved some years ago to Oregon City."

"What's your uncle's name?" Alex asked. "I know quite a few people there."

"Edward Marsh."

Alex nodded. "I do know him, but he's not in Oregon City. At least not at this time. He's gone south to buy cattle."

She looked crestfallen. "Do you know when he'll return?"

"I don't know for certain, but I guess he'll be back by spring. He only left a couple of weeks ago. I saw him at Fort Vancouver."

She nodded and gave a heavy sigh. "I suppose it doesn't matter. We figured to winter here anyway, since Dr. Whitman offered us his hospitality."

Sam nudged Alex. "I came to let you know that I'm heading back to my village. Gabriel's coming with me and said he'd meet you there." He gave a slight nod to Grace. "It was nice to meet you."

Then without even awaiting her reply, he took off in the same direction from which he'd come.

Grace watched the departing Indian for several silent moments. When she looked back to Alex, she found him watching her.

"He was the first Indian I've ever met. He seemed so . . . so . . ."

"Civilized?" Alex asked with a smile. "He is. Most of his people are."

"My husband said the Indians were savages incapable of civilizing themselves without the help of whites. He said they were like children who needed a firm hand of discipline."

Alex frowned. "Your husband was a fool."

Grace was surprised by his comment. "I often concluded as much myself, but why do you say that? Most white men believe the Indians in need of civilizing."

"Most white men are fools." Alex's eyes darkened to a black hue that matched his hair.

"Because they see the Indians in need of help?"

"Because they don't bother to know the people of this land. They have been told stories, and that's all they care to learn. They believe the people are savage and wild—ready to scalp every white man and steal away white women and children."

Grace could hear the anger in his voice. "But you must admit we have reason to believe those things. The Indians *have* scalped white men and stolen away women and children. My father and grandfather fought in many uprisings back east, and I've heard horrific tales. It would benefit the Indian to put aside such murderous ways and take our help."

"Our help? They've lived off the land for hundreds of years without our help. What makes you think they need us now?"

Tightening her hold on her shawl more out of frustration than cold, Grace lifted her chin. "Because we will populate this country. Now that the United States has come to terms with the British regarding the boundaries of the land, the government is urging westward settlement. You surely are aware of that, even if you are a trapper."

His eyes narrowed. "Your prejudice suggests you think me as illiterate and savage as you think the Indians. Your ignorance is insulting, but as a gentleman, I won't respond in such a way as to give credence to your assumptions. However, I would pose a question. Why suggest that the Indian become like the white man? Why not suggest that the white man become more like the Indian? After all, they have successfully lived on this land for generations without the conveniences most whites seem to require."

Grace tried her best not to react to his obvious anger. She shook her head. "The future cannot be reached by living in the past. The Indian may very well have lived here for hundreds of years without our help, but the future will prove most difficult for him if he expects to continue living as he has. I don't say that to be harsh or unfeeling, or even prejudiced, as you suggest. It's simply a fact. The government has determined that this part of the country will be settled, and so they will settle it."

"Even if it costs the lives of every single man who dares to reject that notion?"

Grace shrugged. "I certainly hope it won't come to that. If the Indian is truly as civilized and capable as you suggest, then I would think they could change with the times. However, if they are less capable, as it appears, they will need a great deal of help." With that, she started to walk away.

"It's a pity."

Grace couldn't help but turn back. "What do you mean by that?"

"It's a pity that you can't accept folks for who they are and what they're capable of."

He used her own words against her, then fixed her with a look that dared her to counter his comment. Instead of giving him the satisfaction, however, Grace simply turned and left him to contemplate the matter alone.

It seemed all men in the west were opinionated and full of self-importance.

Sam and Gabe weren't long on their way to the Nez Perce village when Alex caught up to them. Sam could see Alex was in a foul temper, but he wasn't one to pry. Gabe, on the other hand, didn't often keep his thoughts to himself.

"What's eatin' at you?"

Alex shook his head. "Nothing."

"Ain't likely you're tellin' the truth," Gabe countered. "I can see you're het up over somethin'. You and Doc Whitman get into it again?"

"No."

Sam couldn't help but smile. "Last time I saw him, he was talking to a pretty woman."

"Oh, no. Woman troubles are never good."

"I don't have woman troubles," Alex said.

"Sounds to me like she must have read him a page out of the Good Book," Gabe said, looking at Sam.

Sam thought that while it was possible Grace had chewed Alex out, it was more likely his friend was just suffering from having been near a female. They'd been a long time in the mountains trapping.

"I can't see you lettin' yourself get all riled over a woman," Gabe continued. "Personally I'd rather wrestle a grizzly bear than fight with a woman."

"It wasn't a fight—it was more a conflict of views." Alex looked at Gabe and then Sam.

"She's very pretty," Sam said with a teasing tone. "And she's a widow."

Gabe moaned. "That's all we need. It's gonna be a long winter, and I'm too old for this nonsense. I think I'll just head up to the cabin and forego the village." He reined back on his horse and shook his head. "You boys join me when you get this female situation under control. I'm gonna need your help cutting some trees." He nudged the sides of his mount and headed off to the right, disappearing into the trees.

"What's gotten into him?" Alex asked.

Sam shrugged. "Who can say?"

They rode in silence until they stopped to rest the horses and take some food. Chewing on pieces of jerked meat, Sam could see that Alex was still troubled. As long as Sam had known Alex, he had seen his friend given to times of silent contemplation. Alex had a troubled past he couldn't seem to overcome. He'd mentioned a little of it, but mostly he just kept it bottled up inside along with a guarded reserve toward God.

Sam kept his thoughts to himself. "You ready?"

Alex looked up and gave a nod. They remounted but hadn't gone twenty yards when Alex finally offered up a small bit of insight. "Sometimes I'm ashamed to be a white man."

Chapter 4

I think you write beautifully," Hope said as she finished reading from John Sager's journal. She looked at the young man who touched her heart like no one else ever had. "Where do you get such thoughts?"

He shrugged. "I see things and they just spark ideas and words. I can't help but write them down. It always makes me feel like I've accomplished something important."

Hope nodded. "It is important. It's like seeing into your heart."

John smiled. "You aren't like other girls."

She shook her head. "What do you mean?"

"Well, older women like my writing just fine, but when I've shown it to younger ones, they think I'm just being sappy and sentimental."

"Then it's their loss. I think what you write is wonderful. I especially like the part about your folks. I know how hard it is to lose someone you love. Our Da died a long time ago, when I was just about Mercy's age. Then our Mama died last winter. I miss them."

John reached out and squeezed her hand. "It's hard."

Hope thought her heart might beat right out of her chest. She swallowed hard and glanced up at John's sympathetic expression. She couldn't explain the feeling that washed over her. Suddenly all of the men and boys she'd flirted with and teased over the years seemed unimportant. Was this love?

"I need to get back to help Mercy."

"I think it's really wonderful that you care so much about your sisters. My brothers and sisters and I wouldn't have been able to stay together if not for the Whitmans—Father and Mother." He smiled. "They've been real good to us."

Hope nodded. "I never really understood or appreciated all that Grace did for us after Mama died, but coming here has made me see it. You've helped too—with your writing. I hope you keep putting down your thoughts and stories. I want to read them all." She felt her face flush. "That is, if you don't mind."

He rubbed his thumb over the back of her hand, and Hope thought she might well faint. "I don't mind at all. In fact, I like the idea a lot. Maybe after supper we can take a walk together, and I'll tell you more about how I come up with the words."

Hope could barely speak. "Yes, Johnny. I'd like that . . . a lot."

Leaving the mission house was hard, but Hope reminded herself that she would get a chance to be with John again after supper.

Her thoughts were so concentrated on that idea that when she walked straight into a group of Cayuse braves, she let out a little scream. The men laughed and assessed her from head to toe.

"You pretty," one of the men said. "You have man?"

Hope didn't know why, but she nodded. She couldn't begin to speak, however. The stench of their unwashed bodies and their continued study of her made her want to run. She began backing up but kept her eyes on the man who seemed to be in charge.

"You run away like scared doe," he said, laughing. He said something in his native tongue, and when the men around her laughed and ogled her all the more, Hope could no longer stand it. She lit out and ran as fast as her feet would carry her and didn't stop until she was back at the emigrant house and safely behind the closed door.

She held up her trembling hands and tried to force her spirit to calm. There was something very dangerous in the look of those men, and she hoped never to encounter them again. Unfortunately, the Indians were often at the mission, and the likelihood of avoiding them altogether was slim.

As she began to feel her heart slow, Hope felt her tension ease. Tonight after supper she would talk to Johnny about what had happened and see what he thought might be done.

Time had a way of flying by without being noticed. It had been over a week since the Brownings departed the mission, and Grace found that she missed her friend more than she'd anticipated. It had been hard to leave folks behind in Missouri, although Grace could only call to mind three or four who truly mattered, but without Eletta, she felt more alone and vulnerable than she had in a very long time. With most of the remaining wagon train preparing to press on to the west, Grace wondered what the winter might hold in store.

Mercy was still sick. In fact, she was very weak, and Grace couldn't help but worry. Hope helped care for their younger sister and did so without complaint. Perhaps it was a show of maturity or maybe just desperation to avoid doing laundry. Whatever the reason, it had been a tremendous help to Grace.

When Hope wasn't helping with Mercy, she sought out the company of John Sager. John and his six siblings had lost their parents on the journey west some years earlier, and the Whitmans had adopted them to raise as their own. Unfortunately, as with so many others at the mission, several of the Sagers had contracted the measles. Including John. Mrs. Whitman and other women who lived at the mission house helped to care for him, but when Hope wasn't with Mercy, she was at the mission house seeing to John. Grace had been told that Hope could often be found at his side, reading to him.

Dr. Whitman led them in Sunday services, and to Grace's surprise, she found his preaching quite good. She also enjoyed Narcissa's singing. Mrs. Whitman still seemed reserved, but she was kind and generous overall. Harriet Kimball had told Grace how the Whitmans' little daughter, Alice, had drowned years earlier and Narcissa had never recovered from her grief. Narcissa believed it was her fault that Alice had been taken, because she had made her child more important than her work for God. God had seen her heart and knew it to be corrupt. Grace thought it very sad that such a conclusion should be made and even sadder that it should continue to haunt the poor woman. It was little wonder there seemed to be a perpetual sadness about her.

Two of the bachelors at the mission, James Young and Andy Rogers, had taken an interest in Grace. She was first introduced to Andy when he joined Narcissa in singing at church. The Right Reverend would have had a conniption had he been there. As a Congregationalist, he didn't believe in men and women singing together in church services.

James Young lived with his family in the Blue Mountains at the sawmill Dr. Whitman had set up. He made regular trips to the mission to deliver finished wood for the new additions at the gristmill and houses. He was a handsome man of twenty-four, only a year younger than Andy. Both men were easygoing and good conversationalists, unlike the handsome and opinionated trapper who continued to dance around Grace's memories. What was it about Alex Armistead that made her think about him nearly every day?

"You look mighty pretty today, Miss Grace," Andy said, taking a seat across the table from her at the noon meal.

"I'll say," James agreed, sitting down beside Andy. He gave Grace a wide smile.

Grace felt her cheeks warm. "Thank you, Andy, James." She complimented Andy on his singing. "I particularly enjoyed the hymn you shared with us today." She smiled. "And I heard Mrs. Whitman say that you intend to play your violin tonight."

The slender man blushed to the roots of his blond hair. "I do, Miss Grace. I hope you'll join us here at the mission house."

"It will depend on Mercy. Still, I wouldn't like to miss it."

"Miss what?"

To Grace's displeasure, she looked up to find Nigel Grierson approaching the seat to her right. "Mr. Rogers is going to play his violin tonight."

"Wish I could stay to hear it," James said. "I have to head back to the sawmill right after lunch."

Nigel grunted something unintelligible and plopped down beside Grace. "I hope after the meal you'll take a walk with me. I'm leaving with the others tomorrow, and there are a few things we need to discuss."

No doubt he was going to propose again, and Grace had little desire to endure it. However, rather than create a scene at the table, she smiled and nodded. "Very well."

Prayers were offered with special petition on behalf of all who suffered from measles. Grace was particularly concerned about the adults who'd taken the disease. The expectant Mrs. Osborn had taken ill, and everyone feared for her and the unborn baby she carried. Her husband, along with several of the other men and multiple children, had also contracted measles.

Once the prayers concluded, Nigel asked, "Where is Hope?"

Grace kept her gaze on the table in front of her. "She's sitting with Mercy."

"How is your little sister doing?" Andy asked.

Meeting his concerned expression, Grace replied, "She's still very ill. The disease has been particularly hard because she was so exhausted from the trail. She lost so much weight on the trip west, and she was small for her age to begin with." Grace spread some jam on a piece of bread. "Still, I have no reason to doubt she'll recover."

"That's good," Andy said, nodding.

"You're quite the healer." James kept his voice low. "I've heard others talk about how you took care of folks on the wagon train. It's surely a gift from God."

Nigel huffed as if completely disgusted with Grace for speaking to anyone but him. She turned to him. "Is something wrong, Mr. Grierson? You don't seem to be enjoying your meal."

He huffed again and picked up his fork. "I'm just fine."

Once the meal finally concluded, Nigel hurried her away from the others. She protested, telling him she needed to help with the cleanup first, but Harriet Kimball, all smiles, handed Grace her shawl.

"You two go on. We've plenty of help."

Grace took the wrap and returned Harriet's smile with a nod. She had little choice but to go with Nigel unless she wanted to make a scene.

They walked toward where the animals were pastured. The mild day brought to mind early fall rather than its latter days. The temperatures were almost warm, and the breeze actually welcome. Grace carried her shawl instead of wearing it, hugging it close as if it might provide some sort of barrier between her and Mr. Grierson.

"You know I'm leaving in the morning with the others," Grierson began without warning.

Grace nodded. "I do. Hopefully the weather is this nice all the way to Oregon City."

Her reply seemed to confuse him. They walked on until they reached the place where her sheep were happily feeding.

"You refused my proposal," he began again, "but I think you should reconsider. This place isn't all that safe. There's no real protection should the Indians decide to war against the mission."

"I have heard about the dangers," Grace admitted, "but Dr. Whitman said there are always ongoing threats to the settlements and missions. Besides, I have no place in Oregon City for me and my sisters. My uncle is away buying cattle, so he won't be there to help us."

Nigel seemed ready for her answer and quickly continued. "My brothers have a small cabin where we could stay after we married. There's room enough for all of us until I can build a house of our own."

Grace listened patiently, knowing it would do little good to interrupt. He was determined to speak his piece, and she might as well hear it.

"It won't take all that long to build my dairy herd. I already have some good stock, and my brothers have managed to purchase a few additional cows for me. I'll have my dairy up and running before you know it. So I can provide for you and your sisters, and you need not stay here with the Whitmans." To Grace's surprise, he reached out and turned her to face him.

"I want you to marry me." He held up his hand. "I know you don't love me and you fear that will mean a miserable marriage, but I beg to differ. Few people marry for love. Most marry for necessity and learn to love each other. We could be like that. In fact, I'm sure that in time you would come to love me, and I already esteem you, so love can't be far."

"Mr. Grierson, I appreciate your kind offer. I don't want you to think my refusal is out of disregard for you. You are an admirable man and have proven yourself honorable at every turn. However, I have no desire to marry again. I have just buried my husband, and I have my sisters to consider. Mercy is ill and I couldn't consider leaving her, nor could I take her on such an arduous journey. So you see, even if I had a desire to marry, which I don't, I couldn't make that choice."

He studied her face for a moment and finally gave a heavy sigh. "I anticipated this would be your answer, and while I am disappointed, I have another proposition for you."

"Really, Mr. Grierson, I don't think—"

"Please just hear me out."

He looked at her with such pleading that Grace felt obliged to listen for fear he might actually break into tears. "Very well. What is your proposition?"

"I would like to help you in some way, so I thought perhaps you would allow me to take the sheep—*your* sheep with me to Oregon City. The Johnson boys are happy to help me herd them with my cows. I know you're concerned about the Indians stealing your sheep, and Dr. Whitman shouldn't have to worry about feeding extra animals in case the weather turns bad. I could take the sheep with me and care for them until next spring when you come. I could even turn them over to your uncle if you were delayed."

"That is very kind of you. Of course, I insist on compensating you in some way."

"I don't want any recompense," he assured. "I'm offering this so you'll see that I can be of value to you."

Grace shook her head. "Mr. Grierson, if you think taking my sheep to Oregon City will somehow change my mind about marriage, I assure you that isn't going to happen."

The look on his face told Grace she'd figured out his motive. "I will happily allow you to take my sheep along with your cows, but I intend to pay for their upkeep. I can give you money to see to their feed, and come shearing time you could keep the wool or perhaps keep a lamb. Would that be agreeable?"

She could see that he wanted to refuse her, but at the same time he no doubt figured if he had her sheep, he had a better chance of winning her in marriage.

"Very well," he finally answered.

Grace offered him a smile. "Thank you. That will be a tremendous relief to me. I am confident you'll see them safely through the winter."

When Grace finally returned to the emigrant house, she was relieved to find Mercy awake. "Thank you, Hope. You can go rest, if you'd like."

"I want to check on the children at the mission house."

Grace nodded but knew full well that Hope's real interest was John Sager. She waited until Hope was gone before reaching out to brush the hair back from Mercy's face. "How do you feel?"

"My eyes hurt," Mercy said, reaching up to rub them.

Grace took hold of her hands. "Don't touch them. You can damage them. I have some salve that should help them feel better. Let me go mix it up for you."

"Grace, am I going to die?"

Her sister's question startled Grace. "Why do you ask that?"

"I heard the women talking. They said people are dying from the measles."

"It's true, but I have every reason to believe you are well on your way to recovery."

"But I feel so bad. I hurt so much and . . ." Mercy began coughing, and Grace rolled her to one side to pound her back as she continued to gasp for air.

Once the spasm subsided, Grace propped Mercy up with a rolled blanket. "Stay on your side. It will help to keep your lungs clear." She pulled a blanket up around Mercy's shoulders. "As for the pain, I can give you something to help with that as well, but I want you to stop worrying. Measles can be deadly, especially when people refuse to do what is helpful. Dr. Whitman says the Indians are more likely to die because they have not been exposed to the various diseases the Boston men have had." She paused and smiled, hoping she could get Mercy's mind on something else. "They call us Boston men and women. Isn't that funny? As far as I know none of us on the wagon train were from Boston, but that's what they call us."

Mercy nodded and closed her eyes. "I don't want to die."

"I don't want you to die either." Grace looked at her sister with grave concern. "I want you to fight this and to do everything I tell you to do. Will you?"

Mercy reopened her reddened eyes. "I'm so . . . scared."

"You know that God is with you. You made a decision to seek the forgiveness of Jesus and take Him for your Savior. You belong to Him, so don't be afraid. Besides, I'm going to do whatever I can to see you through this. You do believe that, don't you?"

Mercy gave a weak nod. "I know you will."

"And you know that I'm very good at knowing the right remedies to use?"

Again Mercy nodded.

"Good." Grace placed a kiss on Mercy's rash-marked forehead. "Now you rest, and I'll be right back with something that will make you feel better. I love you, Mercy."

"I love you too," the child whispered and closed her eyes with a heavy sigh.

Grace frowned, knowing that Mercy still had a long way to go to recover from the sickness. She was so very weak and fragile. Grace gazed heavenward and whispered a prayer.

Don't take her from us, Lord. Please. I don't want to lose her. Please let her stay with us a little longer.

Hope mopped John's brow with a damp cloth. "Grace says it's important to get the fever down so that your brain doesn't burn. Are you feeling any better at all?"

John closed his eyes. "A little. It makes me feel better just knowing you're here."

"I'm glad." Hope smiled and put the cloth aside. "Would you like me to read to you from the Bible?"

"Not just now."

Hope frowned, worried that he was worse than he let on. "I know Dr. Whitman doesn't like my sister doing things for the sick, but she knows a lot about medicine, and she's helping a lot of folks feel better. I'm going to see if she'll fix you up a tonic. Would that be all right?"

John opened his eyes and gave her a weak smile. "Anything you want to do is all right by me. You . . . you're special to me."

Hope could hardly keep from blurting out her own feelings. She held back, however, knowing there would be time enough for sweet talk later. Right now it was important that John recover and grow strong again.

"I'll be back in the morning, and I'll pray that your rest is peaceful." She stood and held herself in check. She wanted more than anything to kiss his forehead but knew it would be completely inappropriate. "Good night, Johnny."

She looked around the room at the others who were ill. Most were already asleep. Hope felt the weight of their sickness in her spirit. She had already seen so much death and dying. She glanced back at John and whispered the prayer she'd prayed at least a dozen times.

"Please heal Johnny, Lord. Don't let this sickness take him."

The next day was one of great sadness. Grace had no sooner finished helping clean the house and gather the laundry when she heard wailing outside. The women with her heard it as well, and all moved en masse to find its origin.

Outside there was a collection of ten Cayuse. Most were women with children in their arms, but two were braves who were confronting Dr. Whitman. Grace understood little of what was said by the Cayuse even though another man standing with the doctor interpreted. His words were spoken so quietly that it was impossible to hear.

It was the women who drew Grace's attention. They were wailing in sorrow, rocking back and forth with their children held tight against them. Dead children. Grace could tell by the way their limbs flopped like those of a rag doll.

Whitman held up his hands. "I am sorry, my friends, that your children have died. We have had deaths here as well. You may bury them in our cemetery, and I will speak over them." The interpreter relayed his message.

One of the Cayuse men shook his fist at Whitman and countered with words that needed no interpretation. His anger left little question about his thoughts.

Grace watched as the doctor did his best to convince the Indians that he was doing all that could be done. She pitied Whitman in that moment. He was a hard man, arrogant and opinionated, but he did care about these people.

It seemed that the tempers were calming, but not so the grief. Grace had heard women cry like this on the wagon train when they'd lost children. It was an audible sorrow that came from deep within—a sorrow that couldn't be eased with mere words or even kind deeds. Only time would help to diminish their pain, and even then it would never leave them altogether.

And Grace knew the disease had yet to run its course. The mourning had just begun.

Chapter 5

In the days that followed, the Cayuse came to the mission more often for medicine or to bring their children for Dr. Whitman to examine. Grace watched them from afar. The men were lean and formidable. Some wore leather leggings and breechcloths and wrapped themselves in Indian blankets. Others wore buckskin from head to toe as Alex and Sam Two Moons had. The women too wore buckskin made into long dresses with short fringe. All had thick black hair worn long, and their dark, piercing eyes only made their stern expressions more intimidating.

"Grace, will you stir this pot?" Harriet asked.

"Of course." The request brought Grace out of her contemplation, and she stepped to the stove and took the offered wooden spoon. She had come to the mission house kitchen that morning with some of the other women to help dye material and yarn. Dr. Whitman and Narcissa sat to one side, going over an inventory list.

Without warning, several Cayuse men appeared at the open kitchen door and walked in without being invited. The leader was named Kiamasumkin. He was one of the chiefs or subchiefs, but Grace couldn't remember which. Andy had pointed him out to her on another occasion, along with several other important men of the tribe. Kiamasumkin and his men marched straight toward Dr. Whitman.

"You stay here to care for your Boston men and leave my people to die. You give us medicine, and it does not heal but makes my people sick . . . and they die. You are bad tewat."

The word *tewat* had been used enough around the mission that Grace knew this was equivalent to doctor or medicine man. She pressed back further from the gathering to watch, almost mesmerized by the scene.

"I have cared for the Cayuse and Nez Perce as if they were my own family," the doctor assured, getting to his feet to face the men. "I have not wronged you."

Another man stepped forward. "The Boston men lie. They cannot tell us true. My children are dead and it is because of the white man sickness."

Whitman held his own despite the fact that he was only one man against several. "You know that I have cared for the Cayuse and have helped many to wellness. I have given you food and help when it was needed. Most importantly, I have told you about the Great God who died for your sins so that you could be saved from the fires of hell. I would not do that if I did not care about you."

"You will come today and heal our people," Kiamasumkin said, looking directly at Dr. Whitman. He switched from English to Nez Perce and continued speaking.

Grace had no idea what was being said. She had learned very few Nez Perce words. She knew Andy was called *Hushus Muk Muk*, which meant *Yellow Head*, and that *Weyiletpa* was another name for the mission area and meant *place of waving grass*. Apparently when "pa" was put on the end of a word, it signified the place, and when "pu" was used, it meant the people. So *Weyiletpu* indicated the inhabitants of the area.

There were a dozen other words Grace had picked up, but none of them could explain the conversation that was now taking place. Even Whitman relied on the help of a translator.

After a few moments of angry exchange, Dr. Whitman ordered the men from the house. For a moment everyone watched and waited to see if the Indians would obey. Finally, Kiamasumkin nodded and walked from the room. The others followed, and Grace let out a breath she hadn't even realized she'd been holding.

Dr. Whitman turned to his wife. "I'm going to the village to see what I can do."

"Is it safe?" she asked, her face pale.

"Now, wife, we did not come to this place because it was safe. We came to serve." He gave her arm a pat, then gathered up his coat and bag and departed without another word.

Narcissa watched him go with tears in her eyes, and then without speaking to any of the other women present, she gathered her papers and hurried from the kitchen to seek the solace of her bedroom.

Grace looked to the other women, wondering what she should do. After a moment, everyone went quietly about their business until only Grace remained frozen. She felt her heart racing and tried to slow it by drawing in deep breaths. For the first time, she truly feared for their safety.

"Are you ill, Grace?" Mary Saunders asked.

"No. Just frightened. That was most disturbing."

Mary nodded. "Come help me with the yarn. It's best to put your mind to something else."

It might be best for a diversion, Grace thought. But it didn't eliminate the problem.

Alex and Sam arrived at the large Cayuse village on the Umatilla River. They had heard about the rising tension and the gathering of some of the chiefs and subchiefs. Alex hoped he might be able to offer some understanding from a white perspective and be a voice of reason in the midst of angry men. Being French-Canadian as well as a Boston man gave Alex better acceptance than most white men could boast. The Hudson's Bay men were often French-Canadian, and the Cayuse and Nez Perce had maintained a good relationship with them. The forts were willing to accept their furs and trade goods with the Indians in exchange. Since Alex was a trapper and often lived with Sam in his Nez Perce village, he was treated as if he were a member of the tribe. To a point. There was still a very clear line drawn, especially by the Cayuse, who were skeptical that any man of white origin could be faithful to his word.

"Greetings, my honored friends. We have come to parley," Alex said in Nez Perce. "Will you share counsel with us?"

A gathering of four chiefs looked first to one another and then nodded. "Wixsil'iix."

Alex and Sam obeyed the invitation to sit down and waited until Tauitowe, the man in charge, spoke again. Tauitowe, unlike the others, was dressed in white man's clothes—a green suit with a red vest. Atop his head was a blue cloth hat, which he removed in greeting. "You have come to make peace between us and the Boston men at Weyiletpa?"

Alex considered his words carefully. "Is that what you need from me?"

Tauitowe looked to a chief Alex recognized as Camaspelo. The man gave a nod. Turning back to Alex, Tauitowe said, "We were many but now are few. The white man's sickness has taken much from us. There is little we can do to save our people." His expression revealed his grief. "We pray to the white God . . . but still they die."

Alex nodded. "The chief speaks true. These are hard times. Many of the white children have also died. White men and women as well. My heart is full of sorrow for you and the Cayuse and Nez Perce people." He drew in a steady breath. "But you must know that the Boston men have not planned this to harm you. They did not seek your death."

One of the other chiefs grunted and muttered something under his breath.

Alex looked to him. "Five Crows disagrees?"

Five Crows fixed him with a hard look. "I believe the Boston men want the land at no cost to themselves. Every year many white men come and take more and more from my people. They will not stop coming unless we make it so."

Alex had heard this argument around other council fires. "The Great Father of the Boston men has agreed with King George of the Hudson's Bay Company men that the land will belong to America. Because of that, the Boston men will come and settle the land."

"But it was not theirs to give away," Five Crows replied, crossing his arms. "It belongs to the Natítayt—the People. My people."

Alex couldn't help but think back on Grace Martindale's words during their conversation. He hated to admit that she was right in this situation. The Indians would have to change; the whites would never bend. "The Natítayt must find a way to live with the Boston men. They will not stop coming. If you kill them, they will only send more—and not just to settle the land, but to kill you as well."

"Without our land, we are dead," the fourth chief said. Instead of anger, however, his tone held great resignation.

Alex felt sorry for them. They had no idea what they were facing. The Americans were hungry for land, and expansion was all the talk back in the states. Oregon Country's boundaries had only been settled the year before, and now the American government was encouraging citizens to move west with the promise of free land.

"The earth is life to us," Camaspelo said. He looked at Alex and then Sam. "It is life to you as well. When the Boston men come to take all of the land, the beaver will die along with the Natítayt."

Alex nodded. "What you say is true. In the east where the Boston men have their cities, there are few wild animals, yet it is the Boston men who demand the beaver for their hats. They do not understand what they are doing. Or if they do . . . they do not care. But I care. You are my brothers, and I come here to tell you that you must not harm the Boston men."

Sam joined in. "They have great numbers of soldiers with weapons that are far more dangerous than those we carry. If you kill the Boston men, the soldiers will come and kill you and your children. It will be the end of our people."

Five Crows said, "Joe Lewis tells us that Dr. Whitman is poisoning our people. He heard the doctor say that they must kill us all."

"Joe Lewis is a liar." Alex refrained from all the other things he might have called the half-breed Canadian trapper. "He enjoys causing trouble."

"He is not the only one who tells us this," Five Crows answered. "There are others who believe this to be true."

Alex could well imagine. He could name half a dozen men who had done their best to get Whitman and the other missionaries to leave the area. He tried another tactic. "Dr. Whitman has helped you many times. He has journeyed here from his mission to tend your sick."

"And still they die," Camaspelo replied.

"But not all," Alex countered. "If Dr. Whitman meant to wipe out the people, would he not let all of them die?"

Sam spoke up. "Mr. Spaulding has a mission near my village. He has spoken often of his love for our people, and my people love him in return. His words are worthy of trust. He knows that Dr. Whitman came only to share God's love."

"The Black Robes share God's love with us. They came to talk to us and asked to pay for land to build a mission. They give us respect."

"I do not doubt that the priests from the Catholic Church respect you," Alex assured. "But so does Dr. Whitman." Alex wasn't sure he entirely believed that, but he certainly didn't want the Cayuse killing the doctor. "You have a tradition that if the tewat cannot save the sick, then he is killed." The chiefs nodded. "But people will die without the tewats as well as with them. Death is a part of life, is it not?"

"It is, but Dr. Whitman has been heard to say he wants to kill us." Camaspelo's voice rose. "He poisons the medicine and the food he gives us."

"Then do not take Whitman's medicine nor eat the food," Sam said. "Do not allow him to come to the village and treat the people. If he is evil, then have nothing to do with him, but do not kill him. It will be bad for you if you take his life. It will be bad for all of our people."

"We will make it bad for him and his people," the fourth chief offered.

Tauitowe held up his hands to halt the arguing. "We will talk no more about it." He frowned as he met Alex's gaze. "Talk does no good."

Grace took several shirts down from the line where they hung to dry. She thought of Eletta and wondered how her friend was faring so far away. Grace wasn't at all sure she could have managed, despite the fact that she'd convinced the mission board back east that she could. This was such an isolated, lonely life even when there were other people living nearby. Perhaps she would write Eletta a letter later.

She gathered the shirts up and put them in her basket, and when she turned back to retrieve the next piece of clothing, she found herself staring into the scowling face of a Cayuse brave.

"You tewat woman?"

Grace nodded, never taking her gaze from the man's face. She could smell him—a mix of sweat and smoke. It was said the Indians could smell fear, but whether he could smell her fear or merely read it in her face, Grace knew he understood she was afraid.

His expression and tone softened. "You come to village."

She shook her head, slowly at first and then more quickly. "I can't."

"You come," he said, more insistent. "You bring medicine and come."

"Dr. Whitman is the tewat. You need to get him." She pointed to the mission house.

"No. He not there. He go to fort."

Grace licked her lips and took a step back. "I cannot go."

His expression changed to confusion. "There plenty sick in my village. You can help. I hear talk that you can heal."

"I cannot come to your village." Grace stood her ground, but only because her feet were frozen in place. "Go away now." She pointed toward the village. "Go now or I will get the men."

The Cayuse reached for her, and only then could Grace move. Turning to run, she saw the trapper Alex and his Nez Perce friend Sam approaching and hurried to them.

"Please help me. Make him leave." She pointed to the brave.

Alex stopped and took hold of her while Sam moved off to speak to the Cayuse. "What's wrong?"

"He's demanding I come to the village and treat his people.

He heard that I was a tewat. I told him to go get Dr. Whitman, but apparently he's gone to the fort."

"Do you know enough to help him?"

"Of course, but . . ." She looked back over her shoulder.

"But you're too good to help them?"

Grace was surprised by his tone of anger. She fixed her gaze on him. "I'm not too good. Dr. Whitman told us never to go to the village. I'm simply obeying orders." She didn't want to admit that fear was the real reason she refused.

"So you respect Whitman's wishes when it has to do with the Cayuse but not the people here at the mission? I think you believe yourself above them. You don't want to help them because they're savages, as I heard you call them."

His tone and suggestion that she thought herself better were more than Grace could stand. She wasn't about to admit to him that she was simply terrified.

Without waiting for Alex to continue, Grace stalked back toward the Cayuse and Sam. "I will come. Let me get my things."

Both men looked surprised but said nothing.

Grace hurried into the emigrant house, grabbed her bag, and stuffed it with as much vinegar, herbs, and tonics as it would hold, then marched back out to where Alex and Sam stood with the Indian. Without a word to any of them, she headed straight for the village.

Chapter 6

G race was appalled at what she saw in the Cayuse village. The sick lay on thin tule mats, the same material used to create the walls of the teepee-style lodge. Filth, by her standards, was a permanent presence in their lives. The rash-riddled bodies of the Cayuse were filthy, as were their cooking utensils, blankets, and most everything else. The smells of sickness, rancid grease, and unwashed bodies were nearly enough to drive her back out into the fresh air, but she persevered. And to her surprise, so did Alex and Sam. They remained at her side, acting quickly upon her requests for hot water and translation.

She moved from lodge to lodge, doing what she could to make the sick comfortable, but it was clear to her that many would die. Even so, she did her best to prove to Alex that she wasn't afraid, nor was she above helping the Indians. Her anger drove her for the better part of the day, but by the time the skies turned dusky and her body demanded she stop, Grace had no more anger.

The Cayuse were no different than the whites she'd left back at the house. Measles made all men equal.

Using the last of the vinegar she'd brought to the village, Grace gently dabbed the skin of a small Cayuse girl. The child was going to die. Grace told Alex to explain to the girl's mother, and the woman began to wail. Her cries pierced Grace's heart, stirring her compassion for the grieving mother and her people. No matter the color of a person's skin, the loss of a loved one was never easy.

When her supplies were finally exhausted, Grace let Alex and Sam take her back to the mission. The sun was long gone from the sky, and heavy clouds blocked any light from the moon. She said nothing, still reliving the day of death and disease in her mind. Alex and Sam were talking, but the words didn't register. So many of those souls would be dead by morning if God didn't intercede.

"Grace, did you hear me?" Alex stopped directly in front of her and put his hand on her shoulder.

She looked up to see that they'd reached the emigrant house. Light shone from behind the curtains, but she had no idea what time it was. Alex frowned slightly as she finally met his gaze. "No. What did you say?"

"I told you I was sorry for what I said earlier."

She shook her head. "What are you talking about?" A cold wind blew strands of hair into her eyes, but before she could push them back, Alex had done it for her.

"I was harsh and inconsiderate. I knew you were afraid, but I accused you of thinking yourself too good to help the Cayuse. I was wrong, and I'm sorry."

Grace thought again of all she'd seen that day, and exhaustion washed over her in such a way that she wasn't sure she could take another step. She had no desire to talk to Alex or anyone else.

"I'm sorry too." She didn't wait to hear anything more but forced her legs to move and made her way into the house.

Entering the room where Mercy lay sleeping, Grace was surprised to find Hope watching over her. When Hope lifted her head and saw Grace, she burst into tears, jumped up, and wrapped her arms around Grace's weary shoulders.

"I was afraid you weren't coming back." Hope pulled away and her nose crinkled up. "You stink."

"I've no doubt."

"One of the women saw you go off to the village. Why did you go there?"

"I went to help the sick. So many sick." Grace's words trailed off, and with a weary glance she looked around the room. "Where are the others?"

Hope stepped back. "Everybody's gone to bed. It's nearly ten."

Grace nodded. "I need to wash. Is there hot water?"

"I made sure there was some on the hearth. I've been wiping Mercy down and making sure she drinks something every hour—just like you told me."

"Thank you. I . . . you're a good sister." Grace gave Hope a weak smile and felt her knees give way. She sank to the floor. "Maybe I'll just rest for a minute and then wash up."

It was the last thing Grace remembered before she fell into a deep sleep.

When Grace awoke, it was morning. She stretched and frowned at the smell of her own stench. Sitting up, she found Mercy watching her, but Hope was nowhere to be found.

She smiled at Mercy and reached out to touch the younger girl's forehead. "Your fever is gone."

"I feel better," Mercy said, her voice still weak. "But my eyes still hurt."

Grace nodded. "I'll make some more salve. I'm afraid I used up all I had yesterday."

"Hope said you went to help the Indians."

"I did. They're in a bad way. I don't think many of them will live."

"That's so sad," Mercy said, closing her eyes. "I don't like them, but I don't want them to die. You were kind to help them."

"Where's your sister?"

"She went to get food for us. She told me not to wake you unless it was truly necessary."

"I needed the sleep, that's for sure. Now I need to clean up. Will you be all right until I get back?"

Mercy gave a slight nod. "I'm much better, so you don't need to worry."

Grace smiled. "I'm not worried. I knew you would pull through."

Leaving Mercy to rest, Grace made her way to the fireplace, where hot water was waiting for her. She ladled some into a large pitcher and then took it to the privacy of the small room where house residents tended to their personal needs. Grace poured the hot water into a large bowl and began to wash. The heat felt good on her face. She didn't even mind the harsh scent of the lye soap.

She slipped off her filthy gown and hurriedly washed her entire body as best she could. With her bathing complete, she donned her only other dress and put the dirty one to soak in the remaining water. She would see to it later, but first she needed to eat. With all that had happened the day before, she hadn't had a real meal. Alex had given her some dried meat and a hunk of bread at one point, but other than that, Grace had worked through the noon and evening meals.

Thoughts of Alex caused Grace to pause. She remembered a gentleness in him when he'd helped her. He was truly a good-hearted man who cared about people no matter their color. She had been touched when he'd helped her by holding a young boy while Grace bathed him. Alex's dark eyes had betrayed his heart when she whispered that the child was too far gone to help. In that moment she had wanted nothing more than to embrace him and lessen her own sadness along with his.

When she returned to check on Mercy, Hope had come back, and Mercy was already nibbling a biscuit.

"I brought you some biscuits and ham." Hope held out the plate to Grace. "And some berry jam too. I know how you like it."

"Thank you." Grace sat down and began to slather jam on one of the biscuits. "What's the news from the mission house?"

"Not good. Mrs. Osborn had her baby—a little girl—but the baby's bad off. I heard the doctor say he didn't think she would make it. Silvijane is worse too. The whole family is sick in bed with the measles."

Grace nodded. "I wish there was something I could do to help, but at least they have the doctor's care."

"Are you going back to the Indian village?" Hope asked.

"Yes. I want to do whatever I can to help. You'll look after Mercy, won't you?"

"Of course, but Grace . . ." Hope seemed unable to find the right words. She shook her head. "I wish you wouldn't go to the Indians."

"But they need help."

"I know, but they hate us. What if they decide to hurt you? It's so much safer here."

"Try not to worry. I'm doing what I feel God has called me to do—help the sick." She tried to offer a reassuring smile. "Now, see if you can't get Mercy some broth. I know the women made some from a chicken yesterday. Hopefully there's some left."

"I'll get some."

Mercy looked up from her pallet and gave Grace a smile. "Don't worry, Grace. I'm much better."

After restocking her carpetbag, Grace gave one last look at

her sisters. They looked anxious. "Don't you two worry. I'll be fine. Oh, and Hope, if you have a chance, would you wash out my dress? I left it soaking in my wash water."

At Hope's nod, Grace exited the house and blinked at the brilliance of the sun. It looked to be another unusually warm November day.

She cast a quick glance across the yard toward the mission house. There were several people milling about, but Dr. Whitman didn't appear to be one of them. Grace hurried around the house and made her way past the pond, hoping the men working at the gristmill would ignore her. Picking her way through the dried grass, she prayed for her family and friends, as well as Dr. Whitman and his wife.

Lord, these people need your help. I need your help. There's so much sickness, and the people are so weak. She paused, realizing she was not only praying for the mission folks but the Cayuse as well. *We need a miracle—a healing miracle. Please.*

"Grace?"

Her heart skipped a beat as she looked up to find Alex Armistead a few feet away. "I was heading over to the village. Can you come with me to interpret?"

"Of course. Even yesterday I never intended for you to go there alone. It wouldn't be safe or appropriate for a white woman. You should never go by yourself."

She tried to reply in a way that acknowledged the dangers but didn't sound haughty. "I do . . . realize the issues at hand."

Alex began to walk in step with her. Grace was desperate to change the subject.

"Why do you dress as they do?" She looked up to meet his gaze, and he flashed her a smile.

"It's more enduring and comfortable. Even Dr. Whitman understands that and often does likewise."

"It does look comfortable. I can't begin to imagine all the

work that goes into creating such an outfit, though. I've done a lot of sewing in my time, but not with hides."

"You'll have to come with me to Sam's village and have his wife, Sarah, teach you."

Grace kept her voice void of emotion. "I'd like that. I'm really not the snob you think I am. Nor am I unable to learn. For instance, I would love to learn about the vegetation in these parts. I'm sure there are plants here that offer wonderful medicinal helps."

"There are." He gave her a sheepish look and ducked his chin. "I *am* sorry for how I acted yesterday. It was ungentlemanly. I knew you were scared, and I should have done something to reassure you instead of condemning you unfairly."

"Yes, you were unfair." She paused a moment and softened her tone. "However, I appreciate that you are man enough to apologize. A lot of men wouldn't."

"Like your husband?"

Grace shrugged. "The Right Reverend was never wrong and therefore had no need to apologize." She saw Alex frown but offered no further explanation.

Alex said nothing until they'd passed the pond. "I heard the doctor isn't happy with you, and yet you are braving his wrath once again."

"I don't like to upset him purposefully, but the fact is he's too proud to allow that my abilities might help lighten his load. Perhaps it's because he fears being shown up."

"Most likely," Alex countered, "it's because if you prove to be successful, it will only give the Cayuse more ammunition to support their theory that he's trying to kill them."

Grace looked at him in surprise. "Why would they ever think that? Surely the Indians are intelligent enough to know that death comes to all eventually. They can hardly hold the doctor responsible for the measles claiming so many lives."

"But they do. They are intelligent but also fiercely superstitious and set in their ways."

"Still, many of them have accepted Christ as their Savior."

"True enough, but they don't necessarily discard their other beliefs. Some do, like Sam, but even he leans toward the old ways from time to time."

They were nearly to the village, and Grace took a moment to pause. She wanted to ask Alex the question that had troubled her for the past couple weeks. "Would the Cayuse really come and kill us in our sleep?"

Alex stopped and shrugged. "Who can say? They are known to kill when they feel they've been treated badly. They believe that if a tewat is no good, they are justified in killing him. They won't tolerate the threat to their way of life and their people. I've tried to reason with them, but they won't hear a white man's reason."

She nodded and looked out across the lodges of the village. "I wish there could be peace between us."

"So do I."

Chapter
7

The emigrant house was full of the sick, and Grace did her best to stay out of sight when Dr. Whitman came to check on his patients. Once he was gone, however, her presence seemed to comfort the ill. So did Hope's. To Grace's surprise, Hope was given to singing to the children.

"You have the voice of an angel," Harriet Kimball said, smiling at Hope.

"I like to sing. Our mother used to sing."

Grace nodded. "You sound just like her. I was just thinking to myself how much your singing reminded me of her. She had such a beautiful voice, and you do too."

"Do I remind you of her?" Mercy asked.

Turning back to her younger sister, Grace nodded. "You do. You have her smile."

"She's tiny like Mama too," Hope added.

"Indeed she is. She's definitely the smallest of all of us."

"Da used to say Mama was no bigger than a mite and he worried she'd blow away in a good wind," Hope said.

Mercy giggled, making Grace smile.

It was good to hear her sisters sharing lighthearted conversation again. Equally good to hear them sharing happy memories of their parents. Grace could remember the old days when Mama and Da gathered them nightly for supper and to read the Bible. It was a time of joy, and Grace found herself often longing for that gathering once again. Her parents were very much in love when they'd married, and that love never lessened over the years. Grace had always vowed she'd have a love like that one day, and then she'd married the Right Reverend and those ideals seemed lost. Now, however, she couldn't help but wonder if true love might still be had. An image of Alex came to mind, and she was surprised to realize she was coming to care for him. It was nothing more than friendship, she assured herself.

A knock sounded at the front door of the emigrant house, and Grace went to answer it. She found a very worried Alex holding up an older man at the door.

"He's hurt," Alex said in explanation. "I thought maybe you could help."

Grace glanced down and saw that the older man's lower leg was wrapped in a blood-soaked cloth. "What happened?" She motioned Alex inside and led him to the only available spot where she could work.

Alex eased the man to the floor. "He was chopping wood and somehow managed to hit his shin. It's a deep wound. I did what I could with moss and wrapping it, but it needs more."

Smiling at the pale-faced older man, she began to unwrap the leg. "My name is Grace."

"Grace is what I need," the man said weakly, then gave her a wink. "I'm Gabriel, but everyone calls me Gabe."

"I've always loved that name because it's the name of God's angel. At least one of them."

Gabriel gave another weak nod. "My older brother was

named Michael for the archangel. He was always pullin' rank on me."

"My younger sisters would tell you that I do the same." Grace glanced to where Hope stood watching before refocusing on the task at hand. She continued working, doing her best to keep Gabriel talking lest he succumb to shock.

Once she pulled away the last of the bandages, she could see Alex was right. The wound was deep. "It will have to be stitched." She paused, looking up to see Harriet Kimball watching with a frown. "Perhaps we should call for Dr. Whitman to do the work."

"No," Alex said firmly. "We want you. I told Gabe about you."

The old man smiled from behind a thick, graying brown beard. "It's a sight . . . better to have a . . . a pretty gal caring for you. Besides, me and the doctor have banged heads a few times."

Grace looked over her shoulder. "Hope, get my bag." Her sister hurried from the room. Grace reached up and felt Gabriel's neck. His pulse was weak and very rapid.

"Alex, let's move him closer to the fire and get him lying down. I'll hold on to his leg to keep the wound from bleeding more." She took a firm grasp and held fast, even though she could see how much it pained Gabriel.

Before she could suggest anything more, Alex had already scooped up his friend and, with Grace, moved him near the hearth.

Grace grabbed a pillow and put it beneath Gabriel's head. "There. Now you'll be warmer and more comfortable."

Hope returned with her things. She handed Grace the bag, then went to the fireplace mantel and took up the pitcher for water without being asked. As Grace pulled out some of her medicines, Hope ladled water. With that complete, Hope knelt beside her sister.

"What can I do to help?" she asked.

Mercy had moved closer. "I can help too."

"No, you lie back and rest," Grace told her. "I don't want you having a relapse because you've done too much. You still have a long way to go until your strength returns." She uncovered the wound again and turned to Hope. "Are you sure you can deal with this?"

Hope blanched a bit but nodded. "I want to help."

"Very well. We need to clean the wound. We'll start with water and then use a liberal application of wood vinegar." Grace drew off the moss Alex had packed on the wound.

They worked together while Alex continued to talk to Gabriel. Grace had her doubts the wounded man could comprehend much more than the pain, but she was glad for Alex's attempt to distract him.

The gash was deep and long, not to mention full of debris. Sweat trickled down the side of her face, and her shoulders and back began to ache from bending over Gabriel's leg, but she worked on. It was imperative the wound be clean.

Hope assisted as best she could, but Grace knew the ugly wound was difficult for her sister to stomach. When Hope began to hum the hymn "Christ a Redeemer and Friend," Grace knew it was to calm her own spirit.

"Why don't you sing the words, Hope? I remember that was one of Mama's favorites."

Hope nodded and softly sang, "Poor, weak and worthless though I am, I have a rich almighty Friend; Jesus, the Savior, is His Name; He freely loves, and without end."

Gabriel smiled as Hope continued to sing. He seemed to forget everything else. When she concluded, he nodded. "If there really are angels on earth, then I just heard one sing."

Hope blushed and looked away.

"There, all done," Grace said as she tied off the bandage.

"But you must rest." She looked at Alex. "Where are you staying? Gabriel can't go far. I'd suggest here, but we already have so many, and most are sick."

"That's a good question. I hadn't really thought about it."

"I have our tent, but I don't want Gabriel on the cold ground. If you think it would work out, you may use my wagon. Since the others moved on to Oregon City, the doctor had our wagon brought closer to the mission. There's room there to make a bed for you both, now that I've given most of the contents to the doctor and his wife. The canvas is still on and will shelter you from the weather. Oh, and you could use the little cart we have for hauling water to carry Gabriel so he doesn't put pressure on the leg."

"That'll be fine." Alex gave her a look of such gratitude that Grace felt immediately self-conscious.

"Ah . . . Hope and I will go ahead of you and fix things up." She gathered her things and got to her feet. "It'll only take us a few minutes to gather bedding."

Hope looked at Grace oddly. Something about her sister seemed different. Grace was almost uncomfortable around the handsome trapper, Mr. Armistead. But none of that held Hope's attention for long. She had other things on her mind, and she needed her big sister to offer advice. Something that Hope would never have admitted even a month ago.

"Grace, have you ever been in love?"

Grace straightened from where she was creating a resting place for Gabriel on the floor of the wagon. "No. I don't suppose I have. I told Da I would never fall in love unless the man was just like him. Though perhaps less stubborn." She smiled a sad sort of smile that made Hope almost regret having asked the question.

"I think I'm in love."

Grace smiled. "John Sager?"

Hope nodded. "He's a good man."

"He's hardly more than a boy—and you are certainly still a girl, not yet having reached your majority."

"He's not a boy, and I am a woman just as much as you are. You know very well that many people marry younger than me."

"Are you already talking marriage?"

Hope felt her face grow hot. "Well, not exactly. But I find myself thinking about it all the time. I know I've always been a flirt, but I don't want to be one now that I know Johnny—John. I care about him, Grace. More than I thought it was possible to care about someone."

"And I presume from the time you have spent together that he feels the same?"

"He does. He said he liked my happy spirit." Hope remembered his smile when he'd told her. "I'm sure I love him. I feel all funny inside, and none of the other men are of any interest to me."

"Hand me that pillow," Grace ordered, then added, "I think you should move slowly. We'll be here all winter. Take your time and get to know each other better. Make certain he is a God-fearing man."

"Oh, he is. In fact, he's made me want to know God better. We've been reading the Bible together. Well, I've mostly done the reading, since his eyes hurt him, but he's talked to me about God and how we each one of us have to trust Him for our future." Hope picked up the requested pillow and hugged it close. "And, Grace, I want my future to include John."

"Just go slow. You're only seventeen. You have all the time in the world to decide if you want to spend your lives together."

"I suppose Mama would have said the same thing."

"I'm certain she would have." Grace straightened again.

"There, that's ready. At least it will be once you give me that pillow."

Hope handed it over with a frown. "If you've never been in love, how can you be so sure your advice is right?"

Grace laughed. "I've never been bitten by a rattler either, but I know how to look out for them and what to do if I should get bitten. Honestly, Hope, a month ago you were teasing all of the boys and young men and enjoying your status as the most beautiful girl on the wagon train. Now all of a sudden you're talking about giving your heart to one man and spending the rest of your life with him. That's a very quick transition—even for you." Her voice softened and sounded almost motherly. "Don't be in such a rush to grow up, sweet girl."

Alex awoke with a start. He looked out of the wagon and found the light fading from the skies. What time was it? He lit the lantern Grace had left him and checked on Gabriel.

The old man woke up and looked at Alex in momentary confusion. "Where are we?"

Alex smiled. "We're in a wagon. Grace Martindale's wagon, to be exact. She's the one who sewed you up. Do you remember much?"

"I remember the voice of an angel singin' over me. Was that her?"

"No, that was her sister Hope. Grace was the one with the beautiful green eyes."

"Ho ho, you reckon her eyes to be beautiful. Ain't never heard such words come from you before. Next you'll be tellin' me that she's your gal."

"No, I won't." Alex hadn't meant for his tone to sound so irritated. "That's not at all in my plans."

"Well, maybe the Good Lord has other plans. I reckon Him to be in charge, so you just might find yourself tumbling right into love."

Alex stiffened. "That's not going to happen. Now forget about it and tell me how you're feeling."

"It hurts like the dickens." Gabriel shook his head. "Can't figure what the Good Lord has in His plans for somethin' like this to happen. In all my years, I ain't never had an axe slip on me."

"Maybe God's punishing you for keeping company with me."

Gabriel gave him a frown. "Boy, sooner or later you're gonna have to own up to the past and all that's keepin' you and God at odds. You were taught better, and I know you know the truth. You ain't gonna have any peace at all until you yield yourself to God."

"Don't go preaching at me." Alex found himself caught up in the discussion in spite of himself. "If I'm at odds with God, then it's because He allows injustice and suffering in the lives of innocent people."

"Well, as I recall, there was only one innocent person in all of creation, and God let Him die on a cross."

Alex turned away and shook his head. "We don't need to have this conversation again. I know God is up in His heaven, no doubt amused at your tormenting me, but let's talk about something else."

Gabriel tried to sit up, but Alex stopped him. "You have to rest. That gash on your leg was deep. Grace said you have to stay off of it for a few days."

"Bah, I've been wounded before. I ain't never been one to take to my bed."

"Perhaps it's time you gave it a try," Grace said as she peered into the wagon. "I believe my timing is perfect, given that my patient doesn't wish to obey my instructions."

Alex went to help her up, but she extended two plates of food instead. "I thought you could both use some supper."

"Indeed we could." Alex took the food and set it aside. "Let me help you up."

Grace held up her arms and allowed Alex to pull her into the wagon.

The wagon was small and cramped. Grace had to crouch as she moved to Gabriel. Alex tried to press to one side as far as he could, but her nearness left him feeling flushed all over.

"I've come to make sure you aren't feverish or bleeding." She didn't give Gabriel time to protest but immediately started unwrapping his leg. Alex brought the lantern closer as she inspected the wound. She gave a nod and began to rewrap the leg. "The bleeding has stopped, and the stitches held while moving him here." She finished with the leg and reached into her pocket. "But you must stay in bed, or you'll start up bleeding or get it infected."

"Like I was tellin' Alex, I don't think much of layin' around."

"Well, I suppose if you don't mind the idea of losing your leg, you could do pretty much whatever you like." Grace fixed Gabriel with a matter-of-fact stare that made Alex laugh out loud. She produced a small bottle, poured some of the contents on top of Gabriel's food, and handed it to him. "Eat all of this. The herbs will help with the pain."

"I think you've met your match, Gabe."

Gabriel laughed. "I've had me two wives who weren't anywhere near as bossy as you."

Grace smiled. "You were married? Are you still?"

"No. Both of them gone beaver."

Grace frowned and looked to Alex for explanation. "What?"

"They died. That's just another way of sayin' it."

She nodded and turned back to Gabriel. "I'm sorry to hear that. Was that when you came west?"

Gabriel gave her a strange look. "I've lived out this way pert near all my life. Came down from Canada. Married me a Cree woman. She gave me two sons, but they . . . died, and not long after that she died too. Then I married me a Nez Perce. We had a good many years together. But now she's gone beaver too."

"You married Indian women? Why would you do that?"

Alex stiffened. He hadn't expected Grace to ask such a question. Surely she was familiar with the fact that many of the trappers, if not most, married Indian women. White women were scarce in the northwest. He glanced at Gabriel, wondering if the man would be offended, but to his surprise the older man chuckled.

"Ain't no white woman who'd tolerate me." He gave her a toothy grin. "I needed a woman who could keep up with me and do my biddin'. A woman who didn't mind livin' out here and didn't need a lot of foofaraw and geegaws."

"Well, I would think there are a good number of white women who would have agreed to take on the wild country, as well as the wild men in it. Even if it meant leaving geegaws behind." She smiled. "I don't, however, think mixing the races is a good idea. There are too many differences."

"But the differences are what makes it good," Gabriel answered.

Alex leaned back and decided it was best to keep quiet. He knew their ways were strange to Grace. Maybe in time she'd better understand, but now wasn't the time to take her to task.

"Say, Alex, I could sure use a cup of strong coffee." Gabriel looked to Grace. "You suppose Whitman would spare some?"

"I think he would, although I wouldn't say anything about this." She waved her hand over Gabriel's wounded leg. "I doubt he would appreciate the situation."

Alex nodded. "I'll go see what I can round up." He squeezed past Grace in an awkward crouch, then jumped from the wagon.

He glanced back at his friend and the woman who strangely seemed to fill his every thought. "Shouldn't be long."

Without encountering the doctor, Alex managed to secure two mugs of coffee and return to the wagon. As he drew near, he heard Gabriel talking and decided to hold off a moment to listen.

"A great many people think folks should be quartered off for one reason or another. Either because of their religion or the country they came from."

"That's true enough," Grace replied, "but their point is a good one in the sense that we are more comfortable with what we know. So if we stay in a place where people think and live as we do, then we'll get along better."

"I suppose some figure it'd be nice to have things work out that way, but for me, I like knowing and living amongst a lot of different folks. There are some mighty good people out there who are nothing at all like me."

"I'm sure that's right, but I know in the east people are disturbed by such differences. Like the color of a person's skin. Slavery has many people upset."

"It's never sat well with me for one man to own another. Seems to me that you can't be judgin' one man or woman by the color of their skin."

"I don't mean to sound judgmental, and I don't believe that slavery of one race to another is acceptable. I was just taught that we should each keep to our own kind," Grace replied.

"And we should. But that means people keepin' with people. You wouldn't go out there and marry your horse, now would you?"

Grace laughed. "No, I don't suppose I would. But neither would anyone else I know."

"Knew me a man once," Gabriel began in that thoughtful tone Alex had come to recognize. "He doted so much on his dog,

I think he would have married her. But she was mighty good to him, so I can't say as I would have blamed him. She was one of the best hunters I've ever seen. Saved his life more than once."

"Here, have some more jam on your corn bread," Grace offered.

Alex figured their talk was concluded, but Gabriel went on. "Grace, I know what white folks say about me takin' Indian wives. They say it ain't natural, but I married 'em because I loved 'em. Never dishonored them before marryin' 'em proper. They were good women—Christian women too."

"They were Christians?" Grace sounded surprised by this.

"They were. I led 'em to the Lord myself. Told them all about Jesus comin' to earth as a baby and growin' up to teach folks about His Father in heaven. You know the truth of that?"

Alex had to smile. Gabriel had been a good influence on him over the years despite his frustration and anger with God. Gabriel never let him feel sorry for himself or wallow in despair. It was probably to the older man's credit that Alex hadn't given up on life years ago.

"I do," Grace admitted. "My folks were Christians and made sure we read from the Bible every day."

"That's how I did it with my gals. They were always sad about folks killin' Jesus on the cross," Gabriel continued, "but I told 'em He died for us—because He wanted to, not because anybody made Him. Once they knew the full story, they agreed gettin' saved from their sins was the only way to honor the sacrifice Jesus made." He paused for a moment and gave a chuckle. "They was also afraid of going to hell."

"When I agreed to marry the Right Reverend T.S. Martindale," Grace began, "I knew the plan was for us to come west to set up a mission to preach to the Indians. However, the Right Reverend never wanted a wife, and well . . . frankly we never lived as husband and wife. The Right Reverend said he didn't need a wife and certainly didn't need a family. He wanted to be certain there would never be any children, and that was fine by me. I always figured we would come west and probably part company. I wanted only to get me and my sisters to Oregon City, where my uncle lives, and the only way I could join up on a wagon train was to be married. It was never about love."

Gabriel gave a disapproving grunt. "That's one of the saddest things I ever heard anybody say. Ain't right to make vows to the Lord and not mean 'em."

Grace sighed. "I meant them. I had resigned myself to honor and obey. I wouldn't have asked for a divorce, although I always figured the Right Reverend would annul the marriage in time." For a moment neither one said anything, and then Grace continued. "I suppose it wasn't right, but I never meant it as a lie to the Lord. Besides, now the Right Reverend is dead, and I am free. I'm glad you told me about your wives. I'm sorry if I offended you."

"You didn't. You just didn't know better. Now that you do, I wouldn't expect you to say those things."

"And I won't. Ever again. I guess you've helped me to see the Indians in a different light. Alex helped with that too."

"He's a good man. A lonely man, but a good one."

Alex decided to make his presence known. There was no way he wanted Gabriel encouraging Grace to keep Alex from being lonely.

"Here's the coffee," Alex said, holding up the mugs.

Grace took them and gave him a smile. "Smells good. I think I'll leave you now and go see to my own supper." She put the mugs on a wooden barrel and turned back to face Alex.

"Allow me," Alex said, reaching up to help her.

He pulled Grace from the wagon, and when her feet touched the ground, he was hard-pressed to release her. Her nearness was nearly his undoing. He hadn't expected to feel this way, and it only served to make him all the more determined to put some distance between them.

"Thank you," Grace said before he could move. "Please see that Gabriel stays in bed. I can't stress enough how important it is that he stay off the leg."

Alex nodded, looking deep into her eyes.

Grace smiled again and sidestepped him. "I'll be back to check on him tomorrow."

She walked away, leaving Alex to stare after her. For several moments he couldn't move. What was this spell she'd woven over him? One minute she was infuriating him, and the next he wanted to pull her into his arms.

"You gonna climb up here anytime soon so I can have my coffee?"

Alex turned to find Gabriel sitting up, watching him with a grin. "I'm coming," he replied and climbed up to join his friend. "Don't be gettin' all impatient. If you get that leg messed up, Grace will have my hide."

Gabriel gave a snort of laughter. "I think she just might have it anyway."

Chapter
8

When Grace checked on Gabriel the next day, she surprised him with a guest. Mercy was restless but still far too weak to do much, so Grace had bundled her up and brought her along to keep the old man company.

"I see you brought me a visitor. What a pretty little girl," Gabriel said, throwing Mercy a smile.

Mercy blushed and ducked her head. She was the only one of them who could stand up in the wagon. "I'm glad you're doing better, Mr. Gabriel," she murmured.

Gabriel shook his head. "No 'mister'—just Gabriel or even Gabe."

"My name is Mercy. I'm Grace's youngest sister. I was there when Mr. Armistead brought you to be sewed up."

"Well, I'm sorry I can't remember our meetin'."

Mercy shrugged. "Do you like to play checkers?"

"I certainly do. Did you bring a board?"

Mercy went to one of two remaining trunks in the wagon. "We have a set here. I thought we could play a game or two, if you like."

"So long as you don't wear Gabriel out," Grace commanded. "He needs a lot of rest." She began to unwrap his leg. "I thought Mercy might stay with you for a few hours so that Alex could go about his business." She looked at Alex and shrugged. "Whatever that is."

Alex looked annoyed, but Gabriel chuckled. "This time of year it's mostly making sure the traps are in good working order for the spring. The best furs are had in the spring, so we make certain to have everything ready."

"There's more to it than that. We have to lay in meat and wood for the winter. We have to make repairs to our cabin and weapons, make ammunition. There's a lot to do." Alex sounded completely offended by Gabriel's casual answer. Perhaps he feared Grace would think him a lie-about.

Gabriel grimaced as Grace continued to remove the bandages. She hoped she could get his mind off the injury through conversation. She also hoped it would keep her thoughts from focusing on Alex. All through the night, she'd dreamed of him holding her in his arms. It had nearly caused her to seek out Dr. Whitman this morning and turn Gabriel's care over to him. She wasn't at all sure she could endure spending more time in Alex's company. His presence did things to her that she didn't understand.

She forced her thoughts back to the topic at hand. "I must admit that I know nothing about trapping. My Da would sometimes trap coyotes, but usually he just shot them if he saw them." She frowned at the sight of Gabriel's leg. The area around the wound was hot, swollen, and red. "I fear infection has set in." She shook her head and reached into her bag. "I'm going to make a poultice. Hopefully it will draw out the poison."

She took up her mortar and pestle and added herbs from several bottles along with water she'd boiled the night before. Once she had a thick paste, Grace smeared some of the salve directly on the wound. The rest she put in a cheesecloth poultice. With tender care, she applied the poultice directly to the wound and then began to rewrap the leg.

"I'll come check on you both in a couple of hours and change this in about four. We'll need to keep the salve fresh, so Alex, you'll need to change the bandages through the night."

"Surely we don't got to go to that kind of trouble," Gabriel said in protest. "I'm thinkin' it'll be better by mornin'."

"I hope so," Grace said with a smile.

"I'm happy to apply a new poultice in the night." Alex pointed his finger at Gabriel. "And you will be a cooperative patient or else you'll answer to me."

Mercy giggled. "Grace is always saying that."

Alex met Grace's gaze and smiled. "I'm sure she does."

Grace's heart skipped a beat. She looked away. "Mercy, when you finish with the checkers, why don't you read some of the Bible to Gabriel? He knows a great deal about God, and you two could discuss what you read." She started gathering her things. "I'm going back to see what I can do for the sick."

She climbed down from the wagon before Alex could offer her a hand. He jumped down right behind her and followed her as she headed toward the mission house.

"I want to thank you for helping Gabe. He's a good man."

Grace looked at him as he kept pace with her. "I'm sure he is, but I'm very worried about his leg. I fear I didn't get the wound cleaned out well enough." She frowned and looked toward the mission house. There were at least a half dozen Cayuse arguing with Dr. Whitman. "I'd rather we avoid that," she said, stopping abruptly. "I think I'd prefer to return by the river path."

Alex nodded. "I think you're right. No sense in stirring up Whitman's curiosity as to what we're doing." He surprised Grace by taking her elbow to guide her. "So where's your other sister? Hope's her name, right?" He looked at her a moment. "Grace, Hope, and Mercy. It just now dawned on me that you've all been given names based on—"

"Bible verses," Grace interjected. She tried not to think of the warmth of his hand on her elbow and forced a smile. "Da gave them to us. Mine is based on the last verse of the Bible, Revelation twenty-two, verse twenty-one. 'The grace of our Lord Jesus Christ be with you all. Amen.'" She gave him a sidelong glance. "Of course as Da pointed out, there are a great many verses in the Bible that speak of grace, and it pleased him to give me that name. He said I was a gift from the Lord, therefore I was the Lord's Grace. However, he also told me I should work hard to live up to such a name, for grace in and of itself is a treasure."

"Treasured grace," Alex murmured with a slow nod. "I agree."

"And I know you also agree that I haven't been very full of grace when it comes to the Indians, but you and Gabriel have helped me see the error of my ways. I can't say I'm at ease with them and their ways because I don't know them, but I have prayed to have more grace where they are concerned."

"You show more than most folks. Most of the people here would just as soon not have to interact with them at all. You used your skills to give them comfort and aid."

"Fear is what stops most of the people here at the mission." Grace shook her head. "And I cannot find fault with them for that. I too am afraid. It's difficult to hear the rumors without being afraid."

Alex nodded. "These are trying times, to be sure. But with a little wisdom and calm discussions, I believe peace can prevail. But it will take time before we are completely at ease with each other."

Grace wondered for a moment if Alex was still speaking of

the whites and Indians. She stopped as they approached the emigrant house. "And time is a most precious and unpredictable commodity."

"'Time is what we want most, but what we use worst,'" Alex said, smiling. "William Penn said that. I remember hearing my father quote it."

"It's true." Grace glanced back across the mission grounds to where the Indians stood in conversation with Dr. Whitman. It seemed the situation had calmed. Perhaps yet another crisis had been avoided and cooler heads had prevailed.

She looked back at Alex and nodded. "We just need time."

With Alex's help, Grace made another visit to the Cayuse village. More people had died, and unfortunately they had been treated by Dr. Whitman, causing the chiefs to believe more than ever that the doctor was trying to kill them. It didn't help that several of Grace's patients had immediately improved.

"It won't bode well for Whitman," Alex told Grace as they made their way back from the village.

Ahead of them, near the mill pond, Grace saw the man Alex had called Joe Lewis. Grace recognized him as the one who had interpreted for Whitman that day she'd been in the kitchen. He had dark hair and eyes, but where those features made Alex dashingly handsome, they made Lewis look sinister.

"Your friend there makes a better tewat than Whitman," Lewis said, pointing to Grace. "Maybe we'll let her live."

Grace heard a low growl come from Alex. He narrowed his eyes, his expression taking on the look of a man about to engage in a fight.

"I'm not going to tolerate you frightening her," Alex said in a low tone, emphasizing each of his words.

Lewis laughed and gave Grace a leering look, letting his

gaze travel the length of her body. "I don't want to frighten her. In fact, I can think of a whole lot of things I'd rather do to her."

Grace shuddered as Alex stepped forward with his fist raised. "You touch her, and I'll see to it that you never touch anyone ever again."

Another cold shiver ran through Grace as the men squared off. The last thing she wanted was for them to fight over her. There was already enough arguing and threats between the Cayuse and the mission folks. She certainly didn't want another clash starting on her account.

Lewis took another step toward Alex, the smile fading from his face. "You'd better watch yourself, Armistead. You're only tolerated around here because of your brotherhood with Sam Two Moons and the Nez Perce. The Cayuse would just as soon kill you off with the rest of the tiwélqe."

"Enemies? You really think the whites are your enemies?"

"They are, and the Cayuse will not be defeated by them."

Alex shook his head. "And I suppose you've been inciting them to hate all whites."

Lewis shrugged. "I tell them the truth. Whitman wants them all dead."

"If that were true," Grace couldn't help but interject, "then why bother to try to heal the sick or treat the wounded?"

"That's just another way he gives 'em poison," Lewis answered, meeting her gaze. "I pointed out to them that you follow a lot of the Indian ways when it comes to healing. That way has resulted in their people getting better, while Whitman's way is death."

"You can't believe that Dr. Whitman wants to kill the Cayuse." Grace could see by Lewis's expression that he did believe just that. She hurried to continue. "What purpose would it serve? He came here to minister to the Indians, to share the

Word of God and to see that they didn't die without knowing Christ as their Savior."

"The Black Robes already teach about the Great Father in Heaven. We didn't need the Boston men."

"The Catholics aren't the only ones who want to share the Word of God," Grace said. "God would have everyone share the Gospel of Jesus."

"The Black Robes have proven trustworthy," Lewis countered. "They pay for the land they use and don't charge outrageous prices for trading goods. You can't say that about Whitman. He owes the Cayuse money for using their land, but instead of paying, he just takes more and more land."

Grace had no idea what the agreements between the Cayuse and Whitman were. She imagined the doctor would certainly look out for his own needs. Perhaps he did charge them too much for food and other necessities. Maybe he didn't pay for the use of the Cayuse land. It might behoove her to learn the truth before defending him.

Alex put his hand on her arm. Looking up, Grace could see something in his expression that told her to be quiet. At first she considered ignoring it, but as his grip tightened, Grace decided to cooperate. After all, Alex had been among these people a lot longer than she had.

"Lewis, you are always looking for trouble. I know you're the one stirring up the Cayuse. I've heard your name mentioned many times."

Lewis wasn't at all bothered by the accusation. In fact, he smiled. "I won't lie to my brothers, and if you are a true brother to the Nez Perce, you won't lie to them either. The fact is, Dr. Whitman is responsible for bringing more and more Boston men to this land. He wants the white man to take all of the land and make it into farms and ranches. He wants to push the Indian off the land and see him die."

"That's not true, and you know it. I don't believe Whitman or the government wants to see the Indians eliminated or killed off."

Lewis shook his head. "It doesn't matter what you believe. The whites will soon be swept from this land, and the Cayuse and Nez Perce will once again be free of their interference."

"The white man is here to stay," Alex countered. "You might as well get used to it."

A cold, hard laugh came from Lewis, leaving Grace with gooseflesh. This man gave off an overwhelming sensation of evil and doom.

"The white man will stay, all right," Lewis said. "He'll be planted in the ground. We'll kill them all if we have to." He looked at Grace again. "Maybe we'll save a few of the prettiest white women. Maybe I'll take you as my wife."

"Over my dead body," Alex said, pulling Grace behind him. Lewis gave him a smug smile. "That's the idea."

Alex had never been so infuriated in his life. He wanted to bash Lewis's head in. Instead, he felt Grace pull on his arm.

"We must check on Gabriel," she whispered almost too low to hear.

Alex forced down his anger. It had only ever caused him trouble anyway. He certainly didn't need to repeat his mistakes from the past.

After taking several deep breaths, he looked down at the beautiful woman standing next to him. "Yes, you're right. Let's go."

Lewis called out behind them, making further suggestions of what he hoped would happen and how happy he could make Grace. Alex seethed but said nothing until they were back to the wagon where Gabriel was recuperating.

"Don't go back," he said, stopping several yards away. "Whatever you do, don't go back. I think it's best that way." He let out a heavy sigh as he gazed into Grace's frightened face. "I think if Dr. Whitman can just show the chiefs that Joe is a liar, then everything will settle down."

She shook her head. "But those people are dying. They need help, and I want to do what I can."

"No!" Alex all but yelled. He drew a long breath and forced himself to calm down. "I'm sorry. I know you've benefitted them, Grace, and I know I encouraged it, but things have come to a head. If we can let tempers calm, then things will probably go back to the way they were." He looked across the field toward the village. "There's always going to be difficulties between the tribes and the whites so long as there are instigators like Joe Lewis. The trick will be to prove that Lewis is lying about the poisoning of the people. I'll speak to Whitman myself, and I'm sure we can come up with some way to trap Joe in such a manner to prove to the chiefs that he isn't reliable."

When they reached the wagon, Grace checked Gabriel's leg. Alex could see for himself that the wound looked no better.

Grace turned to her sister and smiled. "Thank you for keeping him company, Mercy. You go on back to the house and rest. I'll be along shortly."

Alex helped Mercy from the wagon, sensing that Grace wanted to spare her sister from further exposure to the situation.

Grace bit her lip. "I don't like the looks of this."

"Don't go frettin'," Gabriel said, shaking his head. "The Good Lord won't come for me a minute before my time."

Grace applied salve to the wound, eliciting a moan from Gabriel. "The infection is worse, Gabe."

"These things got to run their course."

Alex edged in closer. "Is there anything I can do?" He could see the worry in her eyes. "I can change the bandage every hour if that will help."

She nodded. "We'll need some hot water and vinegar. It'll

need to be as hot as Gabe can stand. We'll soak the wound, and hopefully that will draw out the infection."

"Bring me the water and vinegar. I'll set a fire just outside the wagon and keep it hot. I can see to the treatment."

"I can stay with him."

Alex took hold of her arm and shook his head. "Too many others need your help. Just tell me what to do, and I'll do it."

Grace found Gabriel little changed by morning. His fever hadn't abated, and his pulse was rapid. An unpleasant odor rose from the bandage. She feared from the looks of the wound that the infection had spread to his blood. If that were the case, she probably couldn't save him. Opening the wound to clean it out again might be their only hope.

"Gabe, I'm sorry, but I think we have to open the wound."

His pale face was pinched in pain, but he nodded. Grace knew he understood the severity of the situation.

She opened her bag and took out several bottles. "I'm going to give you something to help with the pain. It will also make you sleep." She began to mix the concoction, hoping it would be enough to render him unconscious. She knew the shock of enduring the operation awake would be too much. "You'll soon feel very little," she assured him.

Once he'd finished drinking the tonic, Grace put the glass aside and looked at Alex. "I'm going to open the wound and drain out the infection." She looked back at Gabriel. "It won't be easy on you—especially in your weakened condition."

"Do what you must." Gabriel offered them a weak smile. "I'm a tough old bird."

She went back to her carpetbag and retrieved a pair of tweezers and scissors. "I have to cut away the sutures," she said, looking at Alex. "Will you hold his leg steady?"

Alex nodded and took a seat. "What did you give him?"

"Hemlock."

She saw the surprise in Alex's expression. Hemlock was deadly if not administered in just the right dosage, but she knew what she was doing. She had administered the concoction more than once. She went to her bag and searched for the scalpel she'd bought in St. Louis from a local doctor.

Before she could locate it, however, Mercy called out from outside the wagon. "How's Gabe doing?"

Grace didn't want her little sister to witness what was about to take place. "You shouldn't have come without my help. You're still too weak." She located the scalpel, put it alongside the scissors, and drew a needle and thread out of the bag as well. Then she looked to where Mercy waited. "Gabe's very sick. I need you to go back to the house and have Hope bring me the creosote. Can you manage that?"

Mercy's expression grew fearful. "I can do it. I'm strong enough."

"No. Have Hope bring it. I might need her assistance."

Mercy nodded and took off much quicker than Grace expected.

"Alex, do you still have water on the fire?"

"Yes. What do you need?"

She reached for a shallow pan, then added all of her instruments before handing it to Alex. "Put hot water on these. That will make sure they're ready to use."

He disappeared out the back of the wagon.

Meanwhile, Grace laid out rolls of bandages along with several bottles. She whispered a prayer for guidance. She'd never dealt with a wound as bad as this one.

Alex returned, holding the pan with the edge of his buckskin shirt. Grace motioned to place it beside her. "Thank you." She glanced at Gabriel, who was unconscious. "Let's get started."

Alex could see the situation was grave. With the wound re-opened, the smell was even worse. Gabriel had moaned and groaned until the medicine seemed to take a deeper hold of him.

Grace remained unmoved by the horrific scene. Alex thought her strength monumental as bile rose in the back of his throat more than once. Neither of them spoke, and time seemed to stand still. Just as Grace finally seemed satisfied with her cleaning of the wound, Hope arrived. Unfortunately, so did Dr. Whitman.

"What in the world is going on here? Young Mercy said that a man was wounded and Mrs. Martindale had taken it upon herself to help him." Whitman climbed into the wagon and assessed the scene. "Are you trying to kill him?"

Grace looked up. "I'm trying to clean out the infection. Where's the creosote, Hope?"

"I have it," her sister replied.

"Leave it out there," Whitman ordered. He fixed Grace and Alex with a scowl. "Why was I not called?"

Alex saw that the doctor had brought his own bag of tools. "My friend specifically asked for Grace," he replied.

"She is unqualified and very well may cost this man his life. It's my opinion that leg might have to be removed."

"We need to draw the infection out and see if that takes care of it," Grace countered. "We at least owe it to him to try that much before cutting off his leg."

"I want all of you out of here. I will bleed him and then see to closing that wound." Whitman's eyes narrowed. "I am gravely disappointed that you did not heed my commands in these matters. If this man dies, it will be on your conscience."

Grace shook her head. "If you bleed him, he will die. He's already in a weakened state. You will only make matters worse."

"Leave at once. Do not make me call for assistance."

"Grace stays," Alex said without concern for offending the good doctor. "Gabe asked for her help and hers alone."

Whitman refused to be cowed. Alex had seen him take just such a determined stance against the Indians when the need arose. "I am a trained physician," Whitman said, his voice calm and even. "I realize you have done what your friend asked, and I can see that Mrs. Martindale has done her best. Now, however, you need a doctor who has been carefully trained and has known years of experience. If you won't allow me to work, I will get some men to force you to leave."

Gabriel grew restless, whether from the agitated voices around him or the pain. Whatever it was, Alex knew they couldn't continue to argue while his friend needed help. He touched Grace's shoulder. "We might as well let him do what he will and then do what we can to see that Gabriel survives it."

"But bleeding him will kill him."

Alex glanced at Dr. Whitman, who was already tying a belt around Gabriel's arm just above the elbow. He hated conflict and knew his anger was barely under control. If he didn't leave now, there was no telling what might happen.

"Fighting won't help Gabe, and Dr. Whitman will simply bring in others to interfere." Alex felt a heavy burden settle over him as he acknowledged the severity of the situation. He had known ever since uncovering the wound that Gabriel's recovery was questionable.

Grace looked at him with an expression that Alex had once seen on his brother's face when he failed to live up to his expectations. She thought him a coward. Alex wanted to assure her that he wasn't, but now was not the time. He moved to the back of the wagon.

He heard Grace heave a sigh. "Very well, Dr. Whitman. We will do it your way, but at least allow me to stay and assist you.

You will need someone to hand you bandages and such. And if he wakes up, you may appreciate me giving him more hemlock."

"Stay if you must," the doctor replied, "but do nothing unless I tell you to."

With that, Alex departed the wagon. Hope stood just outside. The look on her face was one of grave concern.

"I'm really sorry. I was visiting with John at the mission house when Mercy found me. Dr. Whitman overheard our conversation and demanded I take him to Gabriel. It's all my fault."

Alex shook his head. "No. It's not. It's mine." He glanced back over his shoulder at the wagon. "It's all mine."

Chapter 9

Another day passed with Gabriel barely clinging to life. It was clear to Grace that he would soon be dead. The bleeding had left him weaker than before, and because Whitman wouldn't allow her to further treat his wound, the infection had worsened. The doctor announced he would amputate, but Grace knew it was unnecessary. The blood was poisoned now, and Gabriel's entire body was shutting down.

"I won't let you take off his leg," Alex said emphatically. "We both know he wouldn't live through it, and if he's going to die, he'll do it with both legs."

Whitman shook his head. "You've no one to blame for his condition but yourselves. This is a high price to pay for pride." He climbed down from the wagon, shaking his head. "It's all in God's hands now."

Grace looked down at Gabriel with a sadness she'd not felt with her husband. It was funny that she should feel so attached to this man she'd only just met.

"Lord, it has always been in Your hands, but I do wish You

would let him live. Gabriel seems such a kind man . . . and he loves You." She sighed. Even men who loved the Lord died.

Gabriel awoke from time to time throughout the night, but he was clearly confused and spoke in garbled, nonsensical sentences. Whether the effects were from the infection or the herbal tonic she gave him, she didn't know. All she knew was that life was most unfair.

Alex stirred and opened his eyes. "What time is it?"

"I don't know. Morning."

He stretched and reached out to touch Grace's arm. "Why don't you go have some breakfast? You've hardly eaten in days, and if you don't, you'll come down sick as well."

"No. I don't want to leave him just yet."

For a moment he looked as though he might argue with her, but then he shook his head. "I'll go get you something. I could stand to stretch my legs anyway." He maneuvered past her and out the back of the wagon.

Dipping a cloth in water, Grace shivered. It had stormed the night before, pouring down an icy rain. At dawn the land had been covered in fog, and the sight of it left her feeling strangely unsettled.

She touched the cold cloth to Gabriel's head. "I'm so sorry, Gabe. I wish I could have done more."

The old man opened his eyes, but from the look of it, he had no real understanding of where he was.

Grace offered him a smile. "Would you like a drink of water?"

"Little Bird," he whispered.

Grace looked around, thinking perhaps he saw a bird. Earlier there had been several kingfishers on a nearby fence. Perhaps one of them had lit on the end of the wagon.

"I don't see any birds, Gabriel. It must have flown away."

He surprised her by reaching up to hold her hand. For a dying man, he was surprisingly strong. "Little Bird, I . . . love . . . you."

Grace remembered his Indian wives. Could it be he had mistaken her for one of them? She'd never thought to ask their names.

Gabriel pulled her hand to his chest. "You're . . . my heart."

His words touched her deeply. She couldn't imagine any man feeling such love for her. She found herself almost jealous of a woman who had died long ago.

"Oh, Gabe." Tears came to her eyes, and she did nothing to pull away, even though the damp cloth she held was saturating Gabriel's shirt.

"How's he doing?"

Grace turned to find Sam standing at the end of the wagon. She shook her head, and the tears rolled down her cheeks. "It's not good."

Sam climbed into the wagon. "Alex said he'd be right here." He took a seat at the end of the bed. "Can I do anything?"

"Gabe is dying." She shook her head, and the tears flowed. "I've done everything I can, but he just grows weaker and weaker."

"It's Whitman's fault," Alex declared as he strode up to the wagon. He looked at Grace as if daring her to deny it. "If he hadn't bled Gabe, it might be a different story." He hoisted himself up one-handed and stretched out a small cloth bundle to Grace.

She didn't want there to be any more fighting or tension. She was weary beyond words and sadder than she'd been since losing her mother. "Dr. Whitman only did what he's been trained to do. I think the infection was too far gone. It's my fault. I just didn't realize how bad it was."

Alex's expression softened. His dark-eyed gaze penetrated her heart. "No. You did everything you could." He put the bundle beside Grace, then returned to his place at the head of the bed. "We can stay with him now. Once the end comes . . . Sam and I will take him home and bury him there."

Gabriel had relaxed his hold, so Grace slipped her hand from his. "I don't think it will be long." She wiped her tears with the hem of her apron. "Who is Little Bird?"

Alex gave her a sad smile. "His first wife. Why do you ask?"

"He was talking to her." Grace felt a sob rise up and fought it back. There would be time for tears later. "He thought I was Little Bird."

"He loved both of his wives, but he loved Little Bird more," Alex said, looking back at his friend. "Maybe now he can finally be with her again."

Grace saw Sam nod and remembered that Gabriel had spoken of leading both of his wives to an understanding of eternal life in Christ. She nodded and forced a smile. "It was that way for my mother and Da. My mother never got over losing him."

She got to her feet. "I need to go check on Mercy and some of the others, but I'll be back in a couple of hours. I've given him something to ease the pain, so he shouldn't be too uncomfortable. I don't think it will be long now."

Alex and Sam kept vigil over their friend through the day and into the night. Grace came by from time to time to check on Gabriel, but they all knew there was nothing to be done, and Alex finally told her to go to bed. When she didn't argue, he knew she was as tired as she looked.

Waiting for someone to die wasn't something Alex had any experience with. It wasn't that there hadn't been death in his life. There had been too much, in fact. But those people had died quickly—without even knowing they were breathing their last. At least he hoped it had been that way.

Alex had known Gabriel since first coming west after his Grandfather Armistead died. His grandfather had taught Alex all about trapping, the value of the furs, and the animals who wore them. Gabriel had taken up that teaching and helped Alex overcome his past—at least as much as he could. Gabriel had also encouraged Alex to let go of his anger at God.

"Bein' mad at the Almighty won't change a thing," he had told Alex. "Just like ignorin' Him won't make Him cease to be."

But Alex had tried. Ignoring God had seemed like justice in light of losing his mother and father and having so many people hate him for what he'd done and what he couldn't do. The image of his younger brother, Andre, came to mind. They had called him Andy, and he was only thirteen when their parents died. Alex knew Andy blamed him not only for being unable to go back into the burning house to save them, but for the fire ever happening to begin with. If only—

"I'm . . . I'm . . ."

Alex's thoughts fled as Gabriel struggled to speak. The older man had once again opened his eyes. He looked at Alex, and his lips curled ever so slightly into a smile.

"Gonna check the traps." He held Alex's gaze only a second, then his eyes closed and his lips relaxed.

For several silent minutes, Alex pondered his friend's words. Gabriel's breathing slowed and became more and more shallow, then finally stopped altogether. Bending his ear to Gabriel's chest confirmed what he already knew. Gabriel was dead.

Alex straightened and looked at Sam. His friend gave a slight nod, but for a long time afterward they simply sat there, saying nothing. What could Alex say? What could either of them say?

As the morning sun broke over the Blue Mountains, Alex looked at Sam. "His horse and mine are in the meadow."

"I'll get them," Sam replied.

Once he'd gone, Alex felt more alone than he had in a long while. Gabriel was dead, and Alex's family and friends back in the states would have nothing to do with him. Sam was his only family now.

With great care, Alex wrapped Gabriel's body in the blanket that had covered him. He had just completed this task and climbed out of the wagon to see if Sam had returned when Grace appeared.

She met his gaze and burst into tears. Without thinking, Alex went to her and pulled her into his arms. For several long moments she sobbed with her face buried against his chest.

Alex knew she bore the grief of Gabriel's passing but also of her misplaced guilt. "You did all that you could, Grace. I know that. Gabe knew it too."

"I . . . just . . . I'm so sorry," she managed to say. She lifted her face and met his gaze.

Alex fought the urge to kiss her. She was so beautiful, but that was no reason to yield to his temptation. Especially with Gabriel not even buried. He pushed her aside, trying not to seem too callous.

"Sam went for our horses. I need to finish securing the blanket around Gabe." He climbed back into the wagon and didn't even offer to help when Grace followed suit.

She said nothing, and Alex dared not look back at her for fear of giving in to his emotions. He told himself it was only the grief of the moment that made him even consider kissing her, but in his heart, he knew better.

"I have a few blanket pins. Would that help?" Grace asked almost too softly to be heard.

Alex nodded. "It would. I can bring them back after . . . after we bury him."

Grace maneuvered behind him. Alex heard her open the lid to a jar, and he turned. They were so close—just inches apart. He drew in a sharp breath when her hand touched his.

"Here. I have four. That should allow you to put two down the length and one each for the foot and head."

He nodded and swallowed hard. He wanted nothing as much

as he wanted to feel her in his arms again. Forcing himself to turn aside and focus on finishing the job, Alex chided himself for letting his sadness cause him to think foolish thoughts.

Paying no attention to Grace, he secured the blanket around Gabriel and had just finished with the last pin when Sam poked his head into the wagon.

"Got the horses and borrowed some rope."

"Rope?" Grace asked.

"To tie the body to his horse," Alex said. Then with a grunt, he hoisted Gabriel over his shoulder and walked in a crouch to the back of the wagon. With great care, he handed the body down to Sam.

Sam took the blanket-wrapped Gabriel and headed toward the horses while Alex jumped to the ground. He stood with his back to the wagon, battling his thoughts.

"Where will you take him?" Grace asked from the wagon.

"Home."

She looked beyond him toward the horizon. "Where is that?"

"The mountains. He has a cabin there. He told me once that if he could, he'd never leave it. Now I guess he never has to leave again."

They arrived at the cabin just before the last remnants of the sun faded from the sky. Tasting the threat of snow in the air, they agreed to light lanterns and get on with the burial. If a storm hit in the night, at least the deed would be taken care of.

The ground, however, proved hard, nearly too hard to carve out a grave. Alex and Sam labored for nearly an hour to make a hole deep enough to bury Gabriel without fear of animals digging him back up.

It had been Alex's plan to remove not only the blanket pins but the blanket as well, in order to return them all to Grace, but instead he took only the pins. They placed Gabriel's stiff body in the ground, still wrapped.

"I can buy her another blanket," Alex said, noting Sam's questioning look. "This one's pretty worn anyway."

In truth, Alex had no desire to look upon Gabriel's face again. He felt such confusion and grief and no way to express it. If they'd been back at the Nez Perce village, the women would have wailed in mourning whether they knew Gabriel or not. Tears and wailing weren't for men, yet that was exactly what Alex felt like doing.

Sam went to the small cabin and brought back several items—trinkets and pieces of clothing that Alex knew Gabriel had kept because they belonged to his wives. Carefully, Sam placed them in the grave in Nez Perce tradition.

With that accomplished, the two men shoveled dirt over the body. Next they collected as many large rocks as possible to position atop the grave. When that task was complete, Alex took off the fur cap he'd donned once they'd reached the colder air of the mountains. He stood at the foot of the grave, looking down. The only light came from the bright moon overhead and the two lanterns they'd lit.

"I suppose someone should pray or read some Scripture," he muttered. "It's not like it'll do any good now, but Gabe would have wanted it that way."

Sam went back to the cabin and returned with a Bible. He handed it to Alex with a shrug. "I can speak your language, but my reading isn't as good."

Alex didn't say anything, although he knew Sam could read and write English nearly as well as he could. Apparently Sam thought it necessary for Alex to handle the final words.

Alex opened the Bible to the sixth chapter of Romans. He knew this book to be Gabriel's favorite, and the verses he chose were among those he had often heard Gabriel recite.

"'For if we have been planted together in the likeness of his death, we shall be also in the likeness of his resurrection: Knowing this, that our old man is crucified with him, that the body of sin might be destroyed, that henceforth we should not serve sin. For he that is dead is freed from sin.'" Alex paused to wipe the tears that blurred his vision. "'Now if we be dead with Christ, we believe that we shall also live with him: Knowing that Christ being raised from the dead dieth no more; death hath no more dominion over him. For in that he died, he died unto sin once: but in that he liveth, he liveth unto God. Likewise reckon ye also yourselves to be dead indeed unto sin, but alive unto God through Jesus Christ our Lord.'"

He closed the Bible and forced a prayer. His first in a long, long while. "Gabriel loved you, Lord, and now I would imagine he's in a better place. I wish he could have stayed with us a while longer, but thank You for the time we had. Amen."

"Amen," Sam echoed.

Chapter 10

"Grace says it's important to eat, so I thought I'd bring you this." Hope offered John Sager a plate of roasted venison and potatoes.

Earlier Hope and Narcissa Whitman had helped him sit up in bed. They had propped him up with pillows and encouraged him to drink one of Dr. Whitman's concoctions. Nearly an hour later, John's color did look better. Perhaps the doctor wasn't completely without abilities.

John gave her a weak smile. "That's mighty nice of you. I can't think of anyone's company I'd rather have."

Hope settled the food on his lap and then pulled up a chair. "You look like you feel better."

"I do." He picked up the fork and speared a piece of meat. "But I don't have any strength. Fact is, it's hard just to do this." He lifted the meat to his mouth.

"I could feed it to you," Hope offered.

John scowled. "I'm not helpless. Just tired."

Hope bit her lower lip. She hadn't meant to offend him. Her experience with men other than her father had been limited to flirtations and teasing chatter. John Sager made her want more than that.

For a few minutes, John ate and Hope simply sat at his side. She knew he cared for her, but she couldn't help but wonder if he felt the same deep yearning for something more. It was impossible to express what that something more was, but Hope knew that she wanted to spend every waking moment near John.

"You're looking all thoughtful," he said. "I hope you aren't mad at me. I didn't mean to snap at you."

Hope smiled. "I could never be mad at you, Johnny."

He grinned. "I'll bet after a few years of knowing me, you'll have plenty of chances to be mad at me."

She shook her head. "I don't ever want to be mad at you. I just want to always be with you."

The seriousness of her tone apparently hit a nerve with John, because he put down his fork and extended his hand to her. "I want to always be with you too."

Hope quivered and her heart skipped a beat. Was he proposing they marry? After all, they could hardly spend their lives together if they didn't marry. Still, she couldn't bring herself to ask if that was his intention.

"When I'm well enough to leave this bed," John said with a sigh, "I'm gonna kiss you."

Hope lowered her gaze as a wave of embarrassment washed over her. "And I'm going to let you," she barely whispered.

"My pa always told me that when I found the right woman, nothing else would be quite as important. I feel that way right now, Hope."

She forced herself to meet his gaze. "I've never felt this way about anyone but you, John. It scares me to pieces."

His expression changed to confusion. "Scares you?"

She nodded ever so slightly. "I can't help it. I feel all jumbled up inside. I think about you all the time, and when I'm with you, I'm already thinking about when I can see you again."

"But that's no reason to get scared."

"That's not what scares me." She shrugged, trying to think of how to explain her heart. "I get scared because . . . well . . . what if something happens?"

"Happens?"

"Yes. To separate us. What if Grace decides we need to go to Oregon City? Or what if I get sick and die?"

"You can't be frettin' over something that hasn't even happened," John replied and picked up his fork again. "Ma used to tell the girls that all the time. Must be something girls do."

"I suppose so, but maybe we can't help it. Maybe that's just the way God made us."

"Maybe so." He stabbed a piece of potato and raised it to his lips. He glanced over for just a moment and winked. "I can't say I mind at all how God made you, so you fret if you want, and I'll be brave for the both of us. Deal?"

Hope couldn't help but love him all the more. "Deal."

After a restless night in Gabriel's cabin, Alex slipped out of bed and opened the cabin door. It had snowed in the night, and across the yard he could see the white blanket covering the mounded dirt where Gabriel had been laid to rest.

"Will you go back to the mission now?" Sam asked.

Alex turned to find Sam gathering his things. Alex shook his head. "I don't want to go back there just yet. I need some time to think and . . . mourn. Let's go to your village."

Sam nodded. "Sarah will be glad to see you. The children too."

They rode the miles to where Sam's band of Nez Perce had made winter camp, taking Gabriel's horse with them. Alex suggested Sam keep it for when they went out to set traps and retrieve their kill. The rest of Gabriel's belongings, not that there were many, were left at the cabin. The cabin would be useful when trapping season came, and Alex knew Gabriel would want them to stay there and think of him.

When they reached the Nez Perce settlement, Alex felt a strange sense of relief. Whether it was from the tension between the Cayuse and whites or the heavy gray clouds that had moved in to threaten stormy weather, he didn't know. He just knew that he was glad to be done with the day and hoped for nothing more than a hot meal and a warm bed. Hopefully he'd sleep better tonight than he had last night.

Sarah welcomed him just as Sam had assured. She was due to give Sam another child in a little over a month, but she was happy to have them despite what Alex knew would be extra work.

Sarah led them into their lodge and settled them by the fire. She went to get them both food and quickly returned with a wood platter of smoked fish and potatoes with wild onion.

"Where are your children?" Alex asked.

"Their grandfather took them on a walk. They were afraid when the Cayuse chiefs arrived." With her swollen abdomen, Sarah maneuvered slowly to bring them flatbread.

"The Cayuse are here?" Sam and Alex asked in unison.

Sarah's glance moved from Sam's face to Alex's and then back to her husband. She nodded. "They came yesterday. They wanted to talk to the chiefs here about attacking the mission."

"We want to talk to them as well," Sam said. "We have to find a way to stop them from making war."

"They want our chiefs to join them in getting rid of the whites, but I know our people are not willing."

"That's good. Maybe we can parley with them and show the benefits of remaining peaceful," Alex said, getting to his feet.

Sam jumped up and put a hand on Alex's arm. "Let me go request it of the chiefs. You are my brother, but you're still a white Indian." He grinned. "And since they're talking about killing whites, it's probably better if I do the asking."

Alex realized Sam was right. "Very well." He sat back down on the ground and took up a piece of bread. He looked up at Sarah to find her smiling. Alex returned her smile despite his anxiety. "Never thought of myself as a white Indian."

Sam was gone for some time, and when he returned, his father and children accompanied him.

"Alex!" Esther Sings at Dawn shouted and threw herself into Alex's open arms. Two-year-old Joseph Fire on the Mountain followed suit and forced his way into the embrace. Alex could only laugh and hug them close. It was good medicine and helped lift his spirits.

"Children, come," Sarah called from the far end of the lodge. Even great with child, she managed to lower herself to the matting gracefully. "Your father and grandfather must speak with Alex."

They reluctantly left Alex's embrace but didn't protest their mother's will. Sam and his father came to the fire as Alex got to his feet.

"You are good for my eyes to see," Sam's father said in Nez Perce. He put his hand on Alex's forearm.

Alex turned his arm just enough to take hold of the older man's forearm in return. "It is good to be with you again, Jacob Night Walker."

"My son tells me you have asked to speak to the Cayuse chiefs."

Alex nodded. "Will they hear us?"

"The chiefs have agreed we may join them," Sam said. "We can go now, but let my father speak first. He will ask if we might be allowed to speak our piece."

"I'm certain they will agree," Jacob added.

"I'll do as you say." Alex felt only a modicum of relief. There was no way to know if what he and Sam might say would sway the Cayuse to back down and remain peaceful.

They made their way to the lodge where the chiefs were holding council. Alex let Sam and his father lead the way, but he kept his eyes open for any sign of aggressive behavior on the part of the Cayuse.

Once they were seated, greetings were exchanged, and Jacob was called up to speak. He nodded but asked that his son and Alex be allowed to share his heart.

The chiefs discussed it for a moment, then turned to Jacob. "Will they pledge to speak only truth?" one of the men asked.

Jacob nodded. "They will." He looked to Sam and Alex. Both men nodded.

The chief nodded in return. "Then let us hear your words."

With that established, Sam began to speak. "We are grieved that so many of our brothers have died because of measles. We are sad too that our Cayuse brothers seek to wage war against the Boston men. We have heavy hearts that such a thing should be done. The Boston men are strong and will send many soldiers here if we fail to keep the peace."

"We will kill the soldiers as well," Telokite declared.

"And the Boston men will send more soldiers. There are so many more of them than there are of the Cayuse."

"That is why we need our Nez Perce brothers to fight with us."

"But we have no grievance against them," a Nez Perce chief stated firmly. "I have told my brother this. The King's men have always traded with us and buy our furs. The Boston men have traded with us as well."

"They have given us great sickness too. Are not some in your camp dying also?" The Nez Perce chiefs nodded, and Telokite continued. "Our grievance is shared. The white man will see us dead if we do not kill them first." The other Cayuse nodded in agreement.

Alex could see this would not easily be resolved. "The Cayuse and Nez Perce can learn to live in peace with the Boston men," he said softly. He didn't want any of the men there to think he was challenging their authority. "You know I am white, but I am also a brother to the Nez Perce. I want peace with the Cayuse. I have done good by you and have never sought to harm you. Would you kill me too?"

The chiefs looked at Alex in silence, and then Telokite spoke. "You have been a good brother to us. I would not wish you to die. I do not wish all white men to die, but I don't see that they will leave our land unless we force them to do so." The other Cayuse nodded.

The conversation went on for nearly an hour with Alex pleading the case for peace and Sam and Jacob joining in with their own thoughts on the matter. When Alex found he was merely repeating himself, he decided he had said all that he could say. It was time to leave the matter in the hands of the chiefs.

He sat in silence while the men continued to discuss the situation. To his own surprise, he found himself praying that God would open their hearts and minds to see that not all white men were evil, just as not all Indians were good.

Finally, Telokite held up his hand. "We have heard your counsel. You are right to say that some of the Boston men have been good to us. In our pain and loss, we had forgotten this. We will not make war."

Alex let go a heavy breath. Telokite had always been a man of his word. The other Cayuse would listen to him. Dr. Whitman and the people at the mission would be safe. His relief was such that he hardly heard anything else. They shared food and drink before finally retreating to their individual lodges for sleep. Alex had never felt so weary in all of his life. It had been a very long day.

"You spoke well, Alex," Jacob said. "You will sleep with ease tonight."

"Thank you, my friend. Sleep is what I desire most."

He thought for a moment of Grace and her sisters and knew for the first time in weeks that they would be safe. Maybe now he could remain here with the Nez Perce or even return to the cabin he'd often shared with Gabriel. Either place would be better than returning to Whitman's.

Here he had no risk of losing his heart.

Chapter
11

For days Grace found herself busy with the sick and dying and did her best not to think of Alex. Sharing the loss of Gabriel had connected her to Alex in a way that she couldn't understand. Watching him leave had been hard, but not as hard as wondering if he'd ever return.

Still, there was plenty to do, and Grace plunged into the tasks at hand, hoping—praying—that she could help someone. Losing Gabriel had made her question her abilities as a healer, especially in light of Whitman's accusations.

However, Whitman wasn't doing any better with his patients. The Osborn baby had passed on, as well as her older sister, leaving Margaret Osborn inconsolable. The poor woman could do little but sob.

Mrs. Whitman had shown Silvijane Osborn's body to one of the Cayuse chiefs as proof that white children were dying along with the Cayuse. Word had spread throughout the camp that the Indian had only laughed. Rather than see the truth, he had hoped that the rest of the white children might also die.

Of course, that was just the opinion of one angry man. Grace had learned that he too had lost a child to the measles, and others were still sick. Many Indians had died that week, and everyone at the mission had tried to offer their condolences and help in whatever way possible. Dr. Whitman even encouraged the Cayuse to bury their dead in the little cemetery near the mission. He also graciously conducted services for the mass funerals.

Grace wondered if he thought this would bring reconciliation between him and the Cayuse. For now, it seemed that no one was of a mind to argue or accuse, and the lull was much needed. A great deal of healing needed to go on in both camps.

From time to time, Grace found herself gazing across the yard and pond to where the tule mat lodges stood. She had wanted to go and offer her healing skills, but Alex said it was too dangerous, and something in her spirit told her he was right. Still, the Cayuse were no different than the whites. They needed someone to care for their needs. Seeing them up close and experiencing their lifestyle had made Grace more compassionate toward them.

"I'm going to the mission house," Hope said, coming into the room where Grace was preparing some of her tonics. "John is feeling much better and has started joining the others in the sitting room and kitchen. I want to go keep him company."

"Have you taken care of your other chores?" Grace asked.

Hope nodded. "I washed and hung the laundry. I was up at five." She was all smiles, as if the work had been nothing but a passing inconvenience. "After lunch, I'm going to peel potatoes in the kitchen and help prepare the evening meal. We're having venison stew and cornbread. John loves venison stew."

Grace could only smile. It was clear that her sister was in love with John Sager. And from what Grace had heard from the other women, John returned Hope's interest.

"They're the perfect age to marry," Harriet had whispered in Grace's ear a few nights earlier.

Grace had a feeling that when Uncle Edward came for them, Hope would remain at the mission. "Be sure to take your shawl. There's a chill in the air."

Hope nodded and held up an old brown shawl. "I already thought of it." She wrapped it around her shoulders and all but danced from the room.

Grace turned her attention back to grinding herbs. She wondered what they would do if Uncle Edward didn't return to Oregon City. He might have died on his trip. She'd heard several of the men discussing the fact that the Indians were growing more aggressive all over Oregon Country. What if they'd attacked some of the western settlements and no one had yet received word? Worse still, what if he no longer wanted them to join him? He might have married and would not want to share his home now that he had a new wife.

Not only that, but once Grace and her sisters arrived in Oregon City, what would they do to support themselves? They still had some of the money from the sale of the farm. Grace had managed to hide about seventy dollars from the Right Reverend in the lining of her carpetbag. It would be more than enough to start, but it wouldn't last long no matter how careful she was. She would need some sort of employment. But what? There were such great limitations for women. Grace knew she wasn't smart enough or book-learned enough to teach. She could sew and cook, even keep house if necessary, but she doubted many people in Oregon City needed a maid. Healing was her gift, but no doubt there would already be doctors in place, and they would probably resent a woman coming in with her herbs and remedies. So what could she do? How would she take care of Hope and Mercy as she had promised their mother? There were just so many unanswered questions.

A knock sounded on the threshold behind her. Grace looked

up from her place by the fire to find Andy Rogers at the door with a letter in his hand.

"Andy, come in. I'm just mixing some tonics."

"An Indian runner came from your friend's mission. Said it was important that you get this letter right away."

Grace frowned and put aside her work. She got to her feet and dusted off her apron. "I hope nothing bad has happened." She crossed the room and took the letter from Andy. Opening it, she scanned the page quickly. "Eletta is desperately sick. Mr. Browning asks that I come right away." She looked up at Andy. "Is there someone who can take me?"

He shrugged and gave her a smile. "I'd offer to take you myself, but I'm committed to help Dr. Whitman. We're preparing to kill one of the steers, and butchering will take some time. I'd ask Dr. Whitman to excuse me from it, but he left early this morning to go to Chief Stickus on the Umatilla River to the south."

Grace nodded. She had heard that Dr. Whitman had gone with Reverend Spaulding to help the sick in that village. Earlier in the week, the reverend had come from his mission in Lapwai over one hundred miles away to bring his daughter Eliza to attend the Whitmans' school. Harriet pointed out that peace between the Indians must have been in the works, or he never would have allowed his daughter to stay at the mission. Further support of this was the arrival of one of the Catholic bishops who was well known to have a good rapport with the local Indians. He assured the mission folks that while there were tensions over so much death and sickness, he believed cooler heads would prevail. Even so, no one was willing to completely relax their guard.

"Perhaps the runner could take me." She didn't like the idea of traveling so far with a stranger, but if there was no other choice, it was better than trying to find her way alone.

"No, he's gone to Umatilla to take a message to the doctor."

"Oh."

Andy frowned. "That trapper friend of yours has returned. Maybe he could help you."

She gasped. "Alex? He's back?" Her pulse quickened. Since the death of Gabriel, she'd been able to think of little more than how much the loss had hurt Alex. She had hoped against hope he might return.

"He arrived about an hour ago. He and Sam Two Moons are at the gristmill."

Grace nodded and stuffed the letter in her pocket. "I must go and find out if they can take me to the Brownings." She didn't wait for Andy's response but maneuvered past him and down the hall. She grabbed her shawl from a peg near the door and pulled it on as she crossed the yard.

She found Alex and Sam at the mill just as Andy had said. The mill itself was little more than an exposed housing for the forty-inch grinding stones and a flume coming from the pond. Once there had been an actual building, but fire had destroyed it, and this was what had been rebuilt. Grace had heard great plans for a large millhouse and granary, but additions to the mission house had taken precedence.

Alex and Sam were talking to the miller, while several Cayuse congregated to inspect a bag of grain. The miller appeared to be grinding grain for the Indians, another good sign as far as Grace was concerned. So long as the Cayuse saw how useful Dr. Whitman's people could be to them, they might forget the problems that had been brought by the same.

Alex spotted her as she approached and gave her a nod. "Come join us," he urged.

"Good day, gentlemen." She looked at each of the men and then turned her attention back to Alex. "Might I have a word? With Sam too?"

The men nodded and moved away from the gathering. Grace stopped near the edge of the pond. "My friend Eletta Browning is sick. You must have met them."

"Are they the ones who took a mission to the northeast of here?"

She nodded. "Mr. Browning sent a runner with a letter asking me to come. Could you take me?" She took the missive from her pocket and handed it to Alex.

Alex looked at it. "It's quite a distance. And what about your sisters?"

Grace hadn't really thought of them. "Well, Mercy is still too weak to travel far, and Hope is in love, so I doubt she'd be willing to leave."

Sam smiled. "In love? Who with?"

"John Sager. He's recovering from the measles, and Hope helped nurse him back to health. Hope would sit by his bed and read to him. She said he told her that was better than reading for himself." Grace smiled. "I thought her too young to do much more than flirt, but it would seem she's lost her heart to him."

"Love knows no age," Sam replied.

Grace nodded and looked back to Alex. "I had thought to ask the Indian runner to take me but learned he was off to Umatilla to take a message to Dr. Whitman."

Alex considered the matter for a moment. "I suppose we can take you. Do you have a horse?"

Grace nodded. "Yes. He belonged to the Right Reverend and now belongs to me."

"Very well. Point him out, and Sam and I will retrieve him. I presume you have a saddle for him."

"I do." Grace knew that Sam and Alex rode bareback. "It's in the wagon."

Alex looked to Sam. "Sorry, I didn't mean to speak on your behalf. Is this all right with you?"

Sam smiled. "Sure. It's an easy distance from my village."

"Well, get your things, Grace, and let someone know your plans," Alex said, his attention focused somewhere behind her.

Grace turned to see that even more Cayuse had arrived at the gristmill. She looked at Alex to ascertain if something was wrong, but it was Sam who spoke.

"Walter is grinding wheat for them. He'll be busy with that for the next couple days."

"I had heard that," she admitted. "Perhaps that will make the Cayuse feel more kindly toward the mission folks."

Alex nodded. "The chiefs have promised to be at peace. We spoke to them when we were in Sam's village. I'm hopeful the tensions will ease."

Grace felt a chill rush over her and clutched her shawl tighter. "Perhaps it's not safe to leave the girls here. Maybe I should hitch the wagon and make them come too."

"Do what you like," Alex said, "but it will slow you down considerably, and frankly . . ." He looked at Sam and fell silent.

"I think what Alex is trying to say," Sam continued, "is that if the Cayuse decide to war, they won't be any safer away from the mission than in it."

Taking all of this in, Grace determined that there was little she could do. She would let the girls decide if they wanted to go with her. Grace could ask to borrow a horse for Hope, and Mercy was so small that she could easily ride double with someone.

"I'll go talk to the girls and then meet you both at the emigrant house in twenty minutes." Grace started to leave but then stopped. "The reverend's horse—my horse is the black with four white socks and a blaze on his face."

She hurried away from the men with a growing sense of worry for her friend. Eletta hadn't shown a very strong constitution on the journey west, and Grace feared that she would succumb to whatever ailed her before they could reach the Browning mission. She murmured a prayer that they wouldn't be too late and that she would know exactly how to help.

Throughout her teen years, Grace hadn't allowed herself close friends. She wanted to be single-minded in regard to learning to heal. Hope had thought her silly and reveled in the company of whoever treated her kindly. Mercy had been the same way. Grace had been far more selective, and the thought of possibly losing her only friend made her all the more determined to reach Eletta quickly.

Grace found Hope sitting next to John in the kitchen. She was busy peeling potatoes, while John was winding twine and exchanging hushed conversation with Hope. She giggled and glanced up to see Grace. When Grace motioned for Hope to follow her from the room, she could see her sister's reluctance and displeasure.

"What do you want?" Hope asked, following her outside.

"I have to go to Eletta. She's sick, and Alex and Sam Two Moons have agreed to take me. I wanted to see if you and Mercy want to go with me. I didn't want you to be afraid staying here without me."

Hope laughed. "I'm not afraid. What is there to fear?"

"Well, the Cayuse for one."

"There are more than enough men here if they should try something. Besides, Mrs. Whitman said we're killing a steer on Monday, and the meat will benefit the Cayuse as well as us, so they won't cause too much trouble."

"And you truly aren't worried about staying here without me?"

Hope shook her head. "I'm not. And I figure Mercy won't be afraid either. I'll watch over her and make sure she continues to take her vinegar and the other herbs you've been giving her."

"I planned to see if she wanted to go with us. I don't want either of you to feel I've deserted you."

"Don't worry about it," Hope said. "Just go, and I'll tell Mercy what's happened. You know she's still too weak to be doing much. You said so yourself."

Grace knew it was true and that she had been foolish to think of dragging Mercy along on a seventy-five-mile trip. "Very well. But I'll find her and say good-bye. I want her to know we've discussed the matter."

"If that's all, I need to get back to the potatoes."

"And John?" Grace asked with a smile.

Hope laughed. "Of course. He read some of his stories to me. He's a wonderful writer. Wouldn't it be amazing if his stories were published?"

"Yes. It would be." Grace watched Hope leave. There was no doubt that her sister was happier than Grace had ever seen her. "I love you, Hope."

Her sister turned quickly and smiled. "And I love . . ." She fell silent and laughed again before hurrying back inside.

Mercy was in the emigrant house when Grace came in to pack up her things. She was resting, just as Grace had instructed her to do every afternoon. Quickly, Grace explained her plans.

"I had thought to take you along, but after speaking to Hope, I think it's better if you stay here. I don't want to do anything to compromise your recovery."

"I don't think I should like to be back on the road so soon," Mercy said, stroking one of her long pigtails. "I'll be just fine staying here. Mr. Saunders is going to reopen the school on Monday, and I don't want to miss class." She yawned and gave a little stretch. "You will be careful, won't you?"

Grace couldn't help but smile. She knelt beside Mercy and pulled her into her arms. "Of course I will, you ninny. And you do likewise." She kissed Mercy's forehead. "I love you."

Mercy hugged her tight. "I love you, Grace. Whenever I

miss Mama, I think about how she asked you to take care of us and how much she loved all of us." She let go and eased back to the pillow. She looked sad. "You won't be gone too long, will you?"

Grace shook her head and got to her feet. "No longer than absolutely necessary. It will take us a couple of days to get there, and then I will have to see what needs to be done. The letter didn't explain what type of sickness Eletta has, but I promise I will come back to you and Hope as soon as everyone is settled and on the mend. I wouldn't think it will take more than a week or two. I should be back in plenty of time for Christmas."

Alex watched as Grace exited the house with her carpetbag and bedroll. She had changed clothes and wore a wide-brimmed bonnet and wool coat. The coat was a practical and wise choice given the heavy clouds rolling in.

Taking her bedroll, Alex tied it onto the back of her Spanish saddle. "I hope you don't mind, but I had Sam bring along your tent. We saw it in the wagon, and given the threat of bad weather, it might be wise."

"I'm glad you thought of it," Grace replied as she slung the handles of her carpetbag over the saddle horn. "The girls are staying here as I presumed they would." She stepped back and frowned. "Ah, I hadn't thought about mounting."

"I wondered if you'd considered it wasn't a sidesaddle," Alex said, looking skeptical.

"I did remember that. That's why I'm wearing such a full skirt." She shrugged. "I guess you'll have to help me."

Alex stretched his hands forward. "Step onto my hand while you hold on to the horn. I'll raise you up, and you can throw your leg over the back of the horse and settle onto the saddle."

Grace frowned. "You make it sound so easy."

He laughed and bent lower so that she wouldn't have to lift her leg very high. As she followed his instructions, Alex noted the heavy boots she wore rather than the shoes he'd seen her in earlier. It was nice to see a woman who was sensible. With little effort, he raised her to the saddle and held her foot until she had arranged her skirts and eased into the seat.

"Ready?" he asked.

"I think so." She looked down at her bags and her feet firmly in the stirrups. "Yes," she replied. "I'm ready."

They headed north, making good time before the land became more difficult to navigate. Grace managed well enough and never complained. Alex remembered when she'd first arrived at the mission. He had thought her no different than so many of the other white women who'd passed through the area. Even the women at the mission, although hearty, were still very much creatures of the eastern cities and states where they had grown up. He had often heard them lament the conveniences they'd left behind. But Grace seemed suited to this life.

He smiled to himself, remembering her fear of Sam. Now she seemed almost comfortable with the Nez Perce and Cayuse. Of course, he had noted her uneasiness earlier in the day with the large number of Cayuse braves at the gristmill, but he couldn't fault her for what he felt himself. Even though Telokite had given his word, Alex knew Joe Lewis was still actively stirring up trouble. Not only that, but Telokite had three very sick children. If they died, there was no telling what might happen. But this Alex kept to himself.

They made camp that night just before dark. The tent was barely staked out before the first drops of rain began to fall. Despite his heavy coat, the icy cold chilled Alex to the bone, making him wonder if Grace was warm enough. Alex had told

Grace that he and Sam would sleep outside, but with the weather growing steadily worse, he knew he'd have to broach the subject of them all sharing the tent for the night. He couldn't help but wonder how she would take it.

The wind picked up, and Grace held fast to her wide-brimmed bonnet despite the fact that the ties remained securely fixed under her chin. "You can't sleep out here tonight," she said, raising her voice to be heard above the wind.

Alex nodded, grateful that she'd taken the difficulty out of the matter. "Go ahead and get inside. Sam and I will make sure the horses are secured."

It didn't take but a minute to check on the horses. The trio paid little attention to the elements and instead focused on seeking out what grass could be had. Alex and Sam quickly made their way back to the tent. Once inside the shelter, Alex tied the flaps as tight as possible and then put his back to the opening, hoping to further block out the wind. It was a tight fit with all three of them inside, but it would suffice.

"I'm glad you decided to share the tent," Grace said, her teeth chattering. "I wouldn't have rested a bit knowing you were out in the storm."

Sam shrugged. "It would not be the first time." He unrolled a buffalo hide and smiled. "This would keep me plenty warm."

Alex chuckled and unrolled a similar hide. "We've slept outside in our share of storms. But I will say this is preferable."

The wind rocked the tent, making Alex worry that they might not have staked it as securely as needed. The howling noise was enough to put them all on edge.

Sam broke out some dried fish for their supper while Grace produced a fine loaf of bread.

Alex nodded in approval. "I wondered if you had thought of packing food."

Grace shrugged. "I brought what I could. I have a dozen or so biscuits, a jar of jam, and some cookies. I wasn't sure whether or not you planned to shoot game along the way."

"I'm sure we'll find a rabbit or two," Alex said, smiling. He paused for a moment, then asked, "What kind of cookies?"

Grace laughed and produced four cookies from her bag. She handed two to each man. "Oatmeal. Dr. Whitman laid in a large supply of oats for the winter. Sugar was a little harder to come by. Apparently when he was at Fort Nez Perce he was told that the Hudson's Bay Company supplies coming in from the Sandwich Islands had been delayed. I was stunned to learn that ships regularly travel back and forth from the islands to Oregon Country. There are even natives who've come to work for the company."

Alex chuckled. "Yes, I've met several. They're interesting folks, similar to the Indians in appearance yet very different. They tell wonderful stories about their lives in the Pacific."

"Where do you come from, Alex?" Grace asked, taking him completely off guard.

"Ontario."

She shook her head. "But aren't you American? Where did you live before Canada?"

He swallowed hard. "New Orleans."

She nodded. "I lived just outside of St. Louis, so we shared the Mississippi."

"Indeed."

"What about you, Sam? Have you always lived in this area?"

"Yes." Sam stretched out on his side. "We move when we need to follow the animals or the seasons, but we are never far from here. This land will always be home to the Niimíipuu."

"Such an interesting language. I'd very much like to learn more, but I've never had much of a head for such things. My Da spoke Gaelic, and for a time I did as well. I'm afraid, however, that after he died I didn't use it all that much, and I've forgotten a great deal."

Alex hoped Sam's life and people would captivate Grace's attention and keep her from asking too much about his own life. The hope was short-lived.

"I know that Sam was led to the Lord's salvation at the Catholic mission, but what about you, Alex?"

He tried not to sound uneasy. "My mother. She taught us to read the Bible and how to pray." The memory was only a vague recollection, but it still remained sweet.

"And what of your father?"

"He was involved with brokering cotton, but he too feared God. There were times when he told me that he felt he was at war with God, but never did he not believe in Him."

"And what of you?" Grace asked. Her eyes met his and seemed to burn into his soul.

"I suppose if I'm honest, I'd say we've called a truce to the war between us." In losing Gabriel, Alex had become only too aware of how distant God seemed.

Grace gave him a smile. "Making peace with God is much better than making war. I know this for myself. There have been times of anger and frustration when I was certain God had forsaken me."

Alex stiffened. Her words matched those in his heart. If he wasn't careful, he'd soon be babbling all the details of his sorry past. Taking a cue from Sam, he stretched out and wrapped up in his fur.

"It's probably best if we get some sleep. We'll need to start early tomorrow." The wind had died down, and only the steady beat of rain could be heard.

He watched as Grace maneuvered into her own blanket and then put out the lantern. Relief washed over him as he realized she wasn't going to say anything more. Not that she needed to speak to make him uncomfortable. He was only too aware of her nearness. He could hear her breathing, smell the faded scent of herbs. She always smelled of herbs.

Rolling to his other side and pressing as far into the canvas of the tent as he could, Alex felt his torment acutely. The storm outside wasn't the only one he had to endure that night. And unlike the rain, he couldn't escape this deluge.

Chapter 12

At Grace's insistence they started early and pushed through until dark. By late that day they had arrived at the Browning mission, and Grace was stunned to see that it was hardly more than a tiny cabin and poorly constructed pen for their animals. There appeared to be a stand of trees and a creek running behind the house, but other than the wagon they'd brought west, that was all.

Alex and Sam cared for the horses while Grace went to the cabin. The door opened to reveal a haggard Isaac. "I wasn't sure if you would come."

"Of course I came. You have Alex and Sam Two Moons to thank for that." She motioned over her shoulder. "They're taking care of our horses. Now tell me what's happened."

Isaac ushered her into the tiny cabin and pointed to the corner where Eletta slept on a narrow bed. Grace could hear her ragged breathing. "She's maybe a little better. I'm no judge, but it seems she isn't coughing as much."

Grace motioned to a chair. "Would you bring that? Oh, and a light." She took off her heavy coat and cast it aside but kept her carpetbag close at hand. Once Isaac brought the chair, she pulled it close to the bed and sat down. She put the carpetbag at her feet, then reached out to feel Eletta's head. She was a little warm. No doubt a low fever. Grace felt for her pulse. It was strong and even. Perhaps the worst had come and gone.

The disturbance brought Eletta awake. "Grace?" The single word sent her into a coughing fit.

Isaac brought a lamp and placed it beside the bed on a crude stand. Grace glanced around. "Isaac, do you have hot water?" She'd never used his first name before, but the setting seemed to beg familiarity.

He stepped toward the fireplace. "I do."

"Please put some in a cup and bring it here." She looked at Eletta. "I'll make you something that will calm that cough."

"I'm . . . so . . . afraid," Eletta sputtered. She fell silent except for the terrible cough.

"Hush now. I'll soon have you to rights." Isaac brought the water to Grace. She opened her carpetbag and located a bottle of tonic. "This is an old remedy from my grandmother. The taste isn't all that pleasant, but it works wonders. If you have any honey, it would help considerably."

"We have some," Isaac replied. He moved to the opposite side of the room, which couldn't have been more than ten feet away.

Alex and Sam entered the house. Neither man said a word but simply exchanged nods with Isaac.

Isaac brought the honey to Grace, but his gaze never left Eletta. "She's been sick for about three weeks. It started not long after we got here."

Grace helped Eletta drink the concoction. "How did the sickness begin?"

"It started with the sniffles, and then the cough came. I've done what I could for her, but I know it's not been enough. I wanted to send for you sooner, but no one could take the message. Even then, I hated to bother you."

"I'm glad you did."

Eletta suffered through another bout of coughing, this one a little worse than the last. Grace prayed her tonic would soon help Eletta rest and the cough to abate.

"So what do you think it is?" Alex asked softly. He had come to stand beside Grace, and when she looked at him, she could tell he understood the gravity.

"I'm not entirely sure. Could be influenza or whooping cough."

Eletta began coughing so hard that Grace feared she might vomit.

"Sam," Grace said, looking over her shoulder, "would you bring more water? We need to fill every pot and get it boiling."

Sam nodded and glanced around the room. "Do you have a bucket?"

"There are two just outside the door," Isaac replied. "Creek's behind the cabin."

Grace was grateful Sam needed no further instruction. Time was of the essence. "I'm going to put some herbs in the pots. As the water boils, the steam will help her breathe easier." At least she prayed it would.

Grace reached into her bag and pulled out a long wooden tube. This stethoscope had been modeled after one that a physician in St. Louis carried. Her mother hadn't the money to afford a professional device, so Da had made it for her out of cedarwood after getting the doctor to allow him to look over the piece. It worked perfectly.

"Eletta, I'm going to listen to your lungs. Isaac, I need you to help her sit up so I can put this stethoscope on her back. It's the best way to hear the function of the lungs."

Isaac immediately moved to help his wife.

"Is there anything I can do to help?" Alex asked.

Grace gave him a grateful look. "Build up the fire, and when Sam gets back, help him get the water on."

Alex nodded and went to work as Grace continued her examination. Listening to Eletta's lungs proved Grace's suspicions. No matter how the sickness had started, Eletta now had a great deal of congestion in her lungs. They would need to work fast to keep her from succumbing.

"I never should have brought her west," Isaac said.

Grace put aside her stethoscope. "Let's put her back down."

Eletta began coughing again.

"I'm so sorry, Eletta. If we'd stayed in the east, there would have been doctors and hospitals," Isaac murmured. "We wouldn't have gone three weeks in the wild without help."

Grace knew there would never be any words adequate enough to ease his guilt, but she wanted to try. "There's no point in worrying about what should or shouldn't have been done. Doctors in the east might have been unable to keep this from growing worse. Often that is the case. Now, I'm going to mix some additional medicine for her." Grace looked at Eletta. The coughing was easing up.

Throughout the next twenty-four hours, Grace stayed at Eletta's side. The men suggested she rest, but her fear of losing Eletta wouldn't allow for it. It wasn't until Eletta's fever subsided and her breathing came easier that Grace agreed to take a few minutes to stretch and get some air.

Outside, a chill wind cut Grace to the bone. She hadn't thought to don her coat since she only planned to be outside for a few minutes. She gazed heavenward and could see neither the moon nor stars for the heavy rain clouds. It had rained off and on all day, but for the moment it had ceased. Even so, the low clouds seemed to press down on her.

"Lord, I don't know what tomorrow will bring, but I pray

that you will help my friend recover. I love her so dearly. She's like another sister." Grace sighed. "This land is so beautiful. I prefer it to the cities, but I know that it's dangerous. Just help us—help me to know what to do. Please."

With another heavy sigh, Grace squared her shoulders. When she turned back to the cabin, she found Alex watching her. He was leaning against the doorjamb, just watching and waiting, and somewhere deep inside, Grace felt a sense of being cared for. That was something she'd not known in a very long time.

By the third day, Eletta showed marked improvement, and Isaac began to relax a bit. In another few days, Grace felt certain her friend would be past the worst of it.

At some point, Sam had gone out and managed to shoot a young buck. Grace put some of the meat into a stew, hoping to get some of the strong broth into Eletta. Throughout the next few hours, she checked on the concoction, sampling it from time to time.

Finally, she gave the men a nod. "The stew is ready." She drew off some of the broth into a bowl and took it to Eletta. "I know you haven't any appetite, but you must eat."

Eletta didn't argue but instead let Grace help her to sit up and then eat. "How are things at the mission?" Eletta asked. Her speaking caused the coughing to resume.

Grace waited until the attack passed before answering. "Things are still very tense because of the Cayuse. Sickness, mostly measles, has taken the lives of so many there, but worse, they believe Dr. Whitman is poisoning them."

"Poisoning them? How and why?"

"Apparently Dr. Whitman put out arsenic to poison the wolves that were coming in to steal food. Joe Lewis, a half-Indian man who often translates for the Cayuse, told them that the doctor intended the arsenic to poison the Indians." She gave Eletta another spoonful of broth. "As to why they would believe it, I can only say that they are worried and grieving. There's been so much death. I've seen so many little ones pass on."

For several long moments, neither one spoke. Grace wished with all of her heart that she could have done more for the natives. If only Dr. Whitman had been willing to work with her instead of against her. But after what happened with Gabriel, Grace didn't desire to work with the doctor at all. His interference had been the death of Gabriel. At least as far as she was concerned.

Grace pushed the matter aside and offered Eletta more soup. "On a cheerier note, Hope is in love with young John Sager. I didn't expect her to become quite so serious about him, but it appears to be true love."

Eletta smiled. "I fell in love with Isaac when I was fifteen."

"Hope will be eighteen next March, so I suppose she can hardly be considered a child. I know for certain that men do not look upon her as one, which has been of some concern to me."

"We married when I was sixteen. That's been almost ten years now." Eletta's expression became sad. "I thought things would be so different."

"I remember you saying that you didn't want to come west," Grace said in a low voice. She glanced over her shoulder, happy to see that the men were too preoccupied with eating to care about what was being said between the women. "However, if you hadn't come west, Eletta, I would never have met you and never known the joy of having a dear friend like you." Grace put the nearly empty bowl aside and took hold of Eletta's hand. "I know it's been very hard on you. I want you to know that if Uncle Edward fails to return or should prove to be dead, the girls and I will come and ease your burden. I'll even use some of our money to bring a few things that would make life easier."

Eletta sighed. "I would like that. It's so lonely here. Although I don't wish your uncle dead."

Grace smiled. "Of course you don't. Besides, I can't help but believe things will get better come spring. Sam said the Indians in this area are friendly. They might even help Isaac enlarge your cabin since they helped Mr. Spaulding build it in the first place. Perhaps you and Isaac will have a child."

"I've wanted a baby since we were first wed." Eletta paused and gave in to a spell of coughing.

"Perhaps we should stop talking for now." Grace patted her friend's hand. "It's good for you to cough up the matter closing off your lungs, but I know it causes you great pain."

"I'm all right. I feel so much better in your care and your presence. But I know you're exhausted. For my sake, I wish you would go rest."

Grace nodded. "I've been able to catch a bit of sleep here and there." She met Eletta's frown with a smile. "But don't you worry. I promise to sleep tonight."

She helped Eletta lie back, then took the bowl to the hearth. She thought of getting a bowl of stew for herself, but her state of weariness won out and she made her way to the pallet Alex had prepared for her that first night.

Isaac took out his Bible and turned up the lantern so that he could read. Alex surprised her by suggesting he read aloud. Isaac nodded, opened the Bible, and began to search. While he did this, Grace settled onto the pallet.

"I'll get you some stew," Alex offered.

"No, I just want to rest a few minutes and then I'll eat." Sitting there, leaning against the rough log wall, Grace closed her eyes and listened to the comforting words of the ninety-first Psalm.

"'He that dwelleth in the secret place of the most High shall abide under the shadow of the Almighty. I will say of the Lord, He is my refuge and my fortress: my God; in Him will I trust.'"

Those were the last words Grace remembered. There was a fleeting memory of Alex helping her lie down, but it wasn't until the next morning that Grace had any real conscious thought. Stretching to relieve her stiff muscles, she looked around the one-room cabin and found it deserted except for Eletta, who was sleeping soundly.

Getting to her feet, Grace felt an overwhelming sense of dread. She crossed the room to check on her friend, fearful that she wasn't merely sleeping. To her relief, Grace saw the rhythmic rise and fall of Eletta's chest. Her breathing was no longer labored.

Grace went back to the fire, which had been built up not long before. She saw that someone had made oatmeal and helped herself. She relished the warmth of the fire and food. The cabin was drafty and the dirt floor cold—a far cry from the pleasant home Eletta had described having back east.

As she settled in to eat, Eletta began to rouse. Grace smiled and greeted her. "Good morning—at least I believe it's still morning. I just woke up myself. How do you feel?"

"So much better. The heaviness has lifted from me." Eletta drew in a deep breath. "And it doesn't hurt to breathe. How long have you been here?"

"This is the fourth day—I think. I've lost track. I believe the worst has passed. You'll soon be right as rain—of which we've had a lot the last few days."

Eletta nodded. "I remember hearing it." She sat up a bit, and Grace hurried to help prop her up with pillows. "Where is Isaac?"

Grace shrugged. "I don't know where any of the men have

gone. Like I said, I just woke up and was about to eat. Would you care to join me? We have oatmeal."

"Not just yet." Eletta stretched and smiled. "I'm so glad you came. I'm certain I would be dead by now if not for you. It would seem both Isaac and I owe you our lives. I wish we could repay you."

"You already have with your friendship." Grace began to eat.

"When I first met you on the wagon train, I knew we'd be good friends. I felt it deep inside." Eletta closed her eyes. "I have never had a friend so dear as you, and when we parted and came here, I feared I would die of loneliness. No friends. No babies to fill my arms. Just this empty land and Isaac."

"He loves you so."

Eletta opened her eyes and nodded. "He does, and that means the world to me, but a woman needs more. We need to nurture and share our love." Tears came, but Eletta brushed them aside. "I do wish you could stay, but even more I long for a child of my own. After almost ten years, however, I don't suppose I shall ever be a mother."

"Nonsense. You're only twenty-five. There is plenty of time to have children. Perhaps God has delayed it so you can get better established here with the Indians. We surely can't know the mind of God and why things happen as they do. We can only trust Him."

Hope sat in the kitchen of the mission house alongside her beloved John. She was so happy to see him recovered.

"You'll soon be back out working with the men." She gave his arm a squeeze as he continued winding the twine they would use to make new brooms. "But for now I'm glad to have you right here. I don't think we would ever have gotten to know each other so well if you hadn't taken measles."

"Well, it seems to me to be a hard way to get to know someone." He gave her a wink.

Across the room, Mary Ann Bridger was finishing her lunch. The young girl had become a fast friend of Mercy, who had just left to go back to class in the school section of the house. Hope wasn't certain Mercy should go to school yet, but Mercy said she'd mentioned it to Grace without any negative response. Mr. Saunders, the teacher, had assured Hope that he wouldn't let Mercy overdo it.

"It's a whole lot colder today than yesterday," Mary Ann said with a shiver. She was still recovering from measles, and Mrs. Whitman thought her too weak to attend school.

Hope took that cue to add more wood to the cookstove. "Dr. Whitman said he'd have Frank bring in more wood after they finished with the steer. I don't think he'd mind so much if we made it a little warmer now."

Mary Ann nodded enthusiastically. "Mercy said Teacher is keeping it warm too. He said since so many have been sick, it's the wise thing to do."

"I hope he's not letting Mercy exhaust herself." Hope reclaimed her seat at the table beside John. She'd soon be expected to help with preparations for supper, but for now she just wanted to be near him.

"She said that Teacher isn't letting anyone who's been sick do very much."

A knock on the kitchen door drew their attention. Mary Ann opened the door and drew back a pace when Chief Telokite and another Indian called Tomahas entered the room. Tomahas was the one who had eyed Hope so thoroughly when she'd first come to the mission. He sent her a leering smile, which made Hope feel even more uncomfortable. John had told her his nickname was "The Murderer," and something about Tomahas suggested he was suitably named.

Drawing a deep breath, Hope was determined to show no fear or distaste. Only that morning Dr. Whitman had performed burials for several Cayuse children, including some of Telokite's. She felt sorry for him, but his dark eyes and severe scowl left her unwilling to offer her sympathies. Instead she took hold of John's arm, not understanding the wave of fear and nausea that rushed through her.

"Need doctor to give us medicine," Telokite demanded.

Since she was near the door to the sitting room, Hope nodded and went to see if the doctor was still in the house. She opened the door to see Dr. Whitman reading on the settee while Narcissa Whitman bathed one of John's sisters. Mrs. Osborn had just opened the door to the Indian room, where she and her family were recovering from measles. "Chief Telokite is here with Tomahas. He says he needs medicine."

Whitman looked up with an expression of concern. "Very well. Tell him I'll be right there." She saw the exchange of glances between the doctor and his wife. They looked momentarily terrified.

Hope returned, leaving the door open to the sitting room. The look she'd witnessed on Narcissa's face made her want to flee, but instead she faced Telokite. "He said he'll be right here."

She hurried to return to John's side. She hated being anywhere near the Indians. They always seemed to watch her with unnecessary attention.

Telokite headed for the door just as Dr. Whitman approached. Whitman refused to allow the chief entry into the sitting room and pushed him back. He called out over his shoulder. "Mother, lock this door."

It seemed as if everything slowed down after that. Hope watched as Whitman conversed with Telokite and Tomahas. Telokite was clearly agitated and continued to argue with the doctor in English, but Tomahas seemed content to creep about the room. He smiled at Mary Ann, then came to stand so close to Hope that she could almost feel his breath on her neck.

"This your man?" he asked, nodding at John.

Hope found it impossible to speak and breathed a sigh of relief when John spoke up. "Have you been watching them butcher the steer?"

Tomahas grunted. "No time to stand around." He walked away from the table and maneuvered behind Whitman.

Hope watched as Tomahas dropped the blanket he'd had wrapped around him and pulled his tomahawk. Before she could so much as shout a warning, he buried the blade in the back of the doctor's head, knocking him to the floor.

Tomahas pulled his tomahawk out of Whitman's head in order to hit him again, but the doctor staggered to his feet. Mary Ann began screaming as Telokite joined in to kill Whitman. The doctor fought them as he made his way out the kitchen door. He had unnatural strength for a man who had taken such a vicious blow to the head.

Hope found herself unable to move. She wanted to run, but her body wouldn't cooperate. She glanced across the room to see Mary Ann open the window and throw herself out. Maybe she was going for help, or maybe, like Hope, she just wanted to hide from the gruesome display.

Hope felt John rise. She looked at him, terrified that if he interfered, the Indians would kill him as well. He reached for his pistol, and Hope couldn't help herself.

"No!"

Just then Tomahas turned at the door and fired back at the couple. John clutched his chest and fell to the ground. Hope hurried to his side. Blood poured from his wound.

She pressed her apron against his chest. "Don't die, Johnny. Please don't die."

Outside, gunfire sounded in volley after volley. She heard

the screams of women and children. She felt the warm, sticky blood—John's blood—as she tried to stop his bleeding. "We need to get to safety." But even as she said the words, Hope knew there was no such place.

"Hope," John whispered. He looked at her for just a moment, and then his eyes turned glassy, and Hope knew he was gone.

"No! No! Don't leave me, Johnny. Please don't leave me." She rocked him close, feeling that a part of her had died with him. Gone were all her dreams of love and a life of happiness with this brilliant and gentle soul.

The door to the sitting room opened, and Hope glanced up to see Mrs. Osborn. Her eyes widened at the sight of John lying dead, and she disappeared back into the room she shared with her family. Hope heard someone tell the children to go upstairs and hide.

Hope thought of Mercy. There was nothing she could do to help John, but perhaps she might save Mercy. She gently placed his head back on the floor and picked up his gun. Getting to her feet, she saw that her apron and dress were soaked in blood.

Moving to the open door, Hope looked out upon the ongoing war. Shots rang out, ricocheting off the doorjamb. The screams of men and women alike filled the air. Hope stood rigid. She tried to move, but her feet refused to obey. Just a few feet away, Dr. Whitman moaned as his blood soaked into the ground.

Across the yard, the Indians were stabbing a man. Hope recognized him as the teacher, Mr. Saunders. Perhaps she was already too late and all of the children were dead. Otherwise why would Mr. Saunders have left them?

Mrs. Hays and Mrs. Hall came running from the emigrant house even as Mrs. Whitman pushed past Hope and went to her husband. She took hold of his arms and began pulling.

"Help me get him back in the house!" she cried, looking up at Hope.

Hope pocketed the pistol and stepped forward. Mrs. Hall and Mrs. Hays arrived and took hold of the doctor's legs, and together the four women managed to get him back into the house. They dragged his bleeding frame to the sitting room and maneuvered him onto one of the settees.

Narcissa Whitman pressed her apron to his head. "Do you know me?" she asked, looking into her husband's eyes.

The doctor moaned and murmured, "Yes."

"Can you talk to me?"

Hope wasn't sure why Mrs. Whitman felt this necessary. He was clearly dying.

Andy Rogers burst through the door, bleeding from wounds in his head and arm. He glanced down at Dr. Whitman. "Is he dead?"

The women seemed stunned by Andy's appearance. Before they could speak, Dr. Whitman rallied.

"No, Andy." The doctor gasped for breath and closed his eyes.

"I'm a widow," Mrs. Whitman moaned, and Hope thought for a moment she might faint.

At the sound of more gunshots, John's little sister Elizabeth hurried to the window. "Mother," she called to Mrs. Whitman, "Mother, they are killing Mr. Saunders."

Narcissa left her husband and hurried to the window. "Joe Lewis, are you responsible for this?" she cried.

Hope thought her mad to worry about such things. Why did it matter who was responsible? The fact was they were all going to die.

A shot rang out, hitting Mrs. Whitman under her left arm. Hope thought Mrs. Whitman was dead as she slumped to the floor, but within a moment she was righting herself again. She staggered toward the collection of people who still stood by her husband. "This will kill my poor mother," she murmured.

Nathan Kimball, Harriet's husband, had shown up at some

point, but Hope couldn't say when. Along with Andy, he was suggesting that the women get upstairs.

"At least there we can form a defense," Kimball said.

Hope backed away, inching into the kitchen. She felt numb—no fear, no pain. The sounds of the attack were nothing more than a dull humming in her ears.

Several Indians rushed into the house and pushed Hope back as they made their way into the room. They were calling out, demanding that those who had barely managed to get upstairs come back down.

One of the Indians, named Tamsucky, began to climb the steps. He called out with promises to help Mrs. Whitman and the others. He begged them to come downstairs, as they planned to burn the house to the ground.

Hope crossed the kitchen in a stupor and stepped outside. She pressed her back against the wall of the house. Just a few steps away was the door to where the children met for school. Mercy would be there. Hope inched her way along the wall. She had to know if her sister was still alive.

She hadn't made it far when Andy and Joe Lewis emerged from the house carrying a settee. On it was Mrs. Whitman. Apparently Tamsucky had been able to convince those upstairs to leave the house. Mrs. Hall and Mrs. Hays hurried past the men and headed toward the emigrant house. For what purpose, Hope couldn't imagine. Perhaps the Indians had decided to call a truce and now the killing would stop.

But this thought no sooner came to mind than the Cayuse began firing at Andy Rogers, and Joe Lewis dropped the settee. Mrs. Whitman fell into the mud, and Joe Lewis fired his gun at her writhing body. The other Indians fired at her as well. Andy stumbled against the edge of the house and fell facedown.

Hope slid down against the wall, unable to comprehend what

she was witnessing. It was too much. Her mind couldn't take it in or make any sense of it.

She thought of Johnny lying dead just feet away in the kitchen. It was then that she remembered his pistol. She pulled it from her pocket and cocked it. Da had showed her once how to fire such a weapon. She clutched the piece tight and put the barrel to her chest.

She thought only a moment of Grace and Mercy, then pulled the trigger.

Chapter

13

I think Eletta is well enough that we can head back in the morning," Grace told Alex. Being away from her sisters for nearly a week was starting to weigh heavy on her mind. "She's much stronger, and with the extra help you and Sam gave Isaac in cutting wood and providing venison, they should both be settled for a while."

Alex nodded. "We'll be ready." He looked at Sam. "Are you still planning to head back to your village?"

"Yes. I'll leave you at the place where the river forks. I feel uneasy and want to make sure that Sarah is all right."

Grace broke the news next to the Brownings. Eletta begged her not to leave, but Grace knew she had to go. "I've left my sisters at the mission and need to get back to them. Mercy has just recovered from the measles, and Hope is in love." She smiled and patted Eletta's hand. "Besides, Alex told me last night that there's a definite taste of snow in the air."

"I don't wish to be parted from my one and only friend," Eletta said, fighting back tears.

"Nor do I, but we will write to each other often."

Eletta nodded. "Yes. That shall have to sustain me."

Grace considered for a moment. "You aren't strong enough to travel just yet, but perhaps when you are, you and Isaac could come back to the mission. Maybe in a couple of weeks. You could spend Christmas there. Wouldn't that be nice?"

Eletta looked away and nodded. "I'd like that."

"Good. Then I'll mention it to Isaac."

Grace got to her feet just as the men came in from outside. She knew they were ready for supper, and her own growling stomach begged for the same. Perhaps she would speak to Isaac after they ate.

She smiled at Eletta. "The men will want their supper, and you need yours as well. I'm going to get you a bowl of stew and a biscuit, and I'll expect you to eat every bite."

Eletta laughed. "Perhaps you are more mother than friend to me."

"Perhaps, so you must do as you're told," Grace teased.

Grace moved to the fireplace and began dishing up bowls of stew. She placed three bowls on the table and then went to retrieve the biscuits she'd made that morning. As the men took their places, she returned to the fire and ladled a bowl of stew for Eletta and then one for herself.

Isaac offered a prayer but hadn't even managed to say "amen" when a loud knock sounded on the door of the cabin. Grace crossed the room with Eletta's food just as Isaac admitted a Nez Perce runner. The youth looked absolutely spent.

"Come in and join us for supper," Isaac said. He led the boy to the table. "Grace, would you get food for our visitor?"

She handed Eletta her food, then retrieved the bowl and biscuit she'd set aside for herself. Bringing them to the young Indian, she smiled.

The boy gratefully took the bowl, ignoring the spoon, and began to drink the contents in a hurry. Grace glanced to the corner where Alex and Sam sat cross-legged on the dirt floor, eating their supper. She could see by their expressions that they were just as curious as she was as to what had brought the young runner to the Brownings' mission.

"Do you bring news?" Isaac asked.

The boy finished his stew and put the bowl down on the table. He began speaking in broken English. "Much killing . . . many dead."

Sam got to his feet and turned the boy to face him. They conversed in their native tongue, and Grace saw the look of disbelief that crossed Sam's face. She looked at Alex, who by now had also gotten to his feet.

"What is it?" Grace asked. "Who is dead?"

Alex held her gaze, his dark eyes conveying something she couldn't identify. Was it sorrow?

"Alex—Sam, tell us what has happened."

"Yes, tell us," Isaac insisted.

Grace moved to Alex's side. She felt him stiffen as she put her hand on his arm. "Tell me—no matter how bad it is."

He nodded. "The runner said the mission was attacked and everyone is dead."

"The mission?" Grace couldn't allow herself to believe the worst. Her words were hardly more than a whisper. "Which . . . mission?"

Alex's brow furrowed. "The Whitman Mission."

Sam Two Moons felt a deep sense of dread as he relayed the information in full to the Brownings and Grace. The actions of a handful of Cayuse had just sealed the fate of Indians throughout the area. The United States government would never stand for such a horrific and unwarranted attack. Especially one that involved so many women and children.

It was little wonder he had been uneasy for the past two days. He had always been sensitive—intuitive, even—regarding attacks and other things that threatened the lives of his people. His father told him it was a gift from God, but it didn't feel like a gift when it offered no clear understanding of what was coming.

Grace insisted they return to the mission, but even now Alex was telling her that it was too dangerous, that they couldn't go there. He promised that in the morning they would go to Fort Nez Perce on the Columbia River and get whatever help they could. But this wasn't any comfort to her.

Sam interrupted her pleas. "I'll go to the mission. They won't harm me."

Grace left Alex's side and came to Sam. "Take me with you."

"No. Alex is right. It isn't safe. The Cayuse will be covering the area and most likely will kill any white person they see." Or worse. He knew there were those among the tribe who would think nothing of taking a white woman hostage to use as they pleased.

"But my sisters are there!"

"Grace, Sam is willing to risk his life to get you information regarding what's happened. If Hope and Mercy are . . . if they're . . . still there, he might even be able to talk Telokite into letting them return with him."

"If they were your sisters, you wouldn't be willing to send someone else to do your bidding."

She stormed from the cabin, not even bothering to close the door behind her. The chilled, damp air rushed into the room, leaving Sam feeling even worse.

"She's got to be the most pigheaded woman I've ever known," Alex declared, closing the door.

"Don't be too hard on her," Eletta called from her bed. "She's afraid for her sisters."

Sam nodded. "Alex, you should go comfort her and assure her that I will learn the truth for her. I'll leave at first light and keep going until I reach the mission. Tell her I won't even stop but to rest the horse."

Alex looked at him for a moment. Sam knew without any doubt that his friend had deep feelings for Grace.

Finally, Alex nodded and reached for Grace's coat. "I'll try to talk some sense into her."

It felt as if an iron band had wrapped itself around Grace's chest. She could scarcely draw breath. Why had this happened? Why, when everyone assured her the Cayuse wouldn't attack, had they committed such an atrocity? She knew they were angry at Whitman. Knew that the death of their people from measles had made them certain that Whitman was seeking their annihilation. But why kill innocent women and children?

Images of her sisters lying dead tormented her, and Grace knew that she couldn't just wait for Sam to return with news. She had to go herself. She had to do whatever was left to do to see her sisters cared for. If they were dead, she would bury them with her own hands if necessary. If they were alive and hurt, she would nurse them back to health. If it cost her her own life, then so be it.

"I've helped the Cayuse. Surely they would allow me to live and help my own," she murmured.

"I wouldn't count on that."

She whirled around to see the shadowy form of Alex. With only a sliver of moon in the sky, she couldn't see his face. "Why are you here?" The words came out much harsher than she'd meant them.

"I brought your coat, and I came to help you understand the situation."

Grace let him help her into the warm wool before pulling away. "I already understand the situation."

"I don't think you do. Sam didn't tell you everything the runner said. You need to understand a few things. Telokite's children died. He's not going to think kindly toward you, another healer. Especially since you helped treat his children."

She heard the urgency in his voice and wished she could see his face. "But I also helped so many live."

"It won't matter. Telokite and the others won't even stop to think about that. They will kill you."

"So I'm just to do nothing?"

"You might pray."

Grace could hardly believe Alex was suggesting such a thing. After all, hadn't he told her he was barely on speaking terms with God?

"Pray? You want me to pray when you yourself think it's useless?"

"I never said that, Grace. I said my own anger had made me put God at a distance, but I've had a change of heart. I'm doing my best to seek His forgiveness and rebuild our relationship. Prayer is essential—even I know that."

She felt the wind go out of her sails. "I have been praying, Alex. I've been praying ever since we came west. I've been praying since leaving the mission. I'm still praying." Her voice broke as tears began to fall. "They may be hurt . . . dead."

Alex pulled her into his arms and Grace stiffened. Her heart fought against her thought to pull away. She desperately needed to feel his arms around her—to feel safe—but how could she feel anything but fear and guilt? She had left her sisters to die at the hands of the Cayuse.

She pushed away from him. "Don't! Don't touch me."

"Grace." His voice was low and soothing. "I just want to help."

She began to cry in earnest. "You can't help. I left them there, knowing there were dangers. I left them to die."

He gripped her upper arms. "You aren't to blame. Things looked like they were going to work out. You couldn't know, and if you had stayed . . ." He fell silent.

Grace lowered her head and sobbed. If she had stayed, she'd have faced the same fate. "I should have stayed."

Once again he pulled her into his arms and held her. Grace didn't push him away this time.

"I promise you, Grace, I'll do whatever I can. You are important to me—so are they."

Grace lost track of the time and even of the words Alex said. She clung to him as if he were the only man in the world who could save her from plunging into a deep abyss. In her heart she knew his embrace did nothing to aid her sister's plight, but it helped her own, and for the moment that was all she had strength for.

Eventually Alex led her back to the cabin, where the others had gathered near Eletta's bed to pray. Only the young runner sat alone by the fire. Alex helped Grace to a chair, then went to get her a cup of coffee. Grace began to shiver so violently that when she took hold of the cup, she spilled the hot liquid on her coat.

"Here, let me help you," Alex said, taking the cup back. He held it to her lips.

Grace took a tiny sip and then another. The shaking began to pass, and after several minutes she reached out and took the cup once again. "I'm better now."

Alex looked unconvinced but let her have the coffee. He moved back to the fire and took up a bowl. He dished up some stew and brought it to Grace.

For a moment she wanted to refuse it, but given that she'd just made up her mind as to what she should do, Grace knew she needed to eat. She put the cup of coffee on the table and took the bowl and spoon Alex offered.

"Thank you." She tried to force a smile, but it wouldn't come. Hopefully seeing her calmer would put everyone at ease. Then, with any luck, she could gather what she needed before they retired for the night and be ready to leave once everyone had fallen asleep.

"She's gone," Sam told Alex. "Her horse is gone too, so she must be on her way back to the mission."

Alex growled. "She doesn't even know her way back. What a fool."

Sam motioned to the horses. "We'd best get on our way. She has at least a few hours on us. I'm sure we can track her, but that will slow our progress."

Alex went back into the cabin and gathered his things. Isaac and Eletta watched in silence until he finally turned to bid them good-bye. "I'm sorry. I know you're worried about Grace. When we find her, I'll bring her back here or at least send word."

"Please do," Isaac Browning said, looking to his wife and then to Alex. "She is . . . she can stay with us for as long as she likes." Eletta nodded in confirmation.

Alex knew they had already concluded that Hope and Mercy were dead. He nodded, unable to think of anything more to say. He picked up the leftover biscuits and some cooked venison, which Isaac had wrapped up for them at Eletta's insistence, and went to find Sam.

They followed Grace's tracks. Given the rain that had fallen off and on, they were easy to spot. At first she seemed to have been confused—no doubt the dark had disoriented her. But after a time, the trail became steady. To their surprise, Grace was accurately backtracking the route they'd taken from the mission.

"She's a smart one," Sam said. "I remember that she asked about the landmarks on our way, and it appears she was listening. Most white women couldn't do as well to find their way back."

"Most white women aren't as stubborn and foolish either."

"You're being kind of hard on her, aren't you?"

Alex shrugged. "She's put her life in danger once again. She's ignored our counsel and set off to do as she pleases. She doesn't care how she upsets other people."

"Other people?"

Alex didn't like the teasing in Sam's tone. "Eletta and Isaac are half sick with worry."

"Ah, I see. I thought maybe you were finally going to admit that you've come to care for her."

Alex gritted his teeth and said nothing. He knew his feelings were evident, but he was determined not to give in to them. The last time he'd let a woman have his heart, it had turned out badly. So badly, in fact, that he had to flee or risk being killed.

They rode on through the tall grasses, which glistened as the sun hit the droplets of water on their stalks. The air seemed heavier than it had been, causing Alex to keep a watchful eye on the skies. It was, after all, December.

I should have known she'd try something like this. I should never have allowed myself to sleep. Not when I knew how desperate she was to learn the truth about her sisters.

"Did you hear me?" Sam asked.

Alex shook his head. He hadn't even realized that Sam had dismounted and Alex's own mount had halted. "Sorry. What did you say?"

"I said it looks like she rested here for a bit. I'm guessing not long ago. Maybe she was waiting for it to get fully light before she started off again." Sam jumped onto the back of his horse. "If she's really as good at finding her way home as she seems, my guess is that she'll pick up speed now that the sun is finally up."

"You're probably right." Alex had to admit admiration for Grace. She had clearly paid close attention to their route. "I guess we'd best do the same."

Grace urged her horse forward, knowing the poor animal was exhausted. It had taken them two days to reach the Brownings, but Grace intended to get back to the mission site in one. She knew it wasn't impossible. Difficult, yes. But not impossible.

She rested the horse as often as she dared, but she had no doubt Alex and Sam would be on her trail with the rising of the sun. That meant she had to put as much time and as many miles between them as possible. Otherwise, she knew Alex would force her back to the Brownings' home, and that was something she didn't think she could bear.

Her mind was consumed by thoughts of the mission. The runner had said they were all dead. Grace couldn't fathom that some seventy-six people had been wiped out that easily. The people of the mission were fully capable of defending themselves. Surely some of the men had been able to fight back. But if that were the case and mission folks were still alive, why did the runner say they were all dead?

"They might have managed to get away," she murmured. That was possible. Some people might have escaped from the fighting and sought a place to hide. Hope and Mercy would have known to do the same. They were intelligent young women—at least Hope was. Mercy was young and inexperienced, but she had a good head on her shoulders.

Without thought of food or water, Grace pressed on. She lost track of the time and the miles as she struggled to remember each landmark. It would be very easy to get turned around and find herself in danger. This was wild land—Indian land—and until now she'd given very little thought to the idea that she might encounter some of the native peoples.

"Lord, I need your help and guidance. You know what I'm up against." She looked to the west and saw a dark bank of clouds. A shiver ran through her. The temperature was dropping, and if the clouds were any indication, the rain that had come earlier would give way to snow.

"Father, please be with Hope and Mercy. Help them not to be afraid. Help them to be safe, Lord, wherever they are. I can't bear the idea of them being dead." She thought of some of the others. Mary Saunders with her namesake two-year-old. Harriet Kimball with her brood, the youngest just a year old. Then she thought of the Sager brothers and their sweet little sisters. Had they been killed? It was too much to even imagine.

She looked heavenward. "Oh, God, I can't even bear to think of it."

Hope sat in the emigrant house beside Mercy, the terrible events of the attack running over and over in her mind. John's gun had misfired, leaving her alive to bear witness to all the violence that unfolded that day. She could still see John lying dead in the doorway. His blood still stained her dress and apron. It was all she had left of him.

The Indians had murdered almost all the men. At least that was what she'd heard someone say. After things had calmed down, the Cayuse had herded the women and children together and then argued in front of them as to what they should do next. Eliza Spaulding, the ten-year-old daughter of Reverend Spaulding, was constantly singled out to give interpretation.

She spoke the Indians' language, having learned it at their own mission. It mattered not to the Cayuse whether it was day or night—when they needed Eliza, they came for her. The child was exhausted and even now was sleeping soundly in the corner near Mrs. Hall.

The Indians had forced all of the survivors into the emigrant house, with the exception of Mr. Bewley and Mr. Sales. Both men were ill when the attack came and remained upstairs in their beds at the mission house. Bewley's sister Lorinda had said that perhaps because her brother had always been kind to the Cayuse, they had allowed him to live. But Lorinda was no longer with them. It was whispered among the women that she had been taken to Chief Five Crows's village some distance away and forced to marry him. Hope knew that was only a delicate way of saying he had forced himself on her.

Lorinda wasn't the only one to lose her innocence or be forced against her will. The Cayuse braves chose women at random to take to their beds. Any of the girls over twelve seemed to be fair game, and Hope was grateful that Mercy still looked like a child.

When Tomahas had come for Hope, she had fought him off as long as she could. She knew it was futile, but she wasn't going to show any willingness. When he tired of fighting her, he had slapped her unconscious, and when Hope awakened, he was already having his way with her.

After that, her mind just seemed to stop processing rational thought. She prayed for death. She begged God's intercession, yet none came. At least none that she could see.

She knew that she wasn't the only one to suffer. Many of the other women had endured what she had. Lorinda hadn't even been allowed to stay at the mission. Perhaps they would all be separated and taken to various villages.

The women all seemed to share the same expression—a hollow, vacant look that marked them as victims who had already endured too much. Only the needs of their children kept them alive, and with over thirty children, that job was constant. Hope knew that these women had faced great struggles coming west to live in this wretched land. They were strong. Stronger than her. Hope glanced at Mercy, who was wound up tight in a ball, sleeping. Hope knew Mercy needed her, just as those other children needed their mothers. They desperately needed someone they trusted to assure them that everything would be all right, but Hope couldn't even do so for Mercy's sake. She had nothing left to give. The Cayuse had taken everything.

Hope lost track of time. There was no thought for what day of the week it was or what time of day. The days and nights were marked only by the actions of the Indians. When they were hungry, they forced the women to prepare them food, even though their own women had come and ransacked most of the stored goods kept at the mission. When any of the Cayuse needed something, they demanded it via little Eliza Spaulding.

Tomahas came for Hope time and time again. At first she looked for an opportunity to escape or kill him, but none ever came, and after a while she saw the futility. Even if she could escape—where would she go? And if she killed him, who knew what the Cayuse would do to her—or Mercy?

Every night the Cayuse argued about what to do with the women and children. Always it was suggested that they be killed in the morning. Yet in the morning life went on. Louise Sager and Helen Mar Meek, two little girls sick with measles at the time of the attack, died. Helen was the daughter of Joseph Meek, a law official for the territory. Louise was John's six-year-old sister whom Hope had helped care for prior to the attack. Now they were both gone, and Hope could only wonder who would be next.

As a sort of routine took hold, the women became less silent and started talking to one another, supposing what might happen next. As best they could figure, their husbands and the bachelors and older boys were dead. No one had seen anything of Peter Hall, and Mrs. Hall held fast to the hope that he had escaped to get help. This was what she told her five children over and over, but Hope didn't believe it to be true.

The Osborns were also missing. The entire family had been staying in the Indian room of the mission house. Their sickness was only just passing, and all had still been too weak to be up and about. Since the attack, no one had seen anything of them or their three remaining children. The only one left who was unaccounted for was William Canfield, and Sallie Ann Canfield, like Peter Hall's wife, believed her husband had escaped to get help. It gave the women hope to hold on to.

"Do you think Grace knows what's happened to us?" Mercy asked, nudging Hope.

Hope hadn't realized that Mercy had awakened. "I don't know."

Mercy's expression changed to one of fear. "You don't suppose the Indians killed her?"

"I don't know."

For several long minutes, Mercy said nothing more. Then with a low whisper, she asked, "Do you think they're going to kill us?"

Hope shook her head. "I don't know."

"Hope, have you eaten?" Ellen Canfield, Sallie Ann's sixteen-year-old daughter, squatted down in front of Hope. "I have some bread."

Looking at the young woman, Hope could see the same resignation in her face that the others wore. They were just girls—young women on the threshold of their adulthood. The world had seemed an amazing place just a short time ago. Hope had known love—honest and true love—but now that was gone.

She shook her head. "I'm not hungry."

170

"Mama said we have to eat to keep up our strength." Ellen pushed a chunk of bread into Hope's hands.

"Strength for what?" Hope asked. She handed the bread to Mercy, then leaned back against the wall and closed her eyes. It surely took no strength to die.

Chapter 14

Alex spied Grace's horse first. The mount was feeding, and Grace was nowhere to be seen. For a moment his fears ran rampant. Had she been hurt? Had she been attacked? When she finally came out from a stand of trees, he released the breath he'd been holding.

He and Sam were no more than twenty feet away when Grace looked up and realized they'd caught up with her. She shook her head vehemently and backed away.

"No. No, you can't stop me. I won't let you."

Alex slid off his horse and crossed the short distance between them. He took hold of her shoulders and shook her. "Have you lost all of your senses? This countryside is crawling with Cayuse. Do you really think they'll overlook the fact that you're white and let you live?" Grace pushed at him, but Alex held her fast. "I told you Sam was willing to go. He still is, but you cannot. You and I will wait here for him. Do you understand me?"

"I have to know what's happened. I have to see my sisters—dead or alive."

"You can be far more help to them here. If they are dead,

they need nothing. If they are alive, then Sam will do what he can to bring them to you. For now, the best we can do is wait and keep out of sight."

"You're just afraid to go to the mission. You're a coward!" she declared, pounding her fists against his chest.

Alex froze. The look on her face—a mix of disgust and indignation—was the same look he'd seen on his little brother's face ten years earlier when he wouldn't—*couldn't*—go back into the blazing inferno to save their parents. He dropped his hold and for a moment could only stare at Grace. Her words were like a slap. He wasn't a coward, but he knew what was sensible in this situation.

"Do as you will." He turned and walked away, knowing that he couldn't change her mind if she was determined to have her way. Neither could he make her understand that he wasn't a coward.

Grace hated herself for calling Alex a coward. She could still see the pain in his expression—his eyes. She knew it was only the anger and fear that had caused her to say such a thing, but nevertheless she owed him an apology. Before she could go to him, however, Sam approached her.

"Grace, I know it is hard for you to wait, but if you won't do so willingly, then I will tie you up."

Her eyes widened. "You would really do that?"

"To save your life—yes." Sam looked unhappy, but he didn't back down. "I can't let you risk your life and ours by going to the mission."

"But my sisters—"

"Will be in even more danger if you go in there making demands of people who already bear you a grudge. If they are alive, I can accomplish more—because I share Cayuse blood."

She studied Sam's face for a moment. His expression was stern, but in his dark eyes she saw great compassion. Perhaps she was a fool to think she could just parade onto the mission grounds without consequences, and a worse fool to have hurt Alex.

With a heavy sigh, she nodded. "I'll stay."

Sam reached inside his buckskin shirt to pull out a necklace he wore on a rawhide strip. He took it off and handed it to Grace. A long claw hung from the strip.

"I want you to have this to remind you of your promise to stay."

Grace took the piece and looked up at Sam. "I don't understand."

"I killed this bear when I was thirteen—but not until after he killed my brother." Sam frowned. "My brother was much older than me, and I loved him greatly. When he announced he was going hunting, I wanted to go too. But I had been sick, and my father told me I had to remain in camp. I was angry and determined to prove myself. When my father was busy elsewhere, I snuck out."

He looked away toward the stand of trees. "I easily followed my brother, and when he heard me in the brush, he thought I was an elk or deer. I revealed myself just as he started to shoot. He was scared at first, but then angry. He told me I was a fool and that when our father learned what I had done, I would be severely punished. Distracted with me, he was unprepared when the bear attacked."

Sam returned his gaze to Grace. "The bear killed my brother. Had I not been disobedient, my brother would have been prepared."

"I'm so sorry." She looked at the claw hanging from the end of the necklace. It was longer than she would have thought, and it was easy to see how claws like that could tear a man apart.

Sam continued. "Once I had killed the bear, I ran back to camp for help. The men commended me. My father credited it to my ability to sense trouble or danger before it happened and apologized for having made me stay behind. He blamed himself for my brother's death. I was looked upon as a hero, but I knew the truth, and I took this claw to remind myself of what having my own way had cost me. Years later I confessed to my father that my disobedience had caused my brother's death and that I wasn't a hero at all. He forgave me, but I will always be reminded of what it cost me."

Grace felt the weight of his words. She put the necklace on. "I'll hang on to it for you and let it remind me as well."

He nodded and then gave her a smile. "I told Alex you were a smart woman, and now I see you can also accept correction. That is good. Only a fool refuses correction."

Sam left her and went to Alex, who sat against one of the trees. After a few minutes of discussion, Sam bounded onto his mount and was gone. Grace fingered the bear claw for a moment, then tucked it inside the bodice of her dress. She would go to Alex and beg his forgiveness. It was the right thing to do.

He didn't seem to hear her approach, but when Grace sat down beside him, he moved over without a word to give her the dryer patch of ground.

"I'm sorry, Alex." Those words seemed inadequate, so she continued. "I know you're not a coward, and I know that I hurt you deeply by saying you were. I hope you'll forgive me. It's no excuse, but my fear got the best of me."

"I know," he said, his voice soft and void of anger.

For a moment Grace didn't know what else to say. She hated the silence between them but felt it was important to wait for Alex to speak.

"My brother called me a coward when our parents were

trapped in our burning house and I refused to go inside to rescue them."

She now understood why that single word had caused such pain. "Can you tell me about it?" she asked gently.

He looked at her for the first time since she'd joined him. Grace felt her breath catch and her heart beat faster. She could no longer deny the truth. She was in love with Alex. Seeing him so hurt only made her love him more.

"The fire started after we'd all gone to bed for the night. I woke up to find my room filled with smoke. The stairway and far side of the house were engulfed in flames. I went across the hall to get my brother. He was just thirteen and slept through most anything." He smiled sadly. "Sure enough, he was sound asleep. With the stairs on fire, I knew we'd have to escape by using the window. We got outside without any trouble, although by then both of us were coughing so hard we could hardly stand. I lowered Andy as far as I could and then dropped him. As the fire spread to our side of the house, I jumped to the ground to join him.

"When we moved away from the house, it was easy to see that there would be no going back. However, when we realized our mother and father weren't outside, Andy grew hysterical. He pleaded with me to rescue them."

Alex drew a deep breath and looked toward the grassy meadow. "I wanted to rescue them, but I knew it was too late. I told Andy as much, pointing out that the fire had started on their side of the house and already the roof and walls had given way. He told me I was a coward. I can still see the look on his face. I decided I would risk it and see if our parents could possibly be alive, but when I tried to move—I couldn't. It wasn't fear that held me back. I can't explain it, but I couldn't move."

"Perhaps God sent an angel to hold you back."

He looked again at Grace. "I suppose it's possible, but my

brother never forgave me. By then others had arrived. They had to keep my brother from going back into the house. I finally regained control of my body and went to talk to him, but he refused to have anything more to do with me. The next day we went to stay with our sister, and still he wouldn't speak to me, but I heard him telling my sister what a coward I'd been. Fearing further harm might come to them, I left New Orleans and went to live with my grandfather for a time. He taught me to trap and hunt and . . . that's how I've made my way these last ten years."

She shook her head in confusion. "Why would your being there cause them further harm?"

Alex stiffened. "It's not important." It was clear he didn't intend to say more.

Grace decided not to push him. "I'm so sorry I brought that memory back to you."

He shook his head, and she'd never seen him look sadder. "You didn't bring it back. It's never left me."

Sam approached the Whitman Mission with great caution. For a while he observed the mission grounds from atop the sole hill that stood nearby. He could see numerous Cayuse moving about the area. There were even what appeared to be a couple of white men at the gristmill. Then he caught sight of two white women bringing water from the river. Perhaps the runner's story had been exaggerated and no one had been killed.

As he drew closer, however, Sam could see telltale signs of destruction. Pieces of furniture and dishes were strewn about. Several Cayuse women were wearing clothes that Sam was certain had belonged to Narcissa Whitman. Not far from the mission house was a settee covered in mud and blood.

Several of the Cayuse braves caught sight of Sam and gave a wave of greeting. Sam forced a smile as Tomahas approached.

"How are you, my brother?" Sam asked.

"We have defeated that murderer Whitman. He is dead and will not poison our people again," Tomahas replied.

"And the others?"

"We killed the men who helped Whitman."

"And their women? Their children?"

Tomahas laughed. "They are our hostages. Except for Mrs. Whitman. We killed her too. She thought she was better than us."

Sam shook his head. "You have caused great pain to our people, for the soldiers are sure to come and kill us now."

"They won't dare. We have their women and children. We will keep them prisoners until the white fathers agree to return the land to us and let our people live in peace."

Sam looked toward the mission house. "Where is Telokite? I'd like to speak with him."

Tomahas pointed to the gristmill at the edge of the pond. Sam nodded and without another word made his way across the grounds, ignoring the calls of other braves. When he passed the emigrant house, he could hear the sound of children crying. Apparently the Cayuse were keeping the women and children prisoner there.

Telokite stood arguing with one of the Nez Perce lesser chiefs, who was pleading for the release of Eliza Spaulding to no avail. When the Nez Perce finally left, with tears in his eyes and shoulders slumped, Sam knew it would probably be futile to ask for the release of Hope and Mercy.

"You have come to see our victory?" Telokite asked as he turned to Sam.

"Is it a victory when it will surely spell the end of our people?"

Telokite frowned. "The Boston men will hear our voices now. We will see them gone because they will know we are strong."

Sam shook his head. "I have spent much time in the company

of the Boston men and the Black Robes. I have listened to their stories, and I understand their ways. They will not go. They will simply send more soldiers and more settlers."

"They will make peace with us," Telokite assured. "We have the women and children to ensure that."

"They won't believe you capable of peace." Sam looked to the grinding stone, where two men he recognized as Daniel Young and Joseph Smith were working. Were they truly the only white men left on the mission grounds? Beyond the pond at the Cayuse camp, movement caught Sam's eye, and he saw one of Telokite's sons taking Joseph's fifteen-year-old daughter Mary with him into his lodge. She made no protest. "Your young men are taking the white women against their will?"

Telokite followed Sam's gaze and laughed. "Mary Smith is more than willing. Her father instructed her to go with my son to be his wife. Some of the other women are not so willing, but they have no choice. It is the way of war."

"But you just said you wanted peace. You told Alex and my father that you would not attack the mission and kill these people."

Telokite's eyes narrowed, and Sam knew he had overstepped. "My youngest children died because Whitman poisoned them. Joe Lewis told me he heard this, and when he talked to the Black Robes, they agreed that Whitman would like us all dead."

"Joe has been known to lie."

Telokite shook his head. "Not this time." He sized Sam up for a moment. "Why did you come?"

Sam drew a deep breath. "I am here because of my friend— the white tewat woman who helped you when you asked her to come to the village."

"She was good woman. I did not see her among the prisoners."

"She wasn't here. She had gone to help others who were sick.

Her sisters are here, and she is worried that they are dead. I ask that you let them return with me."

"No. No one will leave. The women and children will stay until the white fathers promise not to punish the Cayuse."

"Can I at least see them so that I can tell Grace that they are all right?"

Telokite seemed to consider this a moment. "I will allow it. They are in the house there." He pointed to the emigrant house. "They are free to come and go, but most are too afraid. Come with me." Telokite started toward the house, and Sam followed.

When the women and children saw the two Indians enter the house, some of them began to weep. It was obvious that they had been sorely misused. Sam immediately spied Hope and Mercy across the room. Mercy had been combing the hair of a much younger child, but the small girl quickly left to join her mother. Mercy tucked up closer to Hope but said nothing. She simply watched Sam and Telokite while Hope stared at the wall. Both girls looked pale, gaunt, and as if they'd seen far too much. Mercy, although dirty, looked all right. Hope, on the other hand, had bruises on her face and blood on the front of her gown. The bodice of her dress was torn but had been tacked back into place. Sam had little doubt she had been molested.

"May I speak to them?" Sam asked respectfully. He hoped Telokite would see that he completely accepted that the chief was in charge.

"Yes." Telokite turned and walked from the house without another word.

With his departure, some of the women seemed to relax. Sam felt certain they recognized him from his previous time spent at the mission. Hopefully they knew he'd had nothing to do with what had happened.

With great care, so as not to cause the women and children

more fear, Sam made his way to where Mercy and Hope sat. Other children scurried away, as did the women who sat near the sisters. Sam squatted down and gave Mercy a smile.

"Do you remember me? I'm Alex's and Gabriel's friend. Grace's too. Remember? Alex and I took her to the Brownings' mission."

Mercy nodded. "Is Grace dead?"

Sam shook his head. "No. She is just fine. She is worried about you and Hope. I tried to get Telokite to let me take you from here, but he would not agree to it."

"He plans to kill us all."

Hope's words surprised Sam. He turned his gaze from Mercy to her older sister and found Hope looking at him with such contempt that it was nearly palpable.

"No." Sam hoped he might at least encourage the hostages with that bit of news. He raised his voice just enough that the women in the room could hear him. "Telokite wants only to keep you here until the government agrees not to punish his people for what they did. If he planned to kill you, you would already be dead."

"Should that make us feel better?" Hope asked sarcastically.

Sam saw the pain in her eyes. "No. Nothing will do that." He reached to touch her hand, and Hope pulled back quickly. "They've hurt you, haven't they?"

By the look on her face, Sam knew she understood what he was asking. Hope said nothing, but in her expression, he could see the truth.

He looked for a moment at Mercy and then back to Hope. "And your sister?"

Hope shook her head. "They haven't touched the younger girls." She barely breathed the words.

Sam nodded just as someone called out to him. He stood and turned to find Tomahas in the doorway. Once again the women cowered closer together and the children began to whimper. He looked back at Hope to see the murderous hatred in her eyes.

"You go now. Telokite said you should go to the fort and speak for us. There are others who will talk for us, but you should go too."

Sam hated to leave the girls but knew he had no choice. He wanted to say something to encourage them, but he knew there were no words that would help. Nothing he could say would ever make this right.

Alex sat by a very small fire, wondering when Sam might return. Grace, exhausted from her emotions, had crawled into the tent and fallen asleep. He had put the tent near the water, where the brush was thick and camouflaged its presence, then made his camp some yards away. He knew it was dangerous to have the fire but hoped that given his friendship with the Indians, they would do him no harm if they should wander across his camp. Besides, this area wasn't along any of the main trails. Always in his past dealings with the Nez Perce and other tribes, Alex had been given friendship because of his French-Canadian ancestry and association with the Hudson's Bay Company. He had no idea if that would be enough to maintain their goodwill now.

While he waited, Alex considered all that had gone on in his life. The loss of his parents and the loss of his brother's and sister's respect had been terrible blows. Even worse were the darker, more tragic origins of why those things had happened. But he wouldn't allow those memories. They weren't worth giving his time to. What continued to return to his thoughts was the question of where God was in all of this. Alex had spent so much time pushing God away. Was it possible that despite Alex wanting to make things right, God had turned His back once and for all?

A part of his mind reasoned that if this were the case, there would be no reconciliation. But his heart told him otherwise.

Weariness washed over him. He was tired. Tired of running from the past and tired of running from God. He glanced at the cloudy black sky.

"I know it doesn't begin to account for my ignoring you, but I am sorry. I've made so many mistakes. I want a fresh start . . . if you'll have me. We both know I'm not doing so good on my own."

He heard the unmistakable sound of someone in the tall grass not far from the camp. He scooted away from the fire and took up his loaded rifle. Waiting, he breathed a sigh of relief when Sam called his name.

"It's me." Sam's voice was hushed.

"Come on over. You must be cold." Alex put down the rifle and drew closer to the fire once again.

Sam joined him, plopping down on the ground in obvious exhaustion. Alex could see the troubled expression on his friend's face.

"Are they dead?" Alex asked in a whisper, praying Grace wouldn't awaken until he had a chance to talk to Sam.

"No. The women and children are alive, except for Mrs. Whitman. They killed her and all the men. I spoke with Telokite. He thinks he can use the hostages to force the government to make peace with his people and not punish them. I told him that would never happen and it would only go worse for them if they continued. He wouldn't listen."

"And he wouldn't allow you to take Hope and Mercy." It was more a statement than a question.

"No. But he let me see them—talk to them."

"And?"

Sam gave him a look that chilled Alex to the bone. "They've hurt so many of the women. Forced them . . ." He left the words unsaid.

Alex felt a deep anger rising. "And Grace's sisters?"

Sam nodded. "Hope."

Alex clenched his fist to keep from taking up his rifle. He knew it would serve no purpose to go storming into camp to avenge the innocence of one young woman. They would simply kill him and add his number to the dead.

For a long time, neither man said anything. The fire died down, and Alex couldn't bring himself to put more wood on it. He had no desire to see Sam's anguished expression, nor to have Sam see his.

When the last flames were gone and only glowing embers remained, Alex drew a deep breath and heaved a heavy sigh. "Say nothing to Grace."

Chapter

15

B ut you saw them, and they were all right?" Grace looked
at Sam, certain that if he lied, she'd know it.

"They live, and they seemed healthy. Telokite would
not allow me to take them because he believes the women and
children will keep the government from sending soldiers in to
take revenge."

"What can we do?" She looked to Alex.

"The best thing we can do is get to Fort Nez Perce. The factor there can send word to the fort in Vancouver, and they can
get word to the governor. We need to move fast. The news may
not have yet reached the fort."

"How can we go and just leave Hope and Mercy at the mission?" Grace knew even as she spoke that there was no other
way. She didn't even wait for an answer. "How far is the fort
from here?"

"About forty miles," Alex replied. "It won't be easy, and we'll
be on our own. Sam needs to get back to his village to tell the
chiefs what he knows. The Spaulding mission in Lapwai may
also have been attacked. We just don't know."

She nodded. "Well, with the horses, we should be able to get there by nightfall."

"We can't take the horses. Sam will take them back with him. Riding would make us too obvious. Sam says there are plenty of Cayuse around the fort. We'll have to go on foot and do most of our traveling at night. Thankfully there's little moonlight."

Grace considered her few supplies. She'd brought her carpetbag with her herbs and the money that was left to her sewn into the lining. She had little else.

"All right." She looked at Alex. "When do we leave?"

They left after sunset when the evening skies darkened with rain clouds. It wasn't long before a light, icy rain fell. Grace felt chilled to the bone but refused to complain. Alex had made it clear they wouldn't be able to have a fire, so she tried to keep her mind fixed on the warmth and comfort that awaited them once they reached the fort.

When dawn came the next morning, Alex found them a hiding place in the bank of the river. A depression worn away by floodwaters over the years would afford them a bit of coverage should anyone pass by.

Grace huddled close to Alex, allowing him to wrap his fur bedroll around their shoulders while Grace's blanket covered their legs. In another time and place, the intimacy would have been completely inappropriate, but given the circumstances, it was their only hope of keeping warm.

When evening came, Alex told Grace that he was almost certain they could make the fort by dawn. She nodded and took up her carpetbag. Alex surprised her by taking it and tying it to the sling he wore that held their bedrolls.

"You don't have to do that," she protested. "I can carry it."

He gave her just a hint of a smile. "I know you can." But he didn't offer it back to her.

They ate jerked meat as they followed the river to the west

and said very little for fear of being overheard. Through the course of the night, a heavy fog moved in and settled like a blanket over the land. They used the mist to their advantage.

Dawn came, and they were still several miles from the fort.

"The fog is thick enough that we'll just risk it and keep going." Alex pulled her close and kept his voice low. "We should be safe enough, but there's no real way of knowing for certain."

"It's all right, Alex. I trust you."

He met her gaze, and without thinking, Grace reached up to touch his cheek. Her action so startled her that she immediately pulled away in embarrassment.

"We should go." She moved off, following the river's edge, not even waiting to see if Alex would follow.

I must guard my thoughts and feelings. This is no time or place to let my heart get the best of me. Grace determined that she would do a better job of maintaining self-control.

Fort Nez Perce was situated on the Columbia River near the place where the Walla Walla River merged with the Columbia. The Hudson's Bay Company fort had been there for a great many years. By the time Alex and Grace reached it, the fog was finally starting to lift. Grace felt disappointed by the lackluster fort. She wasn't sure what she'd expected, but this adobe brick walled fortress wasn't it.

Alex must have sensed her dissatisfaction. "It's not much."

"I'm not sure what I thought it would look like. I suppose maybe I was expecting buildings like in a city." Weariness overwhelmed her and mingled with anguish and fear. "No matter, I am glad it's here."

Alex conversed momentarily with one of the men on guard before leading Grace to the main building, which housed the store. It was there that Grace learned they weren't the first to come. Somehow Peter Hall had managed to get there, as well as the Osborn family. Word had already been sent to Fort Vancouver, and the factor, Mr. McBean, was awaiting news as to what should be done—if anything.

"There's little I can do," McBean said. "I don't have men available. I sent Osborn to see about getting help, and Hall took off on his own to reach Fort Vancouver. I can't be doing anything until I hear from the directors there."

"They could all be dead by then," Grace countered. "I honestly don't know what good it is to have a fort if it offers no safety or help in times of trouble."

Mr. McBean looked sheepish. "This isn't really that kind of fort, ma'am. We're a trading fort, not a soldiering fort. We receive the Indians and white trappers alike to exchange furs and food. We aren't set up with soldiers."

"I can see that." Her frustration was clear in her tone. "Where are Mrs. Osborn and the children? I'll see if I can offer them any medicinal help."

Mr. McBean showed her to the Osborns' lodgings and then told Alex that he and Grace would have to bed down wherever they could find a spot. He didn't have beds for them, but he would lend them additional blankets.

Mrs. Osborn sat in a rocking chair near the fireplace, a blanket wrapped around her for added warmth. The children were still asleep, so Grace tried to be as quiet as possible. She drew up a stool and sat down directly in front of the haggard woman.

"How are you feeling, Margaret?"

"I'm weary of this country—of life," she admitted, her face void of emotion. "I think I shall never feel safe again."

Grace nodded and reached out to squeeze her hand. "I have some herbs with me and vinegar. Is there anything I can do to ease your suffering?"

Margaret looked at Grace and shook her head. "There is nothing to ease this misery. You have no idea what horrors took place that day."

Glancing at the small bed where the three Osborn children slept, Grace gathered her courage. "Maybe it would help if you talked about it. I'd like to know what happened. My sisters are still there."

Margaret looked at Grace oddly for a moment. "I'm sorry. I had forgotten." She closed her eyes and rested her head against the back of the rocker. "I don't know everything that happened, and most of what I do know comes from hearing rather than seeing."

"That's all right. Just tell me what you feel you can."

"My family was in bed in the Indian room. I was feeling a little stronger, so I decided to get up and see how it would be to walk and sit a bit. It was the first time I'd been up in three weeks. I went into the sitting room, where the doctor was reading and Narcissa was bathing little Elizabeth Sager. Poor child. When the killing started, she ran around the room, naked and screaming."

Grace could see it all. She knew what the sitting room looked like. Narcissa would have been bathing Elizabeth by the stove in order to keep her warm. In addition, there were two settees, a sofa, and a bed, the latter necessary for several sick children. There were two outside entrances into the sitting room, as well as one internal door to the Indian room, where the Osborns were staying, and one into the kitchen.

"Did you see either of my sisters?" Grace couldn't help but pose the question. She needed to know what they had endured.

Margaret gave a brief nod. "Hope was in the kitchen with John. It was just after the nooning, and Mary Ann Bridger was there too. I had been there a little earlier to get hot water for tea but had gone back to the Indian room where my family was resting. I left the tea to steep and realized I needed to ask Narcissa about something—I forget what it was, now. I opened the door to the sitting room just as Hope came to tell the doctor that the

Indians were there for medicine. I could see by the look on Narcissa's face that she was afraid. The Indian they called Telokite tried to push his way into the sitting room, but Dr. Whitman prevailed and kept him out." Margaret drew breath and let it go in a long sigh. For several minutes she said nothing.

"I heard raised voices and then a scream. It might have been Hope. I hurried back to the Indian room, and Narcissa called to me to lock the exterior door. At some point, the kitchen door was forced open. My Josiah asked what was happening, and I told him the Indians had risen to kill us. He jumped to his feet, took up a flatiron and some nails, and secured the exterior door so no one could enter.

"The gunfire was deafening and seemed to go on forever. I hadn't thought to close the door to our room. Narcissa again yelled for me to close the kitchen door, and when I went to do so, I saw young John Sager dead on the floor. Your sister was holding him."

Grace gasped and choked back a sob. Tears streamed down her cheeks even though she fought to keep them back.

"There was so much screaming and crying from the children that I thought to go and help, but Josiah called for me to shut the door and come back into the Indian room. I did, and he told me to secure the latch. While I did that, Josiah managed to pry up a few floorboards that weren't yet nailed down and told us all to get under the house. The children were terrified. We all were."

"I'm so sorry." Grace held Margaret's hand, which trembled as she told her story.

"We were no sooner hidden away with the boards back in place when the Indians broke into the room. They were raising such a clatter as they tore the room apart that my Alexander cried out that the Indians were taking all our things. I clamped my hand over his mouth, terrified that they had heard him and would find us, but they didn't."

The children stirred in the bed behind her, and Margaret paused to turn and see if they were all right. When there was no further noise, she looked back at Grace. "After that, it was the sounds that were awful. We could hear the gunfire and screams. We heard people racing through the house as well as those being murdered just outside. Poor Andy Rogers died just beyond our room. I can still hear him as he lay dying. He was praying, calling out to God over and over. 'Come, Lord Jesus, come quickly.'"

Grace's chest tightened in agony at the thought of that gentle soul being murdered. If only he had accompanied her to the Brownings' mission, he might still be alive.

". . . screaming as the Indians forced themselves upon them."

"What?" Grace realized she hadn't fully heard what Margaret was saying.

Margaret shook her head. "The women. They were screaming as the Indians forced them—took them—as wives."

A wave of nausea rose up in Grace and she tasted bile. Hope and Mercy. Had they been so cruelly abused? *Dear Lord, please no.*

"That night after everything was quiet, Josiah said we needed to go. He knew that if we stayed, the Indians would find us in the morning. So we got away—Josiah carrying John on his back and Alexander in his arms. I had Nancy with me. We only got about two miles before I collapsed. Josiah told me to remain hidden with Alexander and Nancy, and then he took John and came to the fort. The next day—no, I think it might have been two . . ." She shook her head. "I can't say, but John and a friendly Indian came and found us. We were riding to the fort when a Cayuse saw us and rode up to kill us. Our Indian talked him out of it, although I don't know what he could have said to change the Cayuse's mind. I was so weary and frightened that I almost wished he would just kill us and be done with it. The constant threat—even here it's maddening." She fell silent, her face still a blank void.

Grace had heard more than enough. She wanted to stay and offer help, but she couldn't. "Thank you for telling me. I needed to know." Without waiting for Margaret's response, Grace nearly ran from the room.

She hurried out of the building, having no idea where to seek comfort. Blinded by tears, she wandered aimlessly around the fort grounds. Her sisters were still at the mercy of the Indians, and there was nothing she could do. She collapsed in a heap at the corner of one of the buildings and gave herself over to mourning. Why had this happened? Why hadn't Whitman known to get them all to safety? But where was safety to be found? Even here at the fort, everyone feared the Indians would attack and continue their war.

"Grace, are you all right?"

She looked up to find Alex not six feet away. She collected herself and got to her feet. He didn't move but watched her with an expression of agony on his face.

"I just heard that Margaret told you about the attack."

"Alex, I want the truth." She came within inches of him. "My sisters . . . were they . . ." She could hardly speak the words. "Were they taken as wives?"

He held her gaze. "Hope told Sam that Mercy was thought to be too young."

Grace realized he was telling her in as delicate a way as he could that Hope had been compromised. She struck out at him, flailing her fists into his chest.

"Why? Why would God let this happen? Why? They're just girls—they did no one any harm."

At first Alex let her rage, but after a few moments, he took hold of her wrists. "Grace, they're alive, and hopefully they'll remain that way. You need to focus on that."

"I failed to keep them safe. I failed my mother and father. They were my responsibility, and I should have made them go with me to the Brownings'."

"You did what you could for them. You carried your responsibility for them in a most admirable way."

She shook her head. "Maybe they'd be better off dead. Think of what they've seen—what they've endured. How can you expect them to live with those memories? How can anyone live with that?" She was close to hysteria.

His arms wrapped around Grace and held her fast. "They are alive. No matter what they've endured, they are alive, and they need you to remain strong. They will need you, Grace."

She calmed and rested her head against his buckskin-clad chest. "I should never have come west. God is punishing me for marrying a man I didn't love—for making vows to love when I knew it would be impossible."

Alex put his hand beneath her jaw and forced her to look up. "I don't know why this happened, but I am sure that this was not God's desire. Why blame Him when the devil is loosed on this world and causes far more harm?"

"I don't know what to believe anymore. I thought being saved spiritually meant that God would keep you from evil. Not that bad things wouldn't happen, like people dying or getting sick, but I figured God would keep away evil things, and this was evil, Alex."

"If we were to be kept completely from evil, He would have to take us out of this world, because it's full of such things."

"I don't know how they're going to bear this." She sought his face, desperate to find an answer in his expression. "I don't know how to help them."

"All we can do is take each minute and get through that. And then another and another."

Chapter 16

S am sat with his father as Cayuse chiefs and subchiefs met at the Umatilla village to discuss what had happened at the Whitman Mission. The Catholic bishop and several priests were also present and demanded an accounting.

Camaspelo, who was in charge of the village that lay between the Whitman mission and the Umatilla village, declared that he had come to protest what had happened. "My words have been stolen," he said to the gathering. "I did not want this killing, and I will not be blamed."

"This was revenge for the doctor's attack on our people," Telokite countered. "My young men were angry at the death Dr. Whitman had caused."

The priests asked questions, and the talk seemed to go on forever. Sam felt certain that very little would be accomplished. Telokite and his men were adamant that what they had done was right in order to keep the doctor from killing even more Cayuse.

Telokite continued to speak, giving a review of the area tribes' history as it related to the arrival of the Boston and King George men. He pointed out numerous wrongs done to the Indians, then finished by speaking to the lessons taught them by the Black Robes. Lessons that focused on the displeasure God had for people who made war and committed murders.

When he finished, his son Edward stood and displayed a Catholic Ladder. The cloth, a pictorial of catechisms used to share the way to heaven, was stained with blood. "Dr. Whitman hated the Black Robes. He said because you had given us this and we allowed priests to be among us, God would cover our country in blood. He told us we would have nothing—but blood."

Edward continued, giving exact details as to what had taken place that day at the mission. "Joe Lewis told us that the doctor intended to see us dead. Just as you have heard from our brother here." He stopped and pointed to a young Cayuse who had actually slept in the Whitman house. "Dr. Whitman planned our murders, giving us poison—taking the life of our people. These things were heard, and we do not lie."

"Did you hear these things yourself?" one of the priests asked.

Edward nodded. "I did. I was there the day before we avenged our people. Mr. Rogers told me that the doctor and his wife, along with Mr. Spaulding, had endeavored for some time to poison us. They had promised to see all of the Cayuse and Nez Perce people dead."

The other Cayuse agreed, and after some further discussion, the priests helped them to put together a letter that might be sent to the governor on their behalf. After that, the priests departed to talk among themselves, and the Cayuse and Nez Perce began to disperse.

Sam knew the whites wouldn't be swayed from revenge by a mere letter. They might declare themselves willing to make peace until they got the women and children to safety, but after that there would be no stopping the soldiers from pursuing the Indians responsible.

"I will return to our people," Jacob Night Walker told Sam. "I will let them know what has taken place here."

"Tell Sarah I will be home when I can. I need to get to Alex at the fort and let him know what has happened."

Alex had never been happier to see Sam than when he arrived back at the fort just a few days before Christmas. The Cayuse chiefs had been summoned to Fort Nez Perce to parley with Mr. Peter Skeen Ogden, one of the directors from Fort Vancouver. Alex hoped that with the goods he'd brought, the Cayuse might be convinced to give up their hostages in trade.

"Do you think this will work?" Grace asked. Alex saw the guarded look on her face and was overwhelmed by the need to reassure her that this ordeal would soon end.

"I think they finally understand that they've caused more problems than they can ever hope to solve," Sam told Alex and Grace. "Ogden is known to many of the chiefs. I think they'll respect him."

"They've always feared and respected the men of the Hudson's Bay Company, especially Dr. McLoughlin," Alex said.

"Yes, but McLoughlin is no longer in charge."

"Who is Dr. McLoughlin?" Grace asked.

"He held control as factor of Fort Vancouver for many years," Alex explained. "Only recently was it decided to have a three-man board in charge rather than a single man."

Grace frowned. "And is Mr. Ogden on that board?"

"Yes, as is McLoughlin, although I think he's finished with the Hudson's Bay Company and may have already resigned. From what I hear, Ogden and a man named James Douglas are making the decisions."

"But if the Indians respect McLoughlin, then couldn't he be prevailed upon to help?" Grace's tone bore a sense of desperation.

Alex wished he could convince her that everything possible was being done. "I think we need to wait and see what Mr. Ogden accomplishes in these negotiations. Meanwhile, I think it would be wise for you to stay out of sight. Telokite knows you, as do his sons. Some of the others might also recognize you."

"I'm not afraid of them," Grace countered.

Alex nodded, but it was Sam who spoke up. "But they know your sisters also. If these negotiations do not fare well, they might remember you were a part of it and harm Hope and Mercy as revenge."

That was all that was needed to convince Grace. She agreed to remain hidden with Mrs. Osborn and her children. Their presence would not be made known to the Cayuse.

When the meeting was finally called, Alex took his place with Sam and waited to hear what Ogden would say. He had to admire the man. He had come of his own accord, bringing goods that he'd paid for himself—all in the hopes of seeing the women and children safely set free.

"It is now thirty years we have been among you," Ogden began. He spoke of how the men of the Hudson's Bay Company had been faithful in trading with the native peoples and had not shed blood but rather had given them ammunition and guns to make their hunting easier. He reiterated over and over that such weapons were never to be used against man.

Then Ogden boldly pointed to Telokite and accused the chiefs of having no control over their people.

Alex held his breath, waiting to see what would happen. The harsh statement was bound to insult the Cayuse.

There was murmuring among the chiefs, but no one spoke, and Ogden continued, explaining that sickness came to both the whites and the Indians. He stressed that only God determined the time of a man's death.

Alex wondered if the Cayuse would accept any value in that statement. Ogden spoke of the white man's God, and while many of them claimed to revere God, Alex knew that others only played along in order to benefit from whatever the missionaries might give them.

While Alex considered this, Ogden continued speaking. The tension remained high, and it was easy to see that Telokite and the other Cayuse were guarded and uncomfortable. Ogden had all but accused them of having broken their pledges. He might as well have called them liars. Finally Ogden fell silent.

The Cayuse chiefs spoke among themselves. Tauitowe looked to Telokite and commented that many of their women were married to the Hudson's Bay men, and because of this they should accept Ogden's help out of respect.

Telokite finally spoke. "We have known you a long time, and you have been a good friend to the Cayuse. We seek to make peace."

Alex exchanged a look with Sam. The relief on his friend's face was mirrored in Alex's soul. Telokite had said many things that Alex didn't believe, but he had also pledged to return the hostages. Hopefully he would honor his word better than he had when he'd promised not to attack the mission.

Alex hurried from the room to find Grace. He prayed the news would give her some peace of mind. When he found her still obediently waiting with Mrs. Osborn, he couldn't help but smile.

He motioned her to come to the door. She whispered something to Mrs. Osborn and followed Alex outside. Alex led her behind the building, hoping to keep her hidden.

"Is it over? Will they let them go?" She looked at him with such an expression of hope that Alex smiled as he nodded.

"Telokite has agreed to release them."

Grace surprised him by wrapping her arms around his neck.

The most logical, most desirable thing in the world was that he should kiss her. Alex lowered his lips to hers and found Grace most receptive. She pulled him closer and returned the kiss with enthusiasm.

For a moment Alex was transported to another place and time—and woman. Caroline. He had proposed marriage and she had accepted, and then everything went wrong.

Startled by the memory, Alex opened his eyes, almost certain he would find Caroline rather than Grace in his arms. A sense of relief washed over him, but just as quickly, panic set in.

Realizing what he'd done, Alex pushed Grace away from him. "I'm sorry. I never meant for that to happen. I know what you're feeling, but I can't . . . won't let you think . . ." He shook his head. "I'm not free to love you."

He saw the hurt on her face—the pain in her eyes. Alex nearly let it be his undoing. Instead he turned and walked away. It was better this way. In time, Grace would get over her feelings for him.

But will I get over mine for her?

Grace was stunned. She had felt Alex's desire in the kiss they shared and knew he cared for her as much as she did for him. So why had he humiliated her that way?

Returning to the front of the building, she saw some Cayuse across the fort commons and hurried to duck inside before they noticed her. Margaret gave her a questioning look when she entered. Grace knew she was wondering what had happened.

"The Cayuse have agreed to release the women and children."

"Praise God," Margaret murmured, hugging her youngest close.

Nodding, Grace moved to the far side of the room. She had

no desire to talk to anyone as she contemplated what had happened with Alex.

It was just a matter of the moment. My feelings got the best of me. It meant nothing.

She was still telling herself that later in the afternoon when Sam came to speak to her. The Osborns were all asleep, so she risked being seen and stepped outside, fearing that should the Osborns awaken to find Sam there, they might be frightened. She motioned Sam to follow her behind the house.

"Sam, Alex told me the chiefs agreed to release the women and children. Have they set a time?"

"It's uncertain. They have agreed to return and load the hostages up immediately. They are even now arranging to borrow wagons from the fort."

She could see a hint of doubt darken his expression. "Do you trust them?"

He shrugged. "I don't see that we have any other choice. They know the trouble they have brought down on our heads."

"Why do you include yourself in their number? You and your people had nothing to do with it."

"Perhaps not, but we will be blamed all the same. We are all the same to the whites. Your people do not see the differences. They only know us to be the enemy."

"No. That isn't true. There are a great many whites who believe otherwise. Mr. Spaulding has spoken highly of the Nez Perce since his arrival here. He wouldn't even have made it here safely had it not been for your people. There are others who will tell the truth of the matter as well."

"And individually people may listen, but collectively they will desire only to rid themselves of what scares them the most."

Grace couldn't argue his point. There was too much truth in what he said. The mob mentality of people could be a very ugly thing to witness.

"I'm sorry, Sam. I've been guilty of judging all Indians by the act of a few. I know it's small consolation, but I have corrected my thinking. Maybe others will too."

"It will be a long time coming. The blood of Whitman and the others will be too bright a stain to ignore." He shook his head sadly. "I fear for my people. The worst is yet to come."

By the next evening, the Cayuse had all departed the fort, and Grace took the opportunity to enjoy a short walk to clear her head. In just two days it would be Christmas. She had thought she and her sisters would celebrate it together at the Whitmans'. Perhaps they might have even heard from their uncle by then. There wouldn't have been gifts to exchange, but they would have shared food and memories of other Christmases before their mother and father had died.

Across the way she spied Alex and Sam near the building where she was staying. They were the last people she wanted to see—especially Alex. His rejection had left her feeling more alone than she'd ever felt. It was important to avoid him for a time. Once she had her emotions under control, she could more easily deal with him and put her memories of their kiss aside.

But that kiss had been unlike anything she'd ever experienced. She couldn't help but remember the feel of Alex's lips upon hers, the warmth of his arms around her. He'd done so much for her when they'd traveled together—eased her load, made her comfortable. He'd been encouraging when she worried about her sisters and what was to be done. He'd held her and consoled her when she'd learned the truth about Hope. She loved him. He was all that she'd ever wanted in a husband.

He cares for me. I know he does.

So why had he pushed her aside and walked away? Why? He said he wasn't free to love her. Did he have an Indian wife like Gabe? Was that the reason he seemed so secretive?

"Grace."

She stiffened at the sound of Alex calling her name. The thought of running away came but left just as quickly. The fort was small, and there was no place to hide. Turning, she saw Alex approaching and squared her shoulders.

"Yes?"

"I think we need to talk."

"No. I don't think that's necessary."

"I owe you an explanation. I think I misled you with that kiss."

"It wasn't important. It meant nothing. I was merely excited about my sisters coming back to me. I would have kissed Sam if he'd brought me the news." She knew it was all a lie, but her pride was wounded, and she couldn't bring herself to show weakness in front of him.

A look of hurt momentarily darkened his expression, but he quickly recovered. "I'm sorry. I do care for you. I really do, and despite what you say, I know you care for me. There are things, however, that won't allow me to . . ." He gave a heavy sigh. "I can't explain it, but you need to know that I'm sorry. If I could allow myself to love anyone, it would be you."

She could hear the pleading in his tone and wrestled with her conscience, knowing that the Christian thing to do was give in and swallow her pride. He'd hurt her—humiliated her, really—but there were so many worthier problems to focus on.

Finally, she replied. "You obviously have your reasons. Reasons that you cannot share. It isn't important." She turned to walk away, but he grabbed her arm and drew her back.

"It is important. I know I hurt you, and that was never my desire."

She hated his nearness as much as she desired it. If she couldn't put some distance between them soon, she was going to make a fool of herself. "I need to go." She pulled free of his hold and hurried across the grounds.

A part of her hoped he'd stop her. She longed to return and make him listen to reason—to hear him say it was all a mistake and that he . . . loved her.

But instead only silence followed, and Grace felt her heart break a little more.

On the twenty-ninth of December the wagons rolled into Fort Nez Perce. Hope held Mercy close, fearful that the entire affair was simply a trick—some heinous joke. The survivors had been mostly silent on the trip. The tension and fear was almost more than they'd known at the mission. Now that they were so close to being free, they were terrified that something might keep it from happening. But as the wagons halted inside the fort and people came to help them down, most of the women and children broke into tears of relief.

Hope saw Grace run from one of the buildings to greet them. She looked haggard—older than Hope remembered. She embraced Mercy first, alternating between hugging and kissing her.

"Oh, I can scarcely believe you're finally here. Oh, my sweet dears, how I have prayed." She let go of Mercy and hugged Hope. "I'm so sorry for what you've endured." She pulled away to look Hope in the eyes. "For what they've stolen from you."

Hope realized that Grace knew about the rapes. Hope knew too that her sister would be sympathetic and generous with her attention and care. But Hope wanted no part of it. She didn't want to be noticed or fussed over. She wanted only to be left alone. If they all forgot that she was even alive, that would be just fine.

"Come on," Grace murmured. "I have a place for you all readied. When I heard that the wagons were just a mile away, I put on hot water so you could wash up. Oh, and I have tonics to help you sleep." Grace directed them to the small room she'd been using. "I have pallets there for you to sleep on, and here's the water."

"Where are the others going to stay?" Mercy asked.

"In the main building. I thought maybe you'd like a little privacy after being forced . . . having to stay with everyone so close together."

"I want to be with Mary Ann. She's been sick," Mercy replied.

"Maybe I can help her. Why don't we check on her after you wash up?"

Mercy shook her head. "No. I want to be with her now." Without another word, Mercy left the room.

Hope could see that Grace had not anticipated this defiance. "She and Mary Ann are very close. They . . . they helped each other to . . . get by."

Grace frowned. "I'm glad she has a friend." She kept her gaze fixed on the door. "Oh, Hope, I wish I'd been there to keep you safe. I feel terrible that you had to bear it alone. Well, I know you weren't alone. God was with you the whole time."

Hope felt rage rise up in her. "Do not speak to me of God. If He was there, then He stood by watching without a single thought for us. I want nothing to do with God."

Grace looked at Hope as if she'd suddenly gone mad. "You don't mean that. I know you're just upset right now. I am too. I hate what's happened, and believe me, I railed at God for letting it happen. But I know He still cares for us—for you. I want to help in any way I can, but I don't know what you need. Help me understand."

A bitter laugh rose up from deep within Hope. She choked it back. "You can't understand. You weren't there. You'll never understand."

Chapter 17

It was a new year, 1848, but no one felt like celebrating. There was very little to celebrate. No one felt safe at Fort Nez Perce—not the company men who'd arrived with Peter Ogden, and certainly not the released women and children. The tension was thick, and it only served to make everyone question when Peter Ogden would get them out of there and to the safety of Fort Vancouver.

Alex watched the rescued hostages from afar. They wanted little to do with anyone, including Grace, although her healing skills were allowed. After having shared the massacre and captivity, it was almost as if they had become one family. They kept to themselves and said very little. When local Indians came in to trade, their fears were evident and the tensions high. The ordeal wasn't over for them. Not yet. Maybe not ever.

Grace did what she could, and Alex knew she was troubled by how these women who had once been her friends now seemed to put a wall between themselves and her. Worse still, Grace's sisters did the same. Since their arrival that first night, they had chosen to stay with the other women and children rather than enjoy the privacy of Grace's room. He knew it hurt her, but she never said a word.

Making his way to a meeting with Ogden and his men, Alex was taken off guard when Hope approached him.

"I know you've been a good friend to my sister," she began.

Alex took a moment to study the once vivacious young woman. He remembered seeing her at the mission—her beauty undeniable, and her zest for life more than evident. She had fallen in love, Grace had said, and she'd seen that same young man killed. She looked at least ten years older. Her eyes, once a vibrant blue, seemed somehow a dull gray—almost void of life. She was pale with dark circles under those lifeless eyes and a grimness to her expression that made Alex all the sadder.

"What can I do for you, Hope?"

"I want your promise on something."

His eyes narrowed. "If I can."

"It's not that difficult." She looked past him to the front gate. Just beyond, a half dozen Cayuse had made camp. They were loud and boisterous, and Alex knew it set the nerves of everyone in the fort on edge.

"Go on." He tried to keep his voice low and gentle.

"We've been hearing that some of the Indians regret trading us so cheaply. I heard a couple of the Hudson's Bay men talking about the threat of the Cayuse bringing more men and attacking the fort to take us back."

"Hope, there are always rumors."

"Well, the Cayuse are here, aren't they? And their numbers are growing. They've been allowed to come into the fort pretty much at will. None of us feel safe."

Alex frowned. He knew there was little he could say to calm her fears. "What can I do?"

"I want your promise that if the Cayuse try to take us again and it looks like they will win, that you will shoot me. I won't go through that again. I can't. If I had my own gun, I'd not worry about it, but since I don't, I'm asking you to help me."

Her words felt like a punch in the gut. He could see in her eyes that she was serious. "Hope . . . I . . . well . . ." He fell silent. What could he say? She was terrified of being taken into captivity again. Terrified of being forced to do the things she'd had to do in order to survive. Without realizing at first what he was doing, Alex began to nod. How could he not promise to keep her from being taken again? "If there's no other way."

He let the statement linger on the crisp morning air. Grace would hate him for this, but a part of him couldn't help but give Hope this tiny bit of assurance.

She released a heavy sigh. "Thank you." She started to go, then turned back. "Don't say anything to Grace. She doesn't understand."

"No, she doesn't, but she does love you more than her own life."

"I know. That's why you can't tell her what you've promised me. She'd never understand—if you have to do it. And . . . if you care anything about her or the others, you'll do the same for them rather than let the Indians take them."

She walked away, leaving Alex more troubled than he'd ever been. He'd been so consumed with his past and the war of emotions going on inside him that the plight of these women had been only a thought on the perimeter of his mind.

Alex considered what he'd just agreed to as he made his way to the meeting. When he arrived, the discussion was well underway.

"We're going to get everyone on the boats and head to Fort Vancouver tomorrow," Peter Ogden announced to his men. When Ogden had come to the rescue, he'd brought three boats and men to man them, along with the trade goods he'd used to ransom the women and children. "I'm sure you know the talk—the rumors about the growing number of Cayuse and other Indians."

"Ain't no rumor," one of the burly, bearded men countered. "I've counted more each day."

Ogden nodded. "As have I. That's why we're leaving. I want to put out no later than noon."

The men gave a nod or grunt of approval.

"We will put women and children as families onto the boats," he instructed. "Try not to separate anyone who wants to stay together. They have been through a great deal, and we don't want to make it worse for them." Again the men nodded, and Ogden continued.

"Make certain the boats are ready—that they haven't been tampered with. I know we've had guards on them continually, but I don't trust those Cayuse not to have found a way to sabotage us. Double the guard tonight and take shifts so that you can still rest up for tomorrow. I want every man to make sure his rifle and pistol are in working order."

Alex stood at the back of the room, waiting for Ogden to complete his speech. He had to speak to him before they departed. Given that Alex wasn't a drinker or a gambler, his Hudson's Bay account still had plenty of credit, and Alex wanted Ogden to see that it benefited Grace and her sisters once they arrived at Fort Vancouver.

As the meeting concluded and the men headed to bed or guard duty, Alex made his way to intercept Ogden.

"I wonder if I might have a word."

Ogden nodded. "Of course, Alex. What is it?"

Alex lowered his voice. "There is a family here . . . three sisters."

"Yes, the oldest was here when I arrived. Mrs. Martindale."

"Yes. Her sisters were at the mission, but Grace was with me and Sam Two Moons at another mission when the attack took place. Anyway, they have very little to their names, especially now."

"None of these women have anything. The Cayuse robbed them of most everything. They're lucky to have the clothes on their backs, and as you saw when they arrived, some of them had very little of that. Supposedly the governor is going to arrange for a militia to go to the mission and retrieve what they can, but for now we're meeting their needs to the best of our ability."

"I know." Alex had been glad to see that Ogden held back some of the supplies he'd brought for trade, instead using them to help feed and clothe the women. He'd also arranged in their negotiations for the Cayuse to bring grain from Whitman's stores to help feed the victims. "Grace and her sisters are special friends of mine."

Ogden smiled. "I've seen the way you act around Mrs. Martindale."

Alex hid his surprise. He had thought himself careful not to reveal his feelings. "My point is that I want them to have my company credit when you get to Vancouver."

This only made Ogden's smile widen. "That's mighty generous of you. Have you told them?"

"No, and I don't intend to. When you arrive, simply tell Grace that credit has been set up for her. If she wants further explanation, tell her that you have none."

"Well, won't she have a good idea? I mean, you'll be right there."

"I'm not going with you. I'm heading back to the Nez Perce village. Sam Two Moons and I are readying our traps for spring."

Ogden lost his smile at this. "Alex, you're a good shot and have a keen eye. I was hoping you'd help me on the return trip. There will be times of portage when we'll be far more vulnerable. I'll need you to scout out things and let us know if any hostiles approach. I'll pay you good money."

Alex knew he couldn't refuse. "I don't need pay to do what's right."

"Then you'll come along?"

Alex blew out a long breath as he remembered his promise to Hope. "I guess so."

"Good. I'll even arrange for you to have free passage back here so you needn't be gone any longer than necessary. Get yourself plenty of powder and balls at the store, and anything else you feel you need. I'll tell McBean to charge the company."

Alex nodded, feeling a sense of trepidation at what he'd just agreed to. He needed to avoid contact with Grace, and yet now he was accompanying her to Fort Vancouver. He walked out of the main hall and crossed the grounds. Overhead, the moon, although half full, was waning. It had been the same the night after the attack. He wondered if the women would notice.

He'd heard the details of the killings at the mission, as well as how Narcissa Whitman had been shot and then later mutilated. In his mind he could see the aftermath—the bodies left out in the moon's dim light. Someone had said that the Indians planned to burn the mission to the ground, and Alex actually thought that would be a good idea. That place would forever bear a sense of loss and sorrow. Better to leave it all in the ashes and let the land—and the people—heal.

But would healing ever come? He had wrestled to find healing these past ten years. He had struggled to make peace with himself and with God. He glanced to the skies again.

"Father, I know I've been wrong to hold such anger . . . at You. Gabriel told me all the time that my anger would only eat away at my heart, and I know that's true. But I also know that You can give me a new heart." He felt his shoulders slump. A weariness unlike any he'd ever known settled on him.

"I'm asking Your forgiveness," he whispered. "I'm asking

You to help me resolve the past. I don't want to go back to New Orleans, but if that's Your will for me, then show me how to do it—how to make peace with those who hate me . . . and those who love me."

By noon on the second of January, the Hudson's Bay Company boats were loaded and heading down the Columbia River. Unfortunately, the growing audience of Cayuse decided to follow along the riverbanks. It left the women weepy and the children clinging to their mothers. Grace did what she could for anyone who needed her tonics and treatments, but medicine could only do so much. After many miles, they finally left the Indians behind, much to everyone's relief.

At night they pulled ashore and camped. Most of the women didn't want to leave the boats, but Ogden insisted. Grace noted that no one moved very far ashore, however. She was grateful that Ogden gave particular attention to posting guards. Even Alex took his turn watching over the camp with the other men. He seemed ever diligent to do his duty and to avoid her.

Grace tried not to let it bother her. She did her best to ignore Alex altogether and focus instead on the women and children. It hurt her more than she could say that they wanted very little to do with her. She had broken bread with them, tended their little ones, and heard their secrets. Now, however, they wanted only to be left alone. Grace was determined not to take their snubbing personally. From what little she'd managed to get out of Hope, Grace knew that having shared and survived the attack on the mission made them different from her. All Grace could do was wait. Maybe, in time, the women would once again allow her into their circle.

After breakfast on their third day, Ogden made an announcement. "Today we'll be on a rather rough part of the river. I don't want anyone to fret, but you'll need to do exactly as you're told or risk losing your life or that of your children. My men will get us through safely and assist you however they can."

There were murmurings among the women, but no one made any real comment. Once they were again on the river and the water became more difficult, many of the women and children became nauseated and vomited over the side of the boats. Grace mixed tonics to help ease their misery, but still they suffered. Even Mercy and Hope were spent from the ordeal. Only Grace and the men seemed to have little difficulty.

"If you drink this, you'll feel better." Grace reached into the bag at her feet and produced a small bottle of tonic and a spoon. She extended it to her sister.

"I don't want it," Hope replied.

"But it's helped the others, and I know it would help you as well. Remember how Mama would give it to us when we were sick?"

Hope glared at Grace. "I don't want or need your remedies. Now leave me alone."

Grace couldn't bear her sister's rejection. "Please, Hope, don't cast me away. I only want to help. I have one remedy that Mama always swore by to calm nerves, and I really think—"

Something in Hope seemed to snap. Before Grace could finish her sentence, Hope pushed her away, scooped up the carpetbag, and threw it into the water.

It made a dull splash and immediately began to sink. Grace lunged for it, nearly throwing herself over the side. Everything they owned was in that bag. Strong arms pulled her back into her seat, and Grace turned to find one of the men looking at her like she was crazy.

"My bag went into the water," she tried to explain. "I need it. It has my medicine and . . . well . . . everything." Rippled rings marked where the bag had entered the river. Even as they moved steadily downstream, Grace could see them. She looked back at the man, knowing there was nothing he could do.

"Sorry. The river has it now. It's way too deep and cold for anyone to go after it." He returned to the job of rowing.

Grace glanced down at her feet, where only moments before the bag had been safely kept. She had no idea what they were going to do now. She had nothing to work with. No herbs to offer for healing. No money to see them resettled.

Looking up, she found Hope watching her. There seemed to be only a hint of regret in her sister's eyes, but that was quickly extinguished, and Hope turned away once again.

Grace looked back at the water and shook her head. "That was all the money we had."

When they finally arrived at the fort on the eighth of January, it was as if everyone knew they were finally safe. The looks on the faces of the survivors held relief. For the widows, that relief was mingled with sorrow. Sadly, Grace knew they'd have little time to grieve. Just as it was on the trail west, women were expected to put aside their anguish and remarry.

"I want to see my husband." Eliza Hall had been told her husband, Peter, had left Fort Nez Perce in hopes of getting armed troops to save the captives.

The man she spoke to shook his head. "Who's your husband?"

"Peter Hall. He escaped the massacre and fled to Fort Nez Perce. Mr. McBean said he then came to this fort in order to get help."

"Nobody came here that I know of." He looked at a couple of men employed by the company. "Any of you fellas seen a Peter Hall?" They shook their heads.

"He has to be here," Eliza countered, her voice sounding

panicked. "He must be. They said he'd come here." Her five children crowded closer, sensing their mother's despair.

The man seemed to realize the situation and smiled. "Look, just because I ain't seen him doesn't mean he hasn't come. Why don't you go rest with the others, and I'll get the word out and see if we can find him?"

Eliza let herself be led away by Mrs. Saunders. The woman talked in hushed tones as they crossed the room and took a seat at one of the tables.

"We have food and drink ready for you," one of the company men announced. "Afterward we will show you where you can clean up and sleep. Your ordeal is over, and you are safe. Tomorrow we'll take you to Portland and then on up the Willamette to Oregon City."

There were murmurs throughout the weary crowd. Grace could see the smirk on Hope's face and knew what her sister was thinking. Their ordeal wouldn't be over for a very long time—if ever.

They took their places at tables filled with plenty of food. Grace thought she'd never smelled anything quite so good as the ham and roasted meat that awaited them. She found herself glancing around the room for Alex, but he was nowhere to be found. She had seen very little of him on their trip, although he'd been with them the entire journey. Having him near made her feel safe, but knowing he purposefully sought to keep his distance made her sad. Perhaps it was for the best. She and her sisters would settle in Oregon City and wait for their uncle to return, while Alex would lose himself somewhere in the wilds.

"Did you know that Alex is going away?" Mercy asked, taking a seat beside Grace.

"Yes. He has to get back to trapping. I heard them say that in another month or so the furs will be at their best." Grace hoped her tone didn't reveal the turmoil in her heart.

"I wish he'd stay," Mercy said.

I wish he would too. Grace didn't speak the words aloud, but she felt them all the same.

"I really like him."

Grace swallowed the lump in her throat. "I know."

And I love him.

They ate in silence, as did most of the women and children. When Hope got up from the table and left the room, Mercy leaned over and hugged Grace.

"I'm sorry she threw away your carpetbag. I know you had all of the stuff Mama gave you and our money."

Grace looked into her sister's blue-green eyes. "Thank you for the hug."

Mercy frowned and looked down at her plate. "I'm sorry that I haven't been a better sister. I didn't mean to hurt your feelings by staying with Mary Ann all the time."

"It's all right. I know you two are good friends, and since you went through so much together, you probably need each other."

"She's all alone. Her papa is far away and her mama's dead. She's scared because she doesn't know where they'll make her go."

"Perhaps she could stay with us, although I have no idea how we're going to survive. I thought we had enough money to get through the winter, but now there's nothing. I can't even make a living with the herbs."

"But you know how to find them and make new tonics and vinegar. You've been making vinegar forever. It shouldn't be too hard."

Grace didn't realize until that moment the depth of her discouragement. "I don't know, Mercy. I doubt I can wait that long."

Mercy looked puzzled. "Then what will you do?"

"I shall probably have to marry someone. All the way on our journey here, the men talked about the fact that none of us need be widows for long. There are at least twenty men for every woman in Oregon Country, and they all want wives because that will allow them to claim additional land and provide someone to help with the work."

"I don't want you to marry one of those men," Mercy said. "Mama said we should only marry for love."

"But that was before." Grace shook her head. "That was a lifetime before."

"Mrs. Martindale, might I have a word?" Peter Ogden helped Grace up from the table and led her away from the others. "I need to let you know something tonight before you leave with the others for Oregon City."

"What is it, Mr. Ogden?"

He smiled. "Good news, for you and your sisters. There is an account here at the fort for you to draw on. The balance is substantial and will help you to re-outfit. We have some dresses on hand that should fit each of you, as well as other things women are fond of."

"An account? How can there be an account?" She shook her head, thinking momentarily of Alex. Had he arranged this? Then just as that thought came to mind, she thought of her uncle. She'd talked at length with Ogden about her uncle when they'd been at Fort Nez Perce. "Did my uncle do this? Does he have an account with the Hudson's Bay Company?"

"Of course he does." Ogden looked sheepish. "The important thing is that you have credit to get some of the things you need. I know you lost your carpetbag and medicines on the river. I think we can set you up with some replacements—bottles and stoppers and such. You can purchase the herbs in Portland and Oregon City, and then come spring, you'll be able to start hunting for your own. This land is rich with resources."

Grace breathed a sigh of relief. The credit wouldn't solve their problem in full, but it would help.

Chapter 18

Alex watched the women and children depart from the fort to head to Oregon City. Dr. McLoughlin had been making arrangements for the victims ever since hearing about their plight. Since he owned most of Oregon City and most folks there were indebted to him, he had the full cooperation of well-established families to help him care for the newly released victims. Alex felt confident that folks would rise up to help. That was the way of things in the west. Everyone tried to be generous, knowing that next time trouble struck, it could be them in the position of need.

Alex knew from Peter Ogden that Grace had taken advantage of the account set up for her at the company store. He also told Alex that she thought her uncle had arranged it. Alex had told him to do nothing to change her mind. Knowing that he had been able to give Grace at least this small thing made Alex feel better. Hopefully it would ease her sadness over the way he'd behaved.

Once the survivors were gone, Alex felt the freedom to let himself be seen at the fort. Volunteers were gathering to answer the call to arms that had gone out when the massacre was announced over a month ago. The attitude of the men made Alex nervous. They were eager to find the Indians responsible and see them hanged. Unfortunately, just as he'd feared, there were a great many who wanted to wipe out the native peoples altogether.

Alex thought of the many friends he'd made among the northwest tribes and the whites who had settled there. Would they always be at odds with one another? The would-be soldiers at the fort had asked Alex to join them, but he declined, telling them he had a prior commitment. He could hardly tell them that he had no stomach for the mass annihilation of a people who for the most part were innocent of what had happened.

Leaving them to their stories of glory and dreams of victory, Alex prepared to leave the fort. He purchased a few things he'd promised to bring Sam and then made plans to board the boat headed back to Fort Nez Perce.

"The territory isn't safe for a white American man to be out on his own right now," Ogden told him as Alex prepared to leave.

"I'm French-Canadian as well as American, and the Nez Perce have welcomed me into their tribe. Many of the other tribes in this part of the country know me and have done business with me. They know me to be honorable in our dealings, so I don't think I'll be in any great peril."

"That remains to be seen. The Indians are riled up. They know the government isn't going to just sit still after what's happened. You can kill a few men and no one thinks much about it, but if you attack a peaceful missionary and his wife, then kill others and take their wives and children hostage, you're going to bear the wrath for your actions. Men have been called up from all over this area. They're heading to the mission as soon as their numbers reach five hundred. They intend to act as militia and bring the Cayuse in for a trial."

"I doubt they'll ever catch up to any of them." Alex looked back at the river. Under the heavy, overcast sky, it looked a dark slate gray. "The Cayuse know this land better than we do. They've also got allies in various tribes at hand."

"As well as some enemies. Especially now. The Nez Perce are on record as having nothing to do with this attack."

"I can vouch for the Nez Perce, as I know Mr. Spaulding has already done. They are peaceful and have proven themselves helpful to us over and over. They escorted Spaulding and his family through hostile territory just to ensure they reached Fort Nez Perce. I think their loyalty is evident. However, I wouldn't call them an enemy to the Cayuse. Many of their families are intermarried, and that makes for a solid bond."

Ogden nodded, then rubbed his chin. "True enough, but I think a strong show of force on our part will coax other Indian tribes to come to our way of thinking."

"Or it may cause the whites to believe all Indians are bad. I fear that if you send five hundred men to the mission, all they will see is the color of Indian skin and judge them all guilty."

"That remains to be seen. We haven't yet put those numbers together. I will warn you, however, that there have been rumors of trouble stirring along the river. The Dalles might be in danger of attack. Whitman's nephew Perrin is there, and in the wake of what happened at the Whitman Mission, no one is taking a chance. They are arming up. Some of the supplies traveling with you will be left there. I think our troubles are just beginning."

Alex hated to admit it, but he couldn't agree more. He extended his hand. "Ogden, you're a good man. I hope you'll be the voice of reason." But even a voice of reason could be drowned out by the enraged rantings of five hundred men.

"Travel with both eyes open," Peter Ogden advised.

Alex reached inside his shirt and pulled out a letter. All night he'd toyed with the idea of sending it. "I wonder if you'd post this east when the mail goes out."

Ogden took the envelope and nodded. "Of course." He glanced down at the address and smiled. "Is this some lady love?"

"My sister," Alex said, still not certain he should send the letter, but before he could say anything more, Ogden had tucked the envelope in his pocket.

Seeking his place on the boat, Alex breathed a sigh of relief when they cast off. He took up an oar to help with the work. It did him good to keep occupied with something other than the threat of attacks and revenge. However, the relief he'd hoped for didn't come. Rowing required no real thought, and that left his mind free to dwell on Grace.

The more he wrestled with his feelings for her, the more he realized that those feelings wouldn't be easily ignored. For both their sakes, he'd do well to stay away for good. At least until he knew for certain what he was facing in New Orleans.

Of course it would take many months before the letter reached Adelina. Then there was the matter of how his own family would respond to hearing from him. It had been ten years. They might be happy to learn of his well-being, but they also might wish to have nothing to do with him.

But I can't have a future with Grace until I've laid to rest the demons of the past.

His thoughts betrayed him. He did want a future with Grace. Since coming west, he'd never considered settling down to marry and raise a family. Even when Sam told him of women in the village who fancied him. The life of a trapper was much too hard on women and children. That meant he'd need to figure out something else to do with his life before he could take a wife.

He gave a heavy sigh. There were so many questions and issues that had to be resolved.

"But everything starts with clearing my name," he muttered.

Dr. John McLoughlin was a giant of a man standing some six feet four inches. His snowy white hair fell to his broad shoulders like a lion's mane. He was treated with great respect and in many cases great affection, although there were also those who resented him, as was true for most men of power.

"I'm glad to have you here in Oregon City," he told Grace and her sisters. He had been working to see all of the hostages settled with small houses of their own or with other established families who had room to spare.

"I'd like to know if my uncle Edward Marsh has returned. I was told he went to California to buy cattle, and we had hoped to find him returned."

The man's piercing blue eyes narrowed. "So you are the nieces of Edward. I must say I'm especially glad to make your acquaintance. We heard you were among the victims from the attack on the mission. But you should know your uncle isn't here at present."

Grace nodded. "I see."

"But you needn't be disappointed. He's only been gone a couple of months, and the trip to bring back cattle will take at least twice that long—maybe longer. He did say to put you into his house at once if you were to arrive before his return."

"He did?" She could have cried. "So he must have received my letter."

"Indeed. I don't recall exactly when it arrived, but I know he was happy to hear that you and your sisters were coming. Then I was notified that you and your sisters were among those at the mission. Knowing you would arrive today, I had the place made ready."

Grace breathed a sigh of relief. "Where is his house?"

"It's a little place on the far side of town just beyond the church. It sits not far from the river. I think you'll be able to make yourselves quite comfortable there."

Grace looked at Hope and Mercy. "Did you hear that? We have a home."

Hope looked away, but Mercy pulled on Grace's sleeve. "Can Mary Ann come and stay with us?"

"She's speaking of Mary Ann Bridger," Grace explained to McLoughlin. "They are good friends, and Mary Ann's father has yet to be notified of her whereabouts."

McLoughlin nodded, but his answer was negative. "No, child. A home has already been provided for her, and as I understand it, she's not been well."

Mercy nodded. "She and I had the measles, but she was still sick when the Indians attacked us. She didn't get much better after that."

"Well, hopefully she will now," McLoughlin replied with a smile. "If you'll come with me, I'll show you to your uncle's house."

"What about the things I purchased at Fort Vancouver?" Grace asked. She hadn't bought all that much, but it was enough that it had been secured in a crate and left at the dock. "It looks like we may get more rain." It had rained off and on since they'd arrived at Fort Vancouver.

"I will see that one of the men brings it over. Now come along."

Grace walked beside McLoughlin while Mercy and Hope followed. Grace asked him a variety of questions about the small town and the safety of the citizens from Indian attack.

"We're well established and have a great many armed men—and women," McLoughlin replied. "From time to time there are threats, but usually the matters are resolved without violence."

Grace wasn't sure his words gave her much comfort, and she decided she would obtain a gun and learn how to handle it.

They walked past a great many houses, a hotel, and other businesses. It wasn't at all a big town, but it was the biggest Grace had seen since coming west. She was surprised to find that most of the buildings were built from finished lumber rather than logs.

"Your buildings aren't what I expected," she told McLoughlin. "I presumed with all the trees, we would find more log cabins."

"We have several lumber mills here. We mill wood and make very fine lumber. We are now selling to people in California, in fact. I ship it down the coast and am met with a very respectable profit."

"I'm sure." She caught sight of the church steeple. "I will enjoy going to church again. It's been such a long time since that was possible."

"We have more than one. If you are of the Catholic faith, as am I, it will be my pleasure to introduce you."

Grace smiled. "I'm not, but thank you. Is there a school?"

"Yes. In fact, we have two. There is a private school that meets in the Methodist church. It's run by Mrs. Thorton. A lot of folks, however, can't afford such luxury and school their children in the public school, while others are taught at home. Education is very important." He picked up his pace, and Grace had to hurry to keep step with him.

"We have most everything we need here," McLoughlin continued. "Stores that provide a wonderful selection of goods, as well as a hotel, boardinghouse, and of course our newspaper, the *Oregon Spectator*. Ah, here we are."

The log house was positioned twenty yards from the river on a little incline. Grace thought it very welcoming. Nothing fancy, just two stories with a small overhang that sheltered the front door. A cold rain began to fall just as McLoughlin escorted them inside.

Grace's first impression was good. The house was simply furnished but homey. A fireplace stood against the far wall of the main room. Someone had laid the fire earlier, and it burned merrily. The heat was a pleasant surprise, and both Hope and Mercy moved closer to warm their hands.

There were two doors to the right of the front door. Both were closed, and McLoughlin ignored them and instead led Grace from the front room through a wide arched opening into the kitchen. There was a small but efficient cookstove, several handmade cupboards, and a long wooden counter where her uncle kept pots, crocks, and utensils, as well as a few dishes and a lantern. A curtained doorway at the end of the room revealed a small but adequate pantry, its shelves lined with jars of preserves and canned vegetables and meat. The only other thing in the room was a small table and two chairs. Grace would have to see about getting a third.

"It looks like it will serve us very well." Grace turned to Hope and Mercy. "Don't you think?"

Mercy nodded and smiled. "Are there beds?"

"I made certain there would be," McLoughlin replied. "Your uncle's bed is big enough that two of you can sleep there. I had another bed built and put upstairs. It's just a rope bed, but I believe you'll find the mattress comfortable. I took it from my own house."

"That was certainly very nice of you, Mr. McLoughlin. I don't know what we would have done without your generosity," Grace said.

"Nonsense. We must help one another out here. If we do not, there is no hope for any of us." He moved back to the main living area, and Grace followed. "As further exploration will prove, there is a bedroom there." He pointed to a

228

door opposite the fireplace. "The door to the right of that one will take you upstairs. I believe your uncle only used the second floor for storage, but it has been cleaned and readied for your arrival."

Again Grace was overwhelmed with gratitude. "Thank you . . . for everything."

"Some of the ladies will bring by a few meals tomorrow. They will also leave you with a few other necessities."

Grace saw him to the door. "I wonder if you know someone who collects herbs. I am a healer, and my collection was lost at the mission and on the way here. I would like to begin learning the vegetation here and restore my collection as best I can. I especially need apples for making vinegar."

"Of course. I will send you several bushels of my own apples. Of course, the entire area is alive with medicinal plants. The local stores will also prove helpful, as they regularly trade with the Indian women." He stepped outside. "I'll be in touch."

The rain was coming in earnest now, but the hardy man didn't seem to mind. He merely pulled his wide-brimmed hat lower and trudged on.

Turning, Grace began to assess the room. This was to be her home for who knew how long. God had anticipated their needs and provided not only her uncle's house but also his account at Fort Vancouver.

"I believe we'll be safe and happy here," she said, touching the back of a sturdy oak rocker. She smiled at Mercy and Hope. Even in the dim light, they looked weary and not at all the happy creatures she had once known. "Come, let's get you two to bed. I'm sure you're exhausted. I'll put you both in Uncle Edward's room." She spied a lamp and candles on the fireplace mantel, as well as several long thin sticks with which to light them.

"I would rather be alone," Hope said.

Grace turned with one of the sticks in hand. Mercy said

nothing, but Grace could see that her sister was hurt. Would they never be a whole family again?

Grace gave Hope a smile. "Very well. You may have the upstairs room. I'm happy to have Mercy in my bed, for I shall cherish her warmth." She put her arm around her little sister's shoulders. "Why don't you go see if it suits us?"

Mercy nodded and left to investigate.

Hope remained in the middle of the room, her expression void of emotion. Grace wanted to say something encouraging, but the words wouldn't come. She gave Hope a smile. "The door to the stairs is just over there. You should leave it open so the warm air will reach your room." She put the stick in the fire, let it catch, then lit one of the candles. She handed it to Hope. "There. Now you'll be able to find your way."

Without a word, Hope crossed to the stairway door. She opened it and headed up, not even pausing to say good night.

Grace frowned. This was going to be so much harder than she'd imagined.

Chapter 19

"He's a fine-looking boy." Alex smiled at the sleeping newborn wrapped tight in his cradleboard.

Sam, ever the proud father, smiled and handed the infant back to Sarah. "He will be strong, I can tell. Already he clasps his fingers around mine."

"What will you call him?"

Sarah answered. "Henry is how we will call him. After the Reverend Spaulding. His full name will be Henry White Owl." She smiled as Sam's father joined them. "We will sleep now," Sarah said, moving to the far side of the lodge where the other two children were already bedded down.

"Your horse is cared for," Jacob told Alex. "Come sit at the fire and tell me of what is happening with the Cayuse."

Alex took a seat. "They are on the run as expected. Well, perhaps *run* is the wrong word. They're hiding, to be sure. When the boats left Fort Nez Perce to take the women and children to safety, several Cayuse followed along the riverbank. I recognized one of Telokite's sons and Tamsucky as well as some of the others. I think Joe Lewis was also with them. McBean said nearly fifty braves showed up just hours after our boats pulled out. They'd come to kill Reverend Spaulding."

"Spaulding is a good man. He has been a friend to us—his wife as well. They have done good work with the Niimíipuu."

"I agree." Alex stifled a yawn. He'd ridden straight through after arriving at Fort Nez Perce and was into his second day without sleep. "However, the Cayuse don't see it that way. Especially the younger men, who are angrier. They equate all white men with Dr. Whitman. McBean and the others at Fort Nez Perce are definitely anxious about the situation and have let their superiors in Fort Vancouver know. The Oregon men are planning to send a full force to locate the Cayuse responsible and bring them to justice."

Jacob nodded. "It is as I feared it would be. The Boston men will never rest until they have avenged the blood of Dr. Whitman and the others."

Sam frowned. "Do you suppose they will even care about locating the actual Cayuse responsible?"

"I fear they'll just kill indiscriminately because of their rage. Just as the young Cayuse would end the lives of the whites, the whites will see only the color of Indian skin and believe the worst of them." Alex closed his eyes, seeing the victims at the mission. "Those women and children were sorely abused, and that's going to stick in the militia's minds as they scout out the Cayuse." He opened his eyes and shook his head. "I will say that the Nez Perce are still regarded as friends to the Hudson's Bay Company and the whites. However, it's possible a few of the men in the militia will feel otherwise. I think it's important you know what has happened. You might want to join up with one of the other bands farther away."

"I will speak to the chiefs and let them know what you have said. We are not cowards to run, however."

"There is nothing cowardly in protecting your women and children."

Jacob nodded. "I will talk to them in the morning. Now I will take my rest, and you should too."

He got to his feet and left Alex and Sam. Sam handed Alex some smoked fish. "Have you eaten or slept recently?"

Alex chuckled and took the fish. He shook his head. "There wasn't time for either one with exception to some jerky I picked up at the fort. I wanted to get here ahead of the militia or the rumors that might go out before them. I'm not overly worried about your people, but I am cautious."

Sam fixed him with a smile. "And what of your Grace?"

"My Grace? She's not mine."

"If you say so. How did she and her sisters do on the trip?"

"It was hard." Alex ate the fish in between sentences as he told Sam about the journey to Fort Vancouver. When he finished the piece of fish, Sam handed him another.

After Alex described how Hope had thrown Grace's carpet-bag—all they had—into the river, Sam asked, "How will they make their way? Has their uncle returned?"

"No. He's still gone. I talked to Ogden about the situation and told him to let Grace use my credit with the company. I asked him to say nothing to her, however, and Ogden told me later that she had the idea her uncle had left it for her. I was glad for that, because I know she'd never have taken it from me."

"What is it the Bible says about pride? That it goes before a fall?" Sam gave Alex a look of amusement. "I've never known two people more prideful than you two."

Alex was taken aback. "I didn't do that out of pride. I just knew she wouldn't take my help. I hurt her feelings and she hasn't gotten over it. Even now I'm sure she's cursing the day she ever met me."

Sam got up and shook his head. "Your mind is asleep, so you might as well let the rest of you join it. Sarah made you a pallet. I'll see you in the morning."

Alex longed for sleep, but throughout the night he dreamed of going back to New Orleans only to be ostracized. Grace's image mingled with those of his little brother, who by now would be twenty and not so little, as well as Alex's sister. Adelina had only been married a short time when Alex left town. By now he imagined she had several children.

When Sam and the others got up, Alex was already tending the fire. After the others had eaten and departed for various tasks, Sam stayed behind.

"You seem to have a lot on your mind," Sam said, eyeing him with the same intense look Alex had seen when Sam was about to shoot an elk or deer.

Alex wasn't sure how to bring up what he needed to say. "I . . . ah . . . figured I'd collect some of the traps and pack 'em out on Gabe's horse. I'm going to the cabin to get things ready for spring. I wasn't sure if you were coming with me or not. I understand if you want to stay here and see what the outcome might be of your father speaking to the council."

"I'm going with you. My father will manage fine without me. What I want to know is what you plan to do about Grace."

His question surprised Alex. Usually Sam wasn't one to pry into personal matters. Alex had always liked that about him. Gabriel thought nothing of pressing for the details, but Sam had been a good friend without needing to know Alex's business. However, now Alex felt he needed Sam's advice, and in order to get it, he would have to explain a few things first.

"I can't do anything about Grace until I tend to the past."

"I've often said as much."

Alex smiled. "So you have, but you don't know in full what that past includes."

With a shrug, Sam sat down next to the fire. "It seems you want to tell me."

"I do." Alex sighed. He wasn't sure where to start. "There was this girl."

"That alone is enough to tell me trouble is coming."

"You're right there. I fell in love with her. At least I thought it was love." Alex shook his head. "Now I'm not sure what it was—youth, lust, loneliness. At the time I wanted her for my wife. Unfortunately, another man felt the same."

Sam smiled. "I had to answer to the challenges of four men for Sarah."

"But you didn't kill any of them, did you?" Alex knew his words would surprise Sam, and he was right.

"You killed the other man?"

Alex drew in a deep breath. "I did. Caroline—that was her name—wouldn't choose between us. She liked being fought over, and by the time I realized that she was toying with both of us, it was too late. My rival . . . his name was Justice, which always struck me as ironic." He paused and shook his head. "Justice challenged me to a duel, and in my hotheaded anger, I accepted. We met and had our appropriate witnesses and seconds. He chose pistols, and we stood back to back. The man officiating counted off our steps, but before he reached the final step, Justice turned and fired on me."

"Were you hit?"

"Grazed. It was hardly even bad enough to bandage, but he had shamed himself, and the official instructed me to take my shot. I was angry and wanted nothing more than to make Justice pay for his action, but I also knew that my mother and father would want me to show mercy. So I fired to the left of him. But as I did, he turned to run like the coward he was. My bullet hit him in the back and killed him then and there. Everyone who witnessed the event knew it to be a fair fight.

Even Justice's family members who'd come knew the truth, but in just a matter of hours, the entire affair was twisted into what amounted to my murdering a helpless man. Suddenly I was the target of their revenge."

"Didn't the official stand up for the truth?"

"No. He was threatened and left the area so that he couldn't be questioned. I tried to defend my actions, pointing out that I had shot wide, but no one seemed to care. My witnesses were considered prejudiced and dismissed."

"Were you arrested?" Sam asked, looking concerned.

"No, but I figured it was just a matter of time. I planned to get a lawyer, but then . . . the fire. I told you about it. I woke up to find our house in flames and was barely able to get my brother to safety before the entire place was engulfed. Our parents died in that fire, and my little brother thought me a coward for not saving them."

He fell silent for a moment. Sam knew about the fire, but he'd never told him the reason for it. "I learned that Justice's brother had started it—he admitted it. Of course, not in front of witnesses. I knew they'd stop at nothing to see me pay for what had happened, so I left. I didn't want my sister or brother to suffer any more for my mistakes."

"And that is why you never went home?"

"Yes. I have, however, sent my sister, Adelina, a letter. I have no way of knowing if she'll ever answer it, but I decided it was the place to start. I've asked her to find out what kind of legal matter I will face."

Sam seemed to consider this for a moment. "I think you did the right thing."

"I hope so. It seems the only thing I could do, short of returning to New Orleans."

A few weeks after they were settled, Grace found Nigel Grierson at her door. His face was sober, but he greeted her with enthusiasm.

"I only just heard that you were here. Why didn't you send me word?"

"We've been very busy trying to get settled."

He nodded and then remembered his hat and quickly took it off. "I apologize. I'm not myself. I know what happened to you at the mission."

"It didn't happen to me. At least not in the sense of having been one of the captives. I was at another mission to help a friend who was ill." She wasn't sure, but it seemed a look of relief flashed in his eyes and then was gone. "My sisters were there. They suffered greatly."

He nodded again. "It's well known. A horrible thing, to be sure. Their innocence is forever gone thanks to the actions of those animals."

Grace countered with a frown. "I know they've endured a great deal, but I believe God can heal them."

"It's a delicate matter to be sure," Nigel said, looking awkward. "But there are men who won't mind that . . . well . . . that they were there."

His implication irritated Grace. "Nigel, I really don't want to talk about it. Why have you come?"

"As I told you, I just heard that you were here. I have your sheep and, well, I thought maybe you would finally agree to marry me after all that has happened."

"Oh really. And are you one of those men who wouldn't mind if I had been at the mission?"

He turned a dark shade of red. "I didn't mean anything by that. Your sisters and the others couldn't help what happened to them. Those savages were to blame. I'm sorry that I sounded so unkind."

Grace took pity on him. "I accept your apology, but not your proposal. I'm not of a mind to marry at this time. My sisters need me, and I need to wait for my uncle's return before I decide what to do."

"You are without money?" he asked.

She hated to admit it to him but knew it would do little good to lie. "I am. My money was lost in the river on the way to Fort Vancouver."

"I could sell your male lambs. If you would allow me to. It would see you through until spring."

Grace thought about it for only a moment. It seemed a logical thing to do and would save her from having to borrow. "That would be very kind of you, Nigel. Thank you."

He smiled for the first time since coming to her door. "I do care about you, Grace. You should know that by now. I've continued to think about you—a lot."

She nodded. "I'm honored that you care, but for now I need to say good-bye and tend to my sisters. I'm sure you understand."

"I do. I'll go arrange for you to have credit at the store. I'll return when it's done to let you know the matter is settled." He donned his hat and turned to go. "It won't take very long," he called over his shoulder.

Grace shook her head and closed the door to find Hope standing behind her. From the look on her face, Grace could tell she'd overheard most of the conversation.

"Mr. Grierson is arranging credit for us at one of the stores. He's offered to sell the male lambs, and I've agreed to it. That will give us money to get through the winter."

"I heard him propose again."

Grace shrugged. "He doesn't seem to understand that I'm not interested. I suppose in time he will, although I'll probably have to endure a dozen more proposals before he gives up."

"Maybe he'll marry one of the women who lost their innocence at the mission," Hope said sarcastically.

"Pay him no mind. He's a ninny."

"Then so is everyone else in Oregon City, for they're all saying the same thing. The women who live here are appalled at the very thought of us. We are filth as far as they are concerned."

"That's not true, Hope."

"Isn't it?" She stepped closer and shook her finger at Grace. "Then why do they avoid us? Why do they look away when we come near? If not for that reason—then why?"

"Fear." Grace had seen the terrified looks the women wore whenever the attack and the newcomers were mentioned. "They're afraid that if it could happen to you, it could happen to them."

Hope seemed surprised by this answer but quickly covered it. "Well, they should be afraid. We are no safer here than we were at the mission. There are still plenty of Indians around, and they hate us. They will do whatever they can to get rid of us." She turned and ran back upstairs.

Grace intended to follow her, but a knock sounded on the door. Surely Nigel hadn't returned already. She opened the door and found Eletta and Isaac.

"Oh!" She put her hand to her mouth and then reached out to embrace Eletta. "Oh, I prayed you would be safely brought here. I am so glad God answered my prayer so quickly. Come in." She stepped back to let the couple enter.

"We were escorted by some of the friendlies. They delivered us to Fort Nez Perce, and then we were brought here. I mentioned your name, and an elderly gentleman told me we'd find you here. I believe his name was McLoughlin."

"Yes, I'm sure it was." Grace closed the door and directed them to warm themselves by the fire. "Mr. McLoughlin is known far and wide. He founded this town, and as I understand it, he's responsible for much more. For years and years he was the chief factor of Fort Vancouver." She paused and assessed the couple standing before her. "Are you hungry?"

"No," Isaac said. "They fed us quite well."

"Please sit. The settee is well-worn but comfortable." They did as instructed, and Grace pulled the rocker closer and took her seat. "Where are you staying? Have they given you a place?"

Again Isaac answered. "They have a room for us at the hotel. It's more than sufficient for the time being."

Grace glanced around the meagerly furnished room. "This is my uncle's house, otherwise I would insist you move in here. As it is, I must wait for his return."

"It's of no matter," Eletta said. Her face looked so pale beneath the shadow of her brown wool bonnet. "All of the missionaries have been called in for fear of attacks at the other missions. We were both relieved to know you were safe—your sisters too."

"Hope and Mercy suffered a great deal, but they are recovering little by little." Grace was uncertain how much to say.

"And are they here?" Eletta asked.

"Hope is resting upstairs, and Mercy has gone to visit her friend. Do you remember little Mary Ann Bridger? She's the little half-breed girl who lived with the Whitmans. Her father left her there for schooling."

"I do remember her. She was a pretty little thing."

"Yes. Unfortunately, she's been unable to regain her health after having the measles. The sick weren't allowed care after the massacre. Two other little girls died. Mary Ann is lucky to have made it so far, and Mercy likes to go over and read to her."

"I'm sure that's a comfort."

Grace nodded. "Any comfort for them is a blessing. They've been through far more than any child should have to endure. I only pray they can soon forget all that happened."

By the middle of February the women and children who'd come to Oregon City seemed to have settled in. As expected, some had married and were making a new life. Whenever Hope saw them, they seemed more at peace—not really happy, but not as conflicted. Even Mercy seemed less inclined to have nightmares, although on occasion Hope still heard her cries in the night.

It wasn't so for Hope. She hated herself for hurting Grace by throwing her bag overboard. She was angry at herself for her weakness and fears. Most of all, she was enraged that a merciful God had allowed the massacre to happen. If God didn't protect missionaries, whose sole purpose was to share the Gospel and help people better know God, then how could anyone else count on His protection? Hope couldn't stop pondering that question.

From time to time, her thoughts went to John Sager. She couldn't stop reliving his death, and the nightmares kept her from ever achieving a restful sleep. Then there was what Tomahas had done to her. That was something she could never forget, because as Nigel Grierson had pointed out, her innocence was forever gone.

It was Monday, so that meant wash day. Grace had managed the wash, but she'd asked Hope to help hang the clothes to dry. Hope didn't really mind, but she wasn't feeling well. Her night had been particularly bad, and even now she felt as though her body were a lead weight. Nevertheless, she joined Grace at the makeshift clothesline to do her part. She hoped her willingness might be seen as an unspoken apology of sorts, for she didn't have the words.

Reaching for a clothespin, Hope fought off a wave of dizziness and closed her eyes for a moment, trying to steady herself.

If Grace knew she was sick, she'd fuss over her, and that was something Hope didn't want.

"Hello!"

Hope and Grace both looked to see who was calling. Eletta Browning gave a wave as she made her way across the yard. "I knocked at the front door, but no one answered, so I thought you might be outside. It's such a beautiful day, even though it's cold."

Grace went to give her friend a hug. "I'm so glad you came to visit. How are you feeling?"

Hope turned back to the line while Grace and Eletta chatted. The sooner she got the laundry hung up, the sooner she could escape the cold and her sister. She secured a clothespin to the end of a sheet just as another wave of dizziness hit. Along with it came the awful nausea she'd been fighting. Without warning, Hope felt the contents of her stomach rise. She ran toward the edge of the river and lost her breakfast. Her vision blurred momentarily, and she collapsed, trying to remain conscious.

Grace was at her side in a flash. She bore the look of concern Hope had so often seen when her sister dealt with the ill.

"Are you all right? Let me feel your head." Grace put her hand to Hope's forehead. "You aren't feverish. That's good."

"I just got dizzy and sick to my stomach. It's been going on all week, so don't fuss over me. I'm fine." Hope pushed Grace away and got to her feet. She didn't feel much better, but she wasn't about to tell her sister.

Eletta joined them and looked at Hope with a strange expression. She whispered something to Grace, making Hope feel as if they were conspiring against her.

She stiffened. "If you two are through talking about me, I would appreciate it if you'd just leave me alone. I can finish hanging the laundry, so why don't you go have tea or take a walk together?"

Grace's face had gone pale. She looked almost frightened. "Hope," she said, then bit her lower lip.

Hope frowned. It wasn't like Grace to act this way. "What? What's wrong now?"

"I must ask you something, but I fear I already know the answer."

"Stop being so dramatic. Ask your question and leave me be."

For a moment she thought Grace had changed her mind, but then her sister stepped forward and asked in a barely audible voice, "When did you last have your monthly bleeding?"

Hope shook her head and shrugged. "I don't know. I haven't . . ." She fell silent as she realized what Grace was implying.

She hadn't bled since before the massacre. Involuntarily her hands went to her stomach. She shook her head. "No. No." She backed away, feeling her chest tighten so much that she could hardly breathe. "I can't be with child. I won't be. I won't have his baby."

She could almost feel Tomahas's hands on her again. She could see his leering face hovering over her. She could hardly bear the thought of what was growing inside her body.

"Make it die," she said, rushing to Grace. She took hold of her sister's shoulders. "Get it out of me." Grace looked shocked, but Hope didn't care. "Either it dies or I will."

Chapter
20

As February came to a close and March roared in with wind and rain, Grace remained troubled. Hope, by her calculations, was three months along. Within the first few days of realizing her condition, Hope had begged almost constantly for Grace to help her miscarry before anyone knew what had happened. Even now, as Grace finished making oatmeal for their breakfast, she knew Hope would appear to beg her help once again.

But what can I do? I cannot murder a baby. No matter its origin.

But Hope had threatened to take her own life, and her actions of late truly worried Grace. She'd heard Hope ask several people about the depth of the river and the danger the falls created. It would be easy for her sister to simply walk out of the house and into the waters of the Willamette. The thought troubled Grace more and more each day. She also wondered if any other women from the mission were in the same situation as Hope.

Mercy came into the kitchen looking morose. Mary Ann Bridger was worsening. Grace wanted nothing more than to shelter her sister from the pain of losing a dear friend, but there was no hope of it. Dr. McLoughlin had told Grace in private that it was unlikely Mary Ann would recover. Grace was doing her best to prepare Mercy for the inevitable.

"Would you like a little coffee this morning?" Grace asked. "It might help you feel better." She brought a half portion in a cup.

Mercy looked at the coffee and frowned. "I don't like it. It's always bitter."

"Well, we can fix that with a little sugar." Grace smiled and retrieved the sugar bowl. She sprinkled in a couple generous spoonfuls and stirred. "There. That ought to help considerably."

Mercy sipped from the cup and nodded. "It's better. Thank you."

Grace dished up three bowls of oatmeal and put them on the table. "Why don't you call Hope, and I'll get the cream." The cream and milk had come compliments of Nigel, and while Grace didn't want to encourage him, Mercy and Hope needed the nourishment.

Mercy got up from the table with a sigh. "She's just going to be mad and tell me to go away."

"We must encourage her to join us."

Mercy shrugged and went to find her sister. Grace brought the cream to the table and had just taken her place when Mercy returned. "She said she'd be here in a minute."

"Truly? Well, that's an improvement." Grace smiled and handed Mercy the small pitcher of cream.

"Grace, I don't understand why Mary Ann isn't getting well. I wish you were her doctor."

"Dr. McLoughlin is very capable. He even uses many of the same remedies I would use." Grace touched Mercy's arm. "Sometimes no matter how much medicine is given, a person . . . can't get well."

Mercy's eyes filled with tears. "But she's my friend."

Grace nodded. "I know."

"It's those Indians' fault. They killed so many people and then wouldn't let the sick ones have any medicine. I hate them."

Grace was surprised by Mercy's uncharacteristic attitude. Usually she was gentle and forgiving of everyone. Of course, she'd gone through a lot at the hands of the Indians. "Hating them won't change anything." Grace reached up to smooth back Mercy's dark brown hair. "Hate is something that hurts the giver more than the one it's intended for. I know it's hard to hear, and I didn't always feel this way, but we need to pray for the Indians instead."

"You didn't see how awful they were, Grace." Mercy leaned back in her chair. "I was in school and we hid up in the loft. The boys helped us get up there. We lay there very quiet, and when the Cayuse came into the room, they didn't know we were there."

Grace sat very still. Mercy had never told her anything about the attack, and she didn't want to do anything to stop her sister from speaking.

"We didn't know what was happening, but we heard the screaming, and Eliza Spaulding said the Indians were probably killing everybody. I started to cry and so did the others. I didn't want them to kill Hope or Mary Ann. I couldn't do anything to help them, though, because they were in the kitchen."

Mercy looked down at her bowl, and tears rolled down her cheeks. "It was so very bad, Grace, and I was so afraid. The Indians came back and told us to come down. They knew we were up there, so we did. They were horrible, and Eliza asked one of them something in their language. He didn't answer but laughed, and I asked her what she said. She'd asked him if he was going to kill us."

"Oh, Mercy." Grace put her hand to her mouth to keep from saying anything more for fear Mercy would stop talking.

"Everything seemed to happen at once, but after most of the shooting stopped, we children were all rounded up and made to stand outside the house. We could see dead bodies in the mud, including Mrs. Whitman. After a long while of standing, the Indians made some of the women join us, including Hope. She had blood on her and I thought she was hurt, but she wasn't. I found out later it was John Sager's blood."

Now that she had started the story, it seemed Mercy couldn't stop. "The Indians grabbed Frank Sager and shot him right there beside us. I just knew they were going to kill me too and I wanted to run, but Hope held on to me. She told me to stand very still and not cry or yell. She told me not to look at the bodies anymore but to close my eyes, so I did. But, Grace, it didn't help. I kept seeing all that blood."

Grace could see it all in her mind. The vivid images did nothing to reassure her that her sisters would quickly recover. No one should ever have to endure such a terrible nightmare. "I'm so sorry, sweetheart. I've wished so many times that I'd insisted you come with me to Eletta's. There isn't anything I wouldn't give to remake that decision."

Mercy didn't seem to hear her. She continued looking at her oatmeal, but Grace had the feeling she was back at the mission, lost in those horrific moments of the massacre. "When the yelling stopped, some of the Indians were arguing. Eliza said they were trying to decide whether to kill us. They decided they would wait and made us go to the emigrant house. Hope and I went to our pallets, and Mary Ann came too. We waited there together, holding on to each other, and I fell asleep. When I woke up the next day, I thought it had all been a bad dream, but then I looked at Hope and saw the blood on her dress, and I knew it had really happened."

Mercy stared blankly across the table, and Grace wanted nothing more than to wipe those memories from her mind. Mercy had seen things no child should ever have to see. Grace prayed God would give her insight—some word or thought that might ease Mercy's sadness.

"All those people were dead," Mercy whispered and finally looked at Grace. "And now Mary Ann is going to die too."

"But you need to remember something." Grace gently touched her sister's wet cheek. "Those people loved God. Mary Ann loves God. I'm sure she's asked Jesus to forgive her of her sins and be her Savior. I know we'll see each other in heaven one day."

"Is that truly all you have to do to go to heaven?"

Grace nodded. "In Romans ten, the Bible says, 'That if thou shalt confess with thy mouth the Lord Jesus, and shalt believe in thine heart that God hath raised him from the dead, thou shalt be saved. For with the heart man believeth unto righteousness; and with the mouth confession is made unto salvation.' I know you understand. You asked God to save you long ago. I know you are a believer of the truth."

"But I remember the Right Reverend saying that even the demons believed in God."

"They do believe in God. They know He exists—it is no question to them. But truly confessing Jesus is more. It's accepting our sin and knowing that His sacrifice on the cross was the only thing that could ever make things right between us and our Heavenly Father. And then we must believe that God raised Jesus from the dead and that if we put our trust in Him—God will raise us from the dead as well."

Mercy considered this a moment. "So those people who died at the mission—they aren't really dead?"

"No, not spiritually." Grace smiled. "And Mary Ann, though her body will fail her, her spirit—if she belongs to Jesus—will live forever with Him."

For the first time in a long while, Mercy smiled. "Then I will make sure she belongs to Jesus."

Hope heard Mercy sharing her story of the massacre and took advantage of the distraction to go into the bedroom her sisters shared and look through Grace's new collection of herbs and medicines. Every day since learning about the child she carried, Hope had contemplated how to take her own life. She had considered many violent acts but felt cowardly when she considered actually following through. But then she remembered what the Indians had said prior to the massacre, that Dr. Whitman was poisoning melons and meat with arsenic to kill them. Everyone knew arsenic was deadly.

She found Grace's bottle of arsenic without any difficulty. Grace had clearly marked each of her tonics and mixtures as she reacquired them. She'd even made new batches of vinegar and forced Hope and Mercy to take their daily dose.

Hope turned the bottle over in her hands for several seconds, wondering if she truly had the strength to take her own life. "Well, it's certain I don't have the strength to live." Exhaustion washed over her. She didn't truly want to die, but she couldn't imagine a future that included bearing the shame and accusing gossip, let alone the child of Tomahas. Why couldn't Grace understand that and help her to miscarry?

Hope looked at the bottle again and knew there was no other answer. She pocketed the arsenic and left the room. With any luck, Grace wouldn't miss the bottle until Hope had a chance to ingest the powder.

She arrived in the kitchen to see Grace and Mercy embracing and Grace telling Mercy how much she was loved.

"No matter what has happened, no matter what you endured,

God loves you and He will help you through this. I love you too, and I will be here to help you also."

"And just how will you help?" Hope asked from the archway.

Grace straightened, and Mercy reclaimed her seat. "I will help in whatever way I'm allowed."

"You refuse to help me." Hope fixed Grace with an accusing expression. She wanted Grace to feel so guilty, so bad, that she would help Hope end the pregnancy. "You talk a lot about helping, but when it comes to actually doing something, you leave us to our own devices."

"Hope, that's not fair. As I told Mercy, I'd give anything—even my own life—to be able to remake that day."

"There's nothing you can give." Hope looked at Mercy and an overwhelming sorrow washed over her. "We already gave it all."

A knock sounded on the door behind her, and Hope glanced over her shoulder but did nothing to answer it.

Mercy got up from the table. "I'll get it. I have to go or I'll be late for school."

"But you haven't eaten," Grace said, getting up to follow her.

"I'm not hungry." Mercy took her coat from a peg by the door. "I'm going to see Mary Ann after school and talk to her about Jesus."

Grace looked as if she might protest, but instead she told Mercy she would bring her something for lunch.

Mercy opened the door, and Eletta Browning gave her a nod. "Good morning, child. How are you today?" She stepped into the house.

"I'm better, Mrs. Browning." Mercy said nothing more as she hurried out the door, leaving Hope wishing she could say the same.

Eletta caught sight of Hope and Grace. "I wonder if we might speak together."

"Of course." Grace smiled and motioned Eletta to the

kitchen. "We're just having breakfast. Hope, your oatmeal is on the table."

"I'm going to my room."

"No, wait," Eletta said, surprising them both. "I want to talk to you too."

Hope wanted no part of it. "I'm tired." She tightly gripped the bottle in her pocket. She needed to leave soon, or she'd lose her nerve.

Eletta nodded and twisted her gloved hands. "Please just hear me out. I think I have a way to help you."

"Help Hope?" Grace asked.

"Yes. Actually, it was Isaac's idea."

Hope had to admit she was intrigued. She walked to the table and plopped into the chair recently vacated by her sister. Grace and Eletta followed suit, taking the other chairs.

Eletta folded her hands in her lap and fixed her gaze on Hope. "I know you're distressed, even desiring death because of the child you carry," she said, wasting no time. "I know how you have suffered."

"You know nothing. You weren't at the massacre."

"Hope, you have no right to speak in such a manner to Eletta. She's come to offer her help."

With a heavy sigh, Hope leaned back in her chair and shook her head. "She can do nothing. You could offer me a solution but refuse. You've failed me." Hope chose those exact words, knowing they would hurt Grace the most.

"Hope, we have no way of knowing why this child has come to be," Eletta said, taking charge. "But only God can create life. It must be His will that this child be born."

A dozen sarcastic comments came to mind, but when Hope opened her mouth to speak, nothing came out.

"Isaac and I have longed for children but seem unable to have them. We're leaving in a few weeks to go to California.

My husband wrote an old friend and yesterday received a reply. There's a small church where Isaac is needed to preach until October. We thought perhaps you might come with us. You could await the birth of the baby, and once the child is born . . . Isaac and I would take it as our own."

"You want to raise a half-breed child? A baby born out of force and such ugliness that I can't even speak of it? Are you mad?"

Eletta looked at Grace and then back to Hope. "My arms are empty, Hope. Where a babe should be nestled against my breast, there is nothing—only that terrible void." Her eyes filled with tears. "I know you have endured more than is fair. I know that you do not want this child, but I do. What happened isn't the babe's fault. The child is innocent of the father's action—just as you are. Would you have someone punish you for what was clearly not your doing? Ending the baby's life won't change what happened. It won't take away those memories."

Until that moment, Hope had never felt even the slightest compassion for the baby in her womb. Until then, the child had been a monster—the creation of a heartless heathen. Eletta's words, however, pierced her heart.

"I know I have no right to ask you to bear this child for me, but I am," Eletta said. "I'm begging, in fact. Please let the baby live, and I will raise it to know love and kindness rather than rejection."

"The baby will be half Cayuse," Hope murmured, still not sure what to think.

"My husband is a quarter Cherokee. The baby's features will seem natural. And the babe could take after you more than the father."

"How would we keep people from knowing?"

"Obviously the folks in California would know that you bore a child. Isaac would explain what had happened to you—that way you wouldn't face condemnation. Once the baby is born, Isaac will see you safely returned to your sisters."

Hope fingered the bottle of arsenic in her pocket. She could choose life or death. It was entirely up to her. She thought again of Eletta's words about the baby being innocent. The baby had no say . . . just as Hope had had no say, and if Hope was ever able to recover from all that had happened, it would be best not to have the guilt of murder on her mind.

"You don't have to make up your mind just now, but we only have a few days before we leave. Dr. McLoughlin is arranging passage for us on one of the ships heading south."

Was death truly preferable to life? Hope thought of John Sager. It seemed as if that part of her life, that happiness, had happened years ago instead of just months. She called to mind something John had written. He spoke of his love of life—of seeing each new sunrise, of breathing deep the scent of newly turned earth. He would reprimand her for her desire to die, because he would never have chosen it for himself. Of course, no one gave him a choice.

After a long, silent moment, Hope looked at her sister and Eletta. She produced the arsenic and placed it in the middle of the table. Grace's eyes widened. She no doubt recognized it.

Silence hung heavy on the air, but Hope knew her decision had been made. She would live—for John Sager's sake. She would live so that his memory would live.

"Very well. I'll go with you."

Chapter
21

LATE MAY, 1848

Alex and Sam sat across the table from several of their fellow trappers. The spring furs were in, and now there would be the short lull of summer to tend to other needs. For now, everyone's thoughts were on the Indians and the growing tensions. For months the Oregon Country men had been out searching for the Cayuse responsible for the Whitman massacre. There had been dozens of conflicts and deaths in their wake.

"Our people realize that the days of peace are gone," Sam said, honing his knife on a whetstone.

"You're a good Indian, Sam. I'm not saying you or your people have caused it, but it seems to me the Indians are all to blame for the upheaval," a grizzled older man said, then put a large plug of tobacco in his mouth.

"My mother often said it takes two to argue or fight." Alex knew these men were far more concerned with their livelihood than with the relationship between the whites and the Indians. "I'm of a mind that both sides aren't without their flaws."

"Maybe not, but I don't see us attackin' helpless Indian villages."

"But Americans have done so," Alex countered. "History proves that well enough. We drove them out of the eastern states, and when they wouldn't go, they were attacked and killed."

"You an Indian lover, Armistead?"

"I happen to believe that God calls us to love everyone. At least that's what I recall my Bible teaching."

A man came to Alex from the back room. He gave Alex a piece of paper. "Is this the place and the person you want me to see the horse and saddle delivered to?"

Alex looked over the paper and nodded. He was finally arranging for Grace to get her horse back. No doubt she could use it. "It looks right. I don't know exactly where she is, but Oregon City was the last place she was known to be. I think she'll still be there. Her uncle lives there, and she was waiting for him. You should add his name to the instructions. Edward Marsh."

The man nodded. "I know Marsh. Didn't know he was an uncle."

Alex smiled and handed back the paper. "Three times over, but the best one is Grace."

The man left, and Alex turned his attention back to the conversation, briefly catching Sam's smirk. No doubt Sam felt Alex was continuing to be foolish for not contacting Grace.

"It's all about power," one of the trappers countered. "Power to control and expand. This is soon to be a territory all its own. I heard from Peter Ogden that a delegation went east to Washington City not long after the massacre. They intend to get the government to name this the Oregon Territory. No doubt after that we'll press on for statehood."

Alex heard a sense of frustration in the trapper's tone. "There are a lot of folks who don't want the government in their business. However, with the coming of settlers, we need a stricter code of law and order. One that can be regulated to keep the peace."

"What I know is that all these people are drivin' out the wildlife, pushin' 'em to the north, and that's where I'm headed. The Company was smart to move their headquarters to Fort Victoria. I know old McLoughlin fought it, but seein' as how the Americans now lay claim to this area, it was the best decision."

One of the other men nodded. "It's just a matter of time until they take this fort for the military."

The old-timer nodded, getting to his feet. He spit and then gathered up his things. "I'm happy for company if any of you boys want to head out with me. It's a good time to gather our gear and head north. We can figure out where to winter and where the best trapping grounds are while the weather holds."

One of the other trappers got to his feet. "I've been thinkin' the same thing. I can't say I enjoy all these people coming around. Gettin' way too crowded for my blood."

Alex smiled but said nothing. Some of these men knew nothing about the bigger cities, where hundreds of thousands of people could be found in close proximity to each other. It was hard to believe that they considered a territory that didn't even hold a hundred thousand people to be crowded.

Once they'd gone, Alex turned to Sam. "So what of you and your village? Will you go north as well?"

Sam shrugged. "It's hard to say. My father has always said the big rivers are life to us. The salmon are needed to sustain us. I think he will want to be wherever the salmon are."

"From what I've heard, they can be had around Fort Victoria as well."

Sam nodded. "If things get bad, there may not even be a chance to go. You know that. The militia has caused more than a little trouble, and I don't see it getting any better for the Nez Perce." He toyed with the knife he'd been sharpening. "I fear my children will know a different world—if they live to see it."

Alex hated the tone of Sam's voice. A sense of defeat already seemed to take hold of him. It was time to change the conversation.

"I've still heard nothing from my sister. I know it's probably too early to get a letter."

"What will you do if she doesn't answer?"

"I honestly don't know. When you started talking about resolving the past in order to have a future, I knew you were right. I know you're still right."

Sam puffed out his chest and crossed his arms. "I'm always right." Alex laughed, and Sam did as well, relaxing his pose.

"You are often right, my friend. Of that there is no doubt. Still, I'd like to know what I was getting myself into before just showing up in New Orleans. That's a long, dangerous trip to make. Costly too."

Sam nodded. "But it would be costly to lose Grace."

"Yes. It would be, but I have to risk that."

"Not if you went to talk to her. You could just take her horse to her. It would be the perfect excuse. Then while you're there, you could tell her what you plan to do and ask if she'll wait for you."

Alex had thought of that again and again, but given the way things were, he didn't think he had the right to ask her to wait. Who knew how bad things might get?

Sam leaned forward. "I know you love her. You can deny it, but that won't change the truth."

"I don't want to deny it—at least not anymore. I just can't expect her to give up her life on the hope that we can have a future together when I may not have a future to give. There are a lot of men out here in search of a wife. Good men who would treat Grace well."

Sam grunted and got up from the table.

Alex looked at him as Sam put his knife back in its sheath. "You headed somewhere?"

"Figured I'd find some company who could speak sense. You aren't making any."

A Nez Perce boy appeared at the door. He looked fourteen or fifteen at the most and was clearly out of breath from running. He spied Sam and came to him immediately. They conversed in a hushed tone for several moments, then the boy took off again. Sam looked worried.

"What's going on?" Alex asked, getting to his feet. "Is something wrong?"

"There's been trouble at my village."

"From the white militia sent to find the Whitman killers?"

Sam shook his head. "No. From some of the Cayuse—probably the killers themselves. My father's been injured."

"Then we need to go. You get our gear, and I'll get the horses. If we ride hard, we can be there by morning."

Grace missed Hope more than she'd thought she would. Despite her sister's negativity and anger, she was still precious to Grace. Mercy missed Hope too. Even more after Mary Ann's death in March. Mercy had told Grace that Mary Ann knew heaven would be a beautiful place and that she would get to see her mother again, because her mother had loved Jesus too. Mercy had hoped their mother might also be close at hand, because she'd asked Mary Ann to give her a message.

"I wanted Mama to know how much we miss her," Mercy had told Grace. "And I want her to be friends with Mary Ann and her mama."

Her words had deeply touched Grace. Mercy had at one time said she hated all Indians, but upon realizing Mary Ann had an Indian mother, she had changed her opinion. Grace was glad, because many Oregon City men had taken Indian wives, and children from those unions were common. Even Dr. McLoughlin's wife was part Cree, and she was most beloved.

Settling into their life in the town hadn't been difficult for Grace. Not like it had been for some. Because of her uncle's generosity and forethought, Grace and her sisters hadn't been forced to seek husbands or indenture themselves, but Grace had no idea how long they could hold out. Surely Uncle Edward would return soon. She had asked Dr. McLoughlin to check into whether her uncle had returned to Fort Vancouver. It was possible—after all, the cattle he went for belonged mostly to the Hudson's Bay Company. The doctor had promised to find out for her.

"Are we going to gather herbs today?" Mercy asked, coming around the corner of the house.

"Yes." Grace looked up from the scrubboard. "I have to finish washing these last few things and then get them hung up before I can do anything else, however. Have you finished with the dusting and sweeping?" She moved the last of the clothes to the rinse water.

Mercy nodded. "We don't make a very big mess."

"That's true enough." Grace smiled. Mercy was finally filling out and looked to have regained her health. Come September she would turn thirteen, and in a very short time she'd be grown. It was hard to imagine her married with children of her own, but Grace knew the day was coming.

"I'd like to go see the falls again. They're so pretty, even with the mills."

Mercy's comment forced Grace to put aside her thoughts. She looked out across the river. "Well, it's a beautiful day, and we can certainly walk that way on our search. I need to find bitterroot, and I know there should be some under the fir trees, so we can go past the falls. Now, if you want to be helpful, would you run to Mrs. Cranston's house and take her that bottle of tonic for her rheumatism I left on the kitchen table? I promised it to her as soon as possible."

"Sure. When I get back, hopefully you'll be ready to go." Mercy disappeared around the corner of the house without another word.

Putting her attention back on the job at hand, Grace quickly rinsed the remaining pieces of clothing and wrung them out. Sunny days without rain came at a premium, and Grace didn't want to waste a single moment of potential drying time.

She began hanging the sheets and thought about Hope and the day she'd realized her sister was with child. Grace could still see the look of horror on Hope's face. She wondered if her sister could ever recover from all that had happened to her.

Eletta had sent a letter saying that Hope was in much better spirits, but that she still tended toward anger and sadness. Grace prayed daily that God would release Hope from those bonds. Her sister had always been such a happy person prior to the massacre, and seeing Mercy gradually recover gave Grace all the more desire for Hope to do so as well.

All I really want for her is to be happy—to find true love and put the ugly things that happened behind her.

This thought led Grace to a place she had tried to avoid. True love. She couldn't think of that without thinking of Alex. He had been gone from her life for months now, without any word. She wondered from time to time where he was and what he was doing. Mostly she wondered if he ever thought of her.

"Mercy told me I'd find you out here," Nigel announced as he made his way to the clothesline. "I put the milk inside the house. There's a lot of cream."

"Thank you," Grace said, forcing Alex's image from her mind. Nigel hadn't stopped by for several weeks, and Grace had begun to hope he'd given up trying to woo her. "I need to make butter."

"I brought you some eggs as well."

Grace smiled. Nigel really was a good man. He worked hard and had a good reputation. He continued to watch over her sheep, given there was no place to keep them here at her uncle's place.

"I have some extra bread I can trade you for the eggs and milk. If I'd known you were coming, I could have had more."

"I'm sorry for not being by sooner. It's been very busy. There are six new lambs."

"In addition to the five that were born earlier?"

"Yes. And most of them are female. I knew you'd be pleased."

Grace nodded. "I am. I see hope for the future."

Nigel shrugged. "You could have a great deal of hope for the future if you would just consent to marry me. You know I've come to care for you deeply."

Yet another proposal. Grace wished he would just give up. She had no desire to marry him, and if necessary she would find someone else to manage her sheep.

"How are your cows doing? Have they all calved?"

Nigel frowned but answered her question. "Yes, they're fine. That's the biggest reason I haven't been around lately. That and the fact that we've been clearing land. My brother sent me here to see about getting a length of chain he ordered as well as new ropes. We have lots of stumps to pull and have worn our ropes clear through."

"I imagine it's not very easy to bring the stumps out." Grace went back to hanging clothes, hoping Nigel would take the hint that she was busy.

"It's hard work," Nigel said, repositioning himself so that

Grace had to look at him. His height made him a head taller than the line. "But it's worth it. This is good land, and it won't be so many years before we have a fine farm."

"I'm sure you're right."

"Grace, I want you to be a part of that farm. My brothers are taking wives. Women are coming from back east to marry them. They'll arrive just before winter, God willing. If you would only consent to marry me, then we would be completely set. Just think of all we could do together."

She gave a heavy sigh. "Nigel, you know I do not love you." She hoped her matter-of-fact statement would discourage him.

He nodded, and as she reached up to pin the end of a sheet to the line, he closed his hand over hers. "I do know that, but I'm convinced that in time you will. For now, I have enough love for us both."

She hated hurting him. He was so kind and always respectful. "I can't marry you. I have to wait for my uncle to return."

"But he may never return. He might even be dead. The Indians have been causing problems to the south of here, and he might well have been captured or killed." He grimaced. "I don't say this to upset you, just to make you think. If he is dead, you will need someone."

She knew he was right. Even when her uncle returned, she couldn't expect him to take care of her forever. She couldn't go on expecting charity, and she wasn't making enough money with her herbs and tonics to provide much in the way of food. Had it not been for the help of the good people around her, Grace knew they'd be in a bad way.

Nigel seemed to sense she saw the truth of his words and pressed on. "I will care for you and your sister. I will care for your other sister as well—should she return."

"She will return. She's currently helping my friends in California, and then she'll come back to join us."

He seemed pleased with her statement. "And I will be able to care for all of you. Me and my brothers. Together we will make good on our dreams."

She pulled her hand away from his. "But they aren't my dreams, Nigel." She saw his crestfallen face and wished there was some way she could force herself to love him and accept his proposal. "I'm sorry. I really must get these things up to dry. Mercy will be back soon, and we have other chores to tend to. Please try to understand."

Grace prayed he wouldn't argue or force her to endure more of his talk of love and dreams. Her dreams were tied to a dark-headed trapper, and even if it seemed unlikely for them to come true, Grace couldn't bring herself to cast them aside.

"Very well. But I don't intend to give up."

Neither do I. She didn't bother to speak, knowing he wouldn't understand.

To her relief, he departed without saying anything more. Grace hurried to get the laundry on the line and was just gathering the basket and leftover clothespins when she spied a stranger coming from the far side of the house. He was in sorry shape. His clothes were well-worn, and his beard and hair were desperately in need of trimming.

"I wonder if you might share a meal with a weary stranger," he said, his head bent toward the ground as if he were ashamed to ask.

Grace felt sorry for him. "Of course. I'll find you something."

He looked up and a smile broke across his face. "Grace Flanagan, don't you recognize me?"

She looked at him. No one here would call her by her maiden name. Recognition dawned and her eyes widened. "Uncle Edward?"

He laughed. "One and the same, although I'm sure I gave you a fright, looking as I do."

Grace dropped the basket and pins and ran to embrace him, mindless of his filthy, unkempt state. "Oh, Uncle Edward, I'm so very glad to see you." Tears came to her eyes as she hugged him close. "You have no idea how happy this makes me." She pulled back and wiped her eyes.

He raised a brow as he studied her for a moment. "I surely didn't expect tears."

"Oh, I'm sorry, but so much has happened that you don't know about. So much tragedy and sorrow, but now that you're here, it all seems unimportant." She hugged him again. "You are an answer to my prayers."

Chapter

22

I can't tell you how good it is to be with family again."
Uncle Edward smiled and reached out to take a hunk
of bread. "Glad to be back and pleased as I can be to have
two of the prettiest girls for nieces." He winked at Mercy. "You
look just like your mama did when she was your age."

"Truly?" Mercy seemed excited by the connection. "I miss
her so much."

"I do too, darlin'. Your mama was a great lady. Loved Jesus
more than most folks—knew Him better too. More than most
preachers I've known, in fact."

Mercy nodded. "Mama always told me that Jesus was the
only one who loved me more than she did."

"I'm bettin' that's true." He sopped gravy from his plate
with the bread. "Grace, you're a fine cook. I can't say when I
had a better meal."

Grace smiled. "Does that mean you're too full for pie?"

Her uncle laughed. "I ain't never been too full for pie. What'd
you make for us?"

"Mrs. Cranston traded some apples she'd canned for a tonic

to help her rheumatism. I thought apple pie would be perfect to welcome you home."

"Been home a week now, but I ain't complainin'," he said, reaching over to tweak Mercy's cheek. "I don't reckon I'll mind it much at all." He leaned back and rubbed his chin. "Sure glad you gave me a haircut and shave, Grace. I almost feel human now."

"You look human too," Mercy said. "Before, you resembled a grizzly bear."

Grace smiled and brought the pie to the table. "But I was happy to see you no matter what you looked like." She cut a big slice of pie and put it on her uncle's plate.

He wasted no time in taking a bite. His look of satisfaction assured Grace that the pie met with his approval. She put a piece on Mercy's plate and then cut a small piece for herself before retrieving the coffeepot to refill her uncle's cup.

She felt a sense of safety and happiness in being reunited with her uncle. She hadn't known him all that well due to him coming west when she'd been younger than Mercy, but they were making up for the lost years.

Mercy quickly consumed her pie, then jumped to her feet. "Can I be excused? I want to go see Beth Cranston."

"She's Mrs. Cranston's granddaughter, isn't she?" Uncle Edward asked.

"Yes. I go to school with her, but since this is Saturday, she invited me to come to her house to help quilt."

"Her pa is a good person. Her mama too. I don't reckon there are much better folks in all of the country."

"Well, with Uncle Edward's approval, I'd be hard-pressed to say no." Grace motioned to Mercy's plate and fork. "Clear those and then you may go."

Once Mercy was gone, Grace decided to speak to her uncle about their situation. "I want to thank you, Uncle Edward, for letting us stay here."

Before she could say more than that, someone knocked on the front door, and she sighed. That conversation would have to wait.

"I'll get it," she said. "You enjoy your coffee. Would you like more pie?"

Uncle Edward gave her a grin. "Does a cat want cream?"

She laughed and left to answer the door. Opening it, she found Nigel smiling back at her. He pulled off his hat with one hand and thrust out a bouquet of wildflowers with the other.

"I thought you might like these. Picked them on my way to town."

Grace forced a smile. "They're pretty. Come on in. I expect you'd like to meet my uncle."

Nigel nodded. "I would. I've heard a great deal about him."

Grace led the way back to the kitchen. "Uncle Edward, this is Nigel Grierson. Nigel, this is my uncle, Edward Marsh." She took the flowers to the counter, uncertain what she could use for a vase.

The two men exchanged handshakes, and Uncle Edward motioned for Nigel to take the chair vacated by Mercy. "Would you like some coffee? Maybe some pie? Grace is quite the cook."

"It smells wonderful. I'd enjoy some of each."

Grace put the flowers in a glass jar. "Let me give these flowers some water first." She wasn't happy to have to entertain Nigel, but she did want her uncle to meet him since Nigel had been so helpful with her sheep.

She took Nigel a cup of coffee, then went back to the counter for a plate and fork. She dished him up a generous portion of pie.

"I hope you enjoy it." She set the plate in front of him and then reclaimed her seat.

"I'd enjoy anything you made."

Grace saw her uncle's raised brow and felt her face flush. She'd have to explain about Nigel after he left, but for now she could at least give her uncle a bit of insight.

"Nigel and his wife were on the wagon train west with us. His wife died, and not long after, my husband passed. When the girls and I decided to stay at the mission and wait to hear from you, Nigel was good enough to bring my sheep here along with his dairy cows."

"I'm glad to meet any friend of Grace's, but especially glad when that friend has done such a kindness."

Nigel looked at Grace. "She's easy to be kind to."

"Well, be that as it may," her uncle continued, "I appreciate what you did for my girls."

"I'd like to do even more," Nigel admitted.

Grace didn't want to give him a chance to explain, so she hurried to continue. "I was glad that he'd taken the sheep. We lost the oxen and the wagon, along with most everything else, when the attack took place."

"Bad business that attack. The Cayuse have never been friendly towards settlers, but I never expected anything like that. I was mighty sorry to hear about it."

"Well, I've no doubt they'll be dealt with," Nigel countered. "We formed up a large number of men to hunt them down. One of my brothers joined the militia. I don't know how that's coming along, but I do hope to see those folks avenged."

Grace wanted to say something about God being the one who should avenge, but she remained silent. She knew her sisters probably felt much the same as Nigel.

Uncle Edward nodded. "We had some trouble in California too. There were some attacks on us as we came north, but we were able to deal with it. The Indians weren't well armed, and each of our men had rifles and pistols."

"Well, it's a relief you're back, Uncle Edward. Once Hope returns from helping the Brownings, I'll feel even better."

The men finished their pie and coffee, and to Grace's surprise, Nigel rose and excused himself. "I have a load of lumber to pick up at the mill and best get to it."

"I'll show you to the door." Grace quickly made her way to the front room so as to give Nigel no time to change his mind. Once he was gone, she made her way back to the kitchen and gave a heavy sigh, which caused her uncle to laugh.

"I can see you're less than interested in that poor lovesick young man."

"He asked me to marry him the same day we buried the Right Reverend Martindale." She sat down at the table. "He continues to propose every time he sees me."

"He seems nice enough."

"He is. But the last thing I want to do is marry him."

Uncle Edward smiled. "Is there someone else?"

Grace flushed. "Well . . . I . . . that is . . . no, not really."

"I don't abide lyin'. You want to try that again, and this time tell me the truth?" His questioning look was emphasized by the raising of his right brow. "Your mama was no better at keepin' stuff from me than you are."

Grace shrugged. "I do have feelings for a man, but he doesn't feel the same for me. So I'm not really lying when I say there's no one else."

"Who is this young man? Do I know him?"

"I believe you do. His name is Alex Armistead. He's a trapper."

Her uncle's smile faded. "I do know Alex. He's a good man. Honorable and trustworthy, but . . ."

Grace felt the uneasiness of her uncle's long pause. What troubled him so much about Alex?

"I don't think he's the type who will ever settle down," Uncle Edward finally said. "He's a troubled soul. I know his friend Gabriel Larquette better than Alex, and Gabe told me there was a lot of sadness and regret in Alex."

"Gabe is dead." Her mouth clicked shut. "I'm sorry. I shouldn't have just blurted it out like that. I was there when he died."

"I'm sorry to hear that. Gabe was a good man. We were friends for a long time, even trapped together for a spell. What happened?"

"He had a wound that festered and then fouled. I tried to treat him, but Dr. Whitman was angry about my interference. He bled Gabe, and in his weakened state, Gabe couldn't recover his strength. I blame myself more than Dr. Whitman. I didn't realize the wound was so infected."

"Well, blame won't bring him back. God rest his soul. I know he knew the Almighty. He was always sharin' his beliefs."

Grace nodded. "He told me Alex was troubled. In fact, Alex told me himself that he has issues in his past. So I'm not completely unaware."

"But you're not giving up on him either." Her uncle smiled at her.

"No. I suppose I'm not. But I'm also not counting on anything to ever come of it. I just know I can't marry Nigel when I love someone else."

"Love's a tricky thing, to be sure."

She couldn't help laughing at his comment. "Are you in love, Uncle Edward?"

"Could be." His grin broadened. "Could be. Just don't ask me to tell you her name. We have an understanding, but I haven't done much about it."

"Very well. Instead I'll pray for you. Oh, and I want to finish what I started to say before Nigel came. I really appreciate that you had the foresight to tell Dr. McLoughlin to let us stay here. I'm so grateful for that and for the credit you left us at Fort Vancouver."

Uncle Edward frowned. "While I did leave word with John to

let you stay here, I'm afraid I had nothing to do with any credit left you at the store. I made 'em pay me out in cash when I went south for the cattle. I wanted to buy a few head for myself."

Grace knew immediately that if her uncle hadn't provided the credit, it must have been Alex. But before she could say as much, another knock sounded on their door.

"Goodness, I've had more company today than in all the years I've been here." Uncle Edward got up and went to the door. After a few minutes, he called to Grace. "You have something here."

She went to the front door, where a stranger stood with her uncle. "You have something for me?"

The man nodded. "I was asked to bring you this horse and saddle. That is, if you're Grace Martindale."

"I am." She stepped outside and saw the Right Reverend's horse. Sam had taken the horse to his village when she and Alex had to go on foot to the fort. She hadn't thought she'd ever get the animal back.

She turned and nodded. "This is my horse and saddle."

The stranger nodded. "I'm glad to get him back to you." He turned to go.

"Wait. Isn't there a letter or something?"

He turned and shook his head. "No. The man just told me to bring the horse to Oregon City and find you. That's all."

"I see." Grace felt a lump in her throat. Why couldn't Alex have at least penned a few words? Did he truly care so little about her?

"Well, it was good of you to come all this way just to return a horse," Uncle Edward said, digging into his pocket. "Have this for your trouble." He flipped the man a coin.

The man caught it but handed it back. "No sir. I've been well paid. Good day to you both." He headed back along the river toward town while Grace stared after him.

"That was mighty nice of Alex," her uncle said. "I'm guessin'

273

I need to build a lean-to and a pen for the horse. Can't have a fine animal like that wandering around."

"No, I suppose not." Grace's thoughts were hardly on the horse's care, however.

"So what are you going to do now?"

She looked at her uncle in confusion. "What do you mean?"

He gave a chuckle. "About Alex."

"I'm not sure, but like I said, I'm not giving up."

Sam walked back to his lodge with Alex. They had buried his father and several others on the hill in keeping with tradition. The faces of the dead had been painted red, the women had wailed and cried, and the shaman had performed the rituals needed to keep the ghosts of the dead from returning. Some of his father's favorite things were laid with him, but he had made Sam promise that no one would kill his horse to be buried with him. Horses were far too needed in the village.

Sam was sorry that Reverend Spaulding hadn't been there. His father had loved the missionary like a brother and had trusted his counsel. He would have appreciated words from the Bible being spoken over him. Instead, Sam and Alex had spoken such words to his father as he was dying. The Scriptures comforted Jacob Night Walker, and for this Sam was glad.

He glanced back up the hill. It was hard to imagine his father was really gone. Sam believed that one day they would all be reunited in God's presence, but for now it would be difficult without him. His father had always been good for advice, and Sam had never known a wiser man.

"I'm going to miss him," Alex said as they walked.

"I buried a part of me with him."

"It's hard not to when you love someone that much. Your father was a good man, and he deserved a better death."

"He told me we should go." Sam stopped and looked out across the valley to where the tule mat lodges were clustered. "He told me it isn't safe here and we should move. He thought all the Nez Perce should join together."

Alex nodded. "I understand his thinking. With the Cayuse causing trouble against their own, it makes sense to have strength in numbers."

"I don't understand why they would hurt my father. He was always fair with Telokite and the others. My father's sister was even married to a Cayuse."

"They're running scared," Alex replied. "They know some of the men sent to capture them have camped out at the mission site, while others are combing the countryside. The Cayuse are nervous, knowing that the men won't rest until they round up the guilty parties. My fear is that they will cause such trouble that the militia will just kill them all."

"Fighting against the Boston men is something I understand. I don't approve, but I understand. Whites have brought sickness and changes to the land." Sam shook his head. "But what happened to my father and friends didn't come at the hand of the Boston men. It happened because they wouldn't give help to the Cayuse. It's hard to see my people fight each other. I remember when I was younger and we were attacked by the Shoshone. I asked my father why we fought, and he told me it was because it was easier to fight than to fix what was wrong."

"There's no doubt the Cayuse feel the same way. To fix what's wrong means giving up the men guilty of attacking the mission and seeing them hanged."

"So they will go on attacking and hurting people—even we who have been their friends and family." Sam shook his head. "This is not a world I want for my children."

Alex put his hand on Sam's shoulder. "Nor I, but it's the world we must live in. We need to seek God's direction on what to do. Fighting and hatred will never resolve this matter—only divine intervention can."

"My father loved you. He would agree with you, no doubt."

"I loved him too. Just as I love you, my brother."

Remembering the brother who had died because of his own disobedience, Sam felt an even deeper sense of loss. Must they all die and be taken from him? His mother—father—brother. All were gone, and now Sarah and the children were all that were left to him. And, of course, Alex. Alex had been the truest of brothers to him and would always be family to Sam, but Alex wasn't Nez Perce. Alex was white, and the changes coming to upend Sam's world were those of the white man. Alex would easily go on living in their world because he belonged there, but Sam and his people did not. They wouldn't be accepted, nor allowed to live in peace.

Sam's father had always said Sam was given a gift of seeing—of knowing when something bad was about to happen. Today that gift seemed more of a curse, for Sam knew that the things to come would spell the end of his people and their way of life.

Today he mourned more than his father's passing.

Chapter 23

Hope put a hand to her rounded abdomen. The baby would be born soon. Eletta had said something about the position of the child having dropped. She'd told Hope that meant the baby was settling in to be delivered. The very idea terrified Hope. The fundamentals of childbirth had been explained, but for the life of her, she couldn't understand why any woman would willingly accept that much pain. One of the women at church who made a point of looking down her nose at Hope had told her the pain would be in keeping with the sin. But this sin wasn't hers, so why should she be the one to bear it?

Her months with the Brownings had, however, softened her heart to a degree. The women of the church had been kind for the most part. They accepted her into their circles and treated her respectably, and because of that, Hope felt her hostility lessen.

Mr. Browning's preaching had also given Hope cause to rethink some of her feelings. Today was no exception, as he was teaching about the suffering of three women in the Bible.

Suffering that had to do with the babies they would bear or had borne.

"These three women," Mr. Browning began, "would bear great sorrow, but not because of anything they had done. Rather it was because of things out of their control."

Hope tried not to appear too interested, but his last sentence held her spellbound. Her own condition was because of things out of her control. Her suffering was great and her sorrow overwhelming at times.

"The first woman I want to discuss is Leah. Leah was given in marriage to Jacob, but this wasn't a love match. Jacob loved her sister, Rachel, but he'd been duped. Leah and Rachel's father tricked him into marrying Leah. And let me tell you, that didn't go well for any of them. You might remember that Jacob fooled his father and lied when it came to stealing his brother's birthright, so some might see this as just deserts for Jacob. But it certainly wasn't for Leah.

"When Jacob realized he'd been fooled, he went to the girls' father, Laban, and asked him why he'd done this and what he intended to do about it. Laban told Jacob that if he worked another seven years for him, he'd give him Rachel as well. Jacob agreed, and Rachel became his wife. And here's the really sad part. Jacob loved Rachel more than he did Leah. In fact, Leah was hated. Look with me in Genesis, the twenty-ninth chapter, verse thirty-one. 'And when the Lord saw that Leah was hated, he opened her womb: but Rachel was barren.'"

He paused for a moment and looked out over the congregation. "God gave Leah a son, and she named him Reuben and said, 'Surely the Lord hath looked upon my affliction; now therefore my husband will love me.' Leah knew that not only was she not loved, she was hated. When she gives birth to another son she says, 'Because the Lord hath heard I was hated, he hath therefore given me this son also.'

"I'm not sure if Leah knew what her father had planned when he tricked Jacob, but I do know that she was punished for it by her husband. She suffered a lack of love, despite being given children while her sister remained barren."

Hope cast her gaze at the floor. She didn't like to think about what Leah had gone through. She'd already convinced herself that no man would ever love her because of what had happened to her, and God knew that she felt the hatred of people who thought her condition was of her own doing.

"Then there's Jochebed, the mother of Moses," Mr. Browning continued. "By the time she had Moses, there was trouble brewing. Pharaoh was starting to worry about the number of Hebrew children being born. He figured sooner or later they were going to take over, so he called the Hebrew midwives and told them that if a boy baby was born, they were to kill it, but to let the baby girls live. These midwives didn't obey, so Pharaoh tells all of his people that if they see a Hebrew boy baby, they were to throw him into the river.

"Jochebed knows that her baby will be thrown into the river as soon as somebody realizes he's been born. So she decides to put him in the river herself—only she makes him a basket, seals it so the water won't get inside, and puts him in the river. She was no doubt deeply saddened by doing this. She loved her baby, and yet she had no choice but to give him up unless she wanted to see him drown. How that must have pierced her heart. She was suffering not from something she'd caused, but because of something demanded of her. Something most unfair and unpleasing to God."

He paused to turn the pages of his Bible, and Hope considered all that he'd just shared and all that she'd endured since coming to stay with the Brownings. They had determined together that they wouldn't lie about Hope's condition. They made it clear she had been misused in the attack and therefore was not to blame. However, that didn't stop people from condemning her. One woman had even told her point-blank that she should kill herself rather than give birth to a savage's child. Hope didn't bother to tell the woman that she'd felt that way once herself. Only Eletta's words about the child's innocence had stayed her hand.

"The last woman I want to talk about is Mary, the mother of Jesus. Mary was just a young girl when the angel came to tell her she was going to bear the Son of God. She wasn't asked ahead of time or given a choice in the matter. She knew that this would cause the legalists of the day to condemn her. She knew that her betrothed husband, Joseph, could order her killed for being unmarried and with child. After all, he knew the baby wasn't his. Mary must have thought of all those things. She would have known people were going to be disappointed in her—even hateful towards her." He glanced at Hope. "They didn't understand.

"And it didn't matter that they didn't understand," he continued, looking back at the congregation. "Mary knew that her Father in heaven loved her. She knew that there would be suffering and sorrow, but she trusted that God had a plan and that she would be blessed because of it. So she told the angel, 'Be it unto me according to thy word.'"

Hope knew that nothing about her condition had anything to do with what Mary went through. She certainly wasn't giving birth to the Son of God. Her child wasn't being born out of God's great love and compassion for mankind but because of the heinous actions of a man who hated her. Yet in each of the examples given, the women suffered—not at their own hand or because of something they'd done wrong—just as she did.

"While I've told you about the suffering these women endured," Mr. Browning said, "I now want to tell you about the blessings they received.

"Leah gave birth to many sons and daughters. She may never have known the love of her husband, or in time Jacob might have learned to love her, we can't say for sure. But we do know that God loved Leah dearly and she loved Him. Jochebed's son Moses lived. He was saved by Pharaoh's daughter, who then paid Jochebed to nurse her own son. Not only did God save Jochebed's child, but He arranged for her to be paid for loving and caring for him. I'm sure some of you ladies out there wish someone would pay you to care for your children."

There were chuckles throughout the congregation.

"Moses went on to lead the Israelites to freedom. How proud Jochebed must have been, but even more, how grateful she must have felt toward God for His mercy. So many of her friends had lost their sons, but she had been allowed to keep hers.

"And of course we know what happened with Mary. She gave birth to Jesus—the Son of God, the Savior of the world. She married Joseph and had other children and no doubt great joy, but she also had great sorrow because the world condemned Jesus and nailed Him to a cross while she could only stand by and watch. But her sorrow is our joy, because without the sacrifice Jesus made, we would be condemned to eternal death. Sometimes the sorrows we bear can be used by God to bring great joy—even deliverance from bondage."

Hope heard little else. Eletta had once said that Hope was giving her a gift that would bring them great joy. For a moment, that thought made Hope angry, just as it had when Eletta had mentioned it. It wasn't fair to make someone bear pain and suffering just to give someone else happiness. How could that be just or good? Yet God was both, so how could she reconcile the matter?

But how can I not?

She was so tired of her own angry, bitter heart. She longed to be with her sisters and to be free from the past and the nightmare of the massacre. She was only eighteen. She should be falling in love and creating a home of her own. Instead she was made to suffer. She could no longer count on any man being willing to overlook her situation.

She thought of her mother, as she often did these days. Mama had said that love covered a multitude of sins. It was in the Bible. Hope missed her mother more than she could say. So many times she'd wished that Mama had been there to talk to—to ask questions. Mama had always been able to help Hope get rid of her anger, reminding Hope that anger and hatred ate a person up from the inside. She said that some folks had even been known to die from being so hateful. Hate destroyed the living part of them until they had nothing of life left in them.

The baby moved within her, and Hope wondered if her anger and bitterness had infected the child. Was it possible for a mother's sorrow and pain to be known by her unborn baby? Had her hate destroyed the child?

Exhaustion washed over her. An exhaustion of the past and its horrors. An exhaustion of the present and the condemnation she had known. If she didn't do something soon, she would also know that same sense of exhaustion for her future.

September in Oregon City brought the end to a beautiful, albeit hot, summer. Grace had enjoyed the warm days. The garden had grown so well that she had been able to put up vegetables to last them the winter. Apples were also in abundance, and John McLoughlin made certain that she had as much as she wanted from his own orchards. Added to this, she had been taught to can and smoke the salmon and other fish abundant in the Willamette River.

Throughout the spring and summer months, she and Mercy had gathered herbs and learned all kinds of remedies from the local women. Some of the Indian medicines were unfamiliar but proved very effective. Even so, Grace couldn't make a living with her healing. Most of the women in the area could see to their own, and when things were too bad for that, there were doctors.

As summer faded, Uncle Edward proposed to his lady love, the widow Mina Andrews. Grace had heard it said about town that most of the men in a fifty-mile radius had been trying to court the widow, but she had been secretly enamored with Edward Marsh.

Grace was happy about her uncle finding love, but at the same time, it would change everything for her and Mercy—Hope too, when she returned. The house obviously wasn't big enough for all of them. Mina Andrews had three young boys small enough to share the upstairs room that Grace and Mercy had been using since their uncle's return. But that meant there'd be no room for Grace and her sisters. When Grace had mentioned this offhandedly at breakfast one morning, her uncle had laughed and agreed the house could never hold them all.

Since then, Grace had tried to discuss it with Uncle Edward, but he was so often gone that she found it impossible. Then even when he was around, so too was Mercy or Mina and the boys, and Grace didn't feel she could bring up the matter in front of them. And so their situation weighed her down all the more. She was, after all, the intruder. She and her sisters could hardly expect their uncle to support them their whole lives. So what was she to do?

Just that day in church, the pastor had spoken of the duty each person owed to the community. He reminded them that without the individual doing his or her part, the people as a whole would fail. He commented on the widowed women putting aside their mourning to marry the men of the community. It was their duty to do so in order to make a better life for everyone.

"We are isolated here," the pastor had said. "Therefore you must do what you can to better the whole. If that means you have to make sacrifices, then so be it. We have all found ourselves in that situation, and you alone are responsible for yielding your will to God's."

But what was God's will? She had prayed for solutions—answers to what she should do. She had come west thinking the answer was to get to Uncle Edward, but now she wasn't so sure. Perhaps she should never have come west. After all, look at all they'd gone through. Had it been her foolishness that brought them to such a fate?

Unable to sleep, Grace slipped downstairs and outside, letting the chilled night air revive her weary spirit. She tugged on the rawhide strip around her neck and pulled Sam Two Moon's bear claw from beneath her bodice. He had said he kept it to remind him of the price he'd paid for having his own way. Was she going to make others pay the price for having things her own way? She looked for a long time at the claw.

She really had no choice but to marry Nigel. There was no other way for her to survive and keep her sisters from having to go elsewhere to live and work for their keep as the orphaned Sager girls had had to do. If she didn't accept the situation for what it was, Hope and Mercy might even find themselves having to marry, and Grace couldn't allow that. Not after how much they'd already suffered. No, if anyone was going to sacrifice, it would be her. It was, after all, only right. Mercy and Hope had endured the massacre and survived. Grace could endure marrying a man she didn't love for their sake. She'd done it once before. She could do it again.

"Lord, You know I've prayed for answers, and nothing seems to come to me except Nigel and his proposals. I suppose I've been wrong to refuse him, but . . ." She sighed and tucked the necklace back inside her blouse. "But maybe this is the answer to my prayers and I've just been too blind to see it. I had all sorts of lofty ideas about marrying a man I truly loved—marrying Alex." Grace shook her head. "Obviously that isn't Your will for me."

She walked to the river's edge and looked out at the water. Surely she could be happy in this country. Surely she could find happiness married to Nigel.

"He's a good man," she said as if trying to convince herself. "He's a God-fearing man, and he has promised to care for my sisters if I marry him."

She gave a heavy sigh and resigned herself to what must be. The weight of her decision left her feeling weary and worn.

"I will marry him and do what I can to be happy . . . and to make him happy."

Chapter
24

H ope bore down, pain ripping her apart inside. She
cried out as the midwife instructed Eletta to mop
Hope's brow. A damp towel wasn't going to make
this any better, and Eletta's tenderness wasn't going to remove
the pain. Hope had been in labor since early that morning, and
now, nearly twelve hours later, she was about to give birth. Or
die. Hope figured either was preferable to what she was going
through.

The pain brought back memories of the rape and all she
had suffered, causing fear to flood her spirit. What if the baby
looked like Tomahas? What if her own hatred had somehow
marred the child?

As the baby slipped from her body, the midwife announced
the birth of a girl. Hope closed her eyes and fought back the
surge of emotion that coursed through her. It was finally done.
Tears came to her eyes, but she couldn't say why. Perhaps it
was just the relief of being able to put aside this part of her
life once and for all.

"I don't want to see her," she said, looking only at Eletta, whose expression could only be described as delighted. She heard the infant give a lusty cry, and for reasons she didn't understand, Hope gave in to her tears. "Please take her away." She sobbed quietly into her hands. Thoughts of John Sager came to mind, and she couldn't help mourning his loss all over again.

The sounds of the baby's cries diminished as Eletta took her from the room. Pain surged through Hope's body as the midwife bore down on her tender abdomen. "What are you doing?"

"Delivering the afterbirth. You don't know much about these things, do you?"

Hope shook her head. Would this nightmare never end?

It was nearly an hour later when the midwife had finally completed her duties. All Hope wanted to do was sleep, but as she dozed, the baby's shrill cries kept jarring her back awake. Finally, exhaustion took over, and Hope fell into a deep, dreamless sleep. Her first since the massacre.

When she awoke, Hope was surprised to find it was light outside. Worse still, the baby was crying. Had she cried all through the night?

Easing up in the bed, Hope sat against the headboard and tried not to be moved by the infant's distress. Eletta was new to having a baby, so no doubt there would be a time of adjustment for her. Hope just wished the child would stop crying.

Hope sat alone, pondering what would happen next, when Eletta appeared at the door. She looked exhausted but smiled. "You're awake. I'm so glad. How do you feel?"

"Tired and sore. You look as though you might feel the same. What time is it?"

"Nearly four in the afternoon."

"I didn't realize I'd slept so long." Hope glanced toward the door. "And . . . what about . . . her? She keeps crying." She found herself torn between the need to know and the desire to forget. "Is she . . . all right?"

"She's hungry, and the cow's milk doesn't sit well. We're going to try goat's milk next. Isaac has gone to get some from a man down the road."

Hope pushed aside the sense of guilt. "Did you name her?"

"Yes. We agreed to keep to what your mother started and will call her Faith."

"Faith," Hope whispered. It seemed strange that a child of her misery would have such an encouraging name.

The baby's cries grew louder, and Eletta excused herself. Hope felt a strange tingling sensation in her breasts. What was happening to her? She crossed her arms against her chest, hoping to ease the sensation. It did little to help.

Eletta returned after ten minutes or so with food. "I know you must be famished, just as she is. I kept this warm for you." She left the tray and hurried from the room.

The bowl contained a generous portion of ham, potatoes, and green beans, which had been cooked together. Beside this was a thick slice of bread slathered in butter. The aroma alone drew Hope's attention. Digging in, she began to calculate how long it might be before she could return to Oregon City. That in turn had her pondering what she would do once she was there.

Still feeling exhausted, Hope finished eating and put the tray aside. She slid back down in the bed, intending to rest for just a little while, and instead fell asleep. In her dreams she heard a baby crying and went in search. She looked through room after room in a dimly lit house that she didn't recognize. She awoke at one point and found her room dark and the house strangely quiet. Not knowing what time of day or night it was, Hope allowed herself to drift off once again. When next she opened her eyes, it was light.

Yawning, Hope again eased herself up in the bed. She adjusted her nightgown, surprised by the firmness in her breasts.

She hadn't even considered that this was a natural occurrence. Most mothers would expect to nurse their babies.

From somewhere in the house, she heard Faith crying—more of a whimper, as if the child had exhausted herself. Hope again felt the strange tingling and crossed her arms. How long would this last?

Faith's cries grew increasingly desperate. Hope heard Eletta doing what she could to soothe the baby, but she was beyond soothing. Determined to pay no attention to what was happening, Hope instead decided to get up and open a window. The room was stuffy and in need of fresh air.

"I don't have to worry about this," she told herself over and over. "Eletta is Faith's mother. She'll know what to do for her."

But it didn't seem like this was the case, and after nearly ten minutes of constant cries, Hope felt like joining in with her own tears. Why couldn't the child be silent? She put her hands over her ears, but that did little to block the noise.

She needs to nurse.

It was as if someone had spoken the words aloud. Hope even looked toward the door, certain she would find Eletta standing there. But the doorway was empty.

The tingling sensation in her breasts increased, and Hope knew that even her body was trying to force the issue.

"But I want nothing to do with her." She gritted her teeth. Surely God wouldn't be so cruel as to force her to nurse the baby.

But now her suffering comes from my hands.

That thought pricked Hope's conscience in a way nothing else could. She was causing the baby pain and misery because of her own selfish need.

Thoughts of God still made her uncomfortable, but Hope put aside that discomfort for the moment and looked toward the ceiling. "Can't You make her stop crying? Can't You fix things so that she can drink the cow's milk?"

Hope heard talking and realized that Mr. Browning was try-ing to help. She held her breath as the baby's cries momentarily subsided. But even as she prayed that God would allow the child to feed without Hope's help, the infant began to wail once again, and this time Eletta began to cry too. Mr. Browning spoke in a soothing tone, but that seemed only to cause Eletta and the baby to cry all the more. Mr. Browning apparently found the situation impossible, because Hope heard the front door slam. Glancing out her widow, she saw him hurrying down the front walk.

Then to her surprise, Eletta showed up at the open doorway of Hope's room, babe in arms. She looked at Hope with plead-ing in her eyes. "Please, help her."

To refuse would make Hope cruel, yet the pain of seeing the child and remembering her father was almost too much.

"Please," Eletta said again. "She'll die otherwise. She's not been able to take any nourishment without throwing it back up."

Hope moved to the bed and sat down. She had once wanted this child dead, but facing the idea of being the cause of Faith's demise, Hope could bear it no longer. She drew a deep breath and unbuttoned the top of her gown. Eletta sobbed in gratitude and hurried to the bedside.

"Thank you, Hope. I know what this is costing you. Truly I do, but God will bless you for your kindness."

Eletta placed the baby in Hope's arms, and for a moment Hope couldn't bring herself to look at the child. She positioned the baby to her breast and startled when Faith latched on and began to suck.

Hope's breathing quickened, and without stopping to think, she looked down. The baby seemed so small and perfect. She was no monster and looked nothing like the man who had forced himself on Hope. She didn't look any different than other babies Hope had seen.

"She's pretty, don't you think?" Eletta asked.

"Yes." Hope barely breathed the word. She touched the baby's dark hair, then let her finger trail down the infant's cheek.

The baby nursed while Hope marveled. How could something so beautiful and precious come from such an ugly beginning?

"Eletta," Mr. Browning called, "is everything all right?"

Hope quickly drew the blanket over herself and the baby. Eletta dried her eyes and gave Hope's shoulder a pat. "I'll be right back."

Hope knew enough about babies and nursing that after ten or fifteen minutes, she put the infant to her shoulder. After a few gentle pats, the baby burped. Hope switched Faith to her other breast, uncertain if the child was full. Again the sensation of Faith latching on caught Hope by surprise. It was all so very strange and new.

As Faith began to fall asleep, the sucking lessened and lessened until she finally stopped altogether. Hope was uncertain what to do next. Should she burp her again? Should she just let her sleep? She wanted to call for Eletta but didn't want to wake the sleeping baby. In the other room, she could hear Eletta and Mr. Browning talking. For a moment Hope thought they might even be arguing. When Eletta returned a few minutes later, she was frowning, and Hope knew she'd been right.

"What's wrong?"

Eletta looked as if she wouldn't answer for a moment. She sank down on the bed beside Hope. "Isaac thinks I was foolish to ask you to nurse the baby."

"Why?"

The older woman looked uncomfortable. "Well . . . he's afraid." She paused and shook her head. "He's afraid that you'll grow attached to the child and won't be willing to give her up."

Hope shook her head. "There's no chance of that. I see that

she isn't the monster I feared she'd be—in fact, she's lighter than I thought and doesn't look that different from the white infants I've seen. But . . ." She fell silent for a moment, then shook her head. "I'm not ready to be a mother. And . . . I can't forget what happened."

Eletta's expression changed from anxious to relieved. "I know he'll be comforted to know that you don't mean to change your mind. I hadn't realized until now how much he wanted Faith. I think he's longed for a child just as much as I have."

"Then put his mind at ease. Better yet, call him here and I will." Hope handed the sleeping baby to Eletta. She felt strangely empty as Eletta stood and left the room with Faith in her arms. Hope did up her buttons and was prim and proper when Eletta returned with Mr. Browning.

Hope could see the look of worry on Mr. Browning's face. "I know you're concerned that I will change my mind about the baby, but I assure you that I won't. I will nurse her until you can work out something else, but I want to go home as soon as possible."

"Are you certain? I'm sure you know how much Faith means to us. We've . . . we've truly looked forward to her arrival."

"I know that and I'm very certain." Hope smiled for the first time in a long while at the sight of the couple holding the baby. "I know this is what is right. I'm not sure if I could ever love . . . Faith. Not like you can. She needs you—not me."

"We'll check into whether there's someone in the area who could nurse her," Eletta said. "There are several women with newborns."

A memory came to Hope. "I recall when we were coming west that one of the women couldn't nurse. Grace mixed water with cow's milk to weaken it and added a little sugar. Then they spoon-fed the baby. Perhaps that would work for Faith if you can't find another woman to help."

Eletta nodded, looking down at the sleeping infant. "I think both of us are exhausted."

"You should sleep while you can," Mr. Browning said. He gave Hope a hesitant smile. "I'll see if I can find someone to help us, but in the meantime . . ." He fell silent and turned his gaze to the floor.

"I will nurse her as you need me to." Hope saw the flash of gratitude as he looked back up.

Once they'd gone, she eased back against the pillows and pondered the situation. She had never planned to see her baby—Eletta and Isaac's baby—but for reasons she couldn't understand, it had actually given her comfort. Knowing that the child appeared healthy and undamaged from Hope's anger and desires to put an end to its life was a relief.

Maybe now she could finally put the massacre and all that had happened behind her. Maybe she could finally forget what she had lost that day and look to the future.

Alex kicked mud off his boots. He and Sam had just turned in their fall cache of furs at Fort Nez Perce. Word had it there had been some violence between tribes to the south of them, but here things had been fairly quiet.

"So what now?" Sam asked Alex.

For days Alex had contemplated that very question. "A bath. A long, hot bath. I can't abide my own stench."

Sam laughed. "Me either, but I was talking about Grace."

Alex could see Sam wasn't going to drop it. "I'm going to Fort Vancouver to check the mail."

"Do you suppose you'll have a letter from your sister?"

"I don't know. I hope so. There's been more than enough time to send one. I figure Adelina must have received mine by summer. She might have been able to have a letter transferred west via the fort stops. I heard from Peter Ogden that they've organized regular mail runs between the forts."

"And if there isn't a letter?"

Alex had already determined what to do, but he kept rethinking the matter in his head. "I'm going to find Grace and talk to her."

"It's about time," Sam said, untying his horse. "You should have gone to see her months ago."

"I couldn't. I'm not even sure I can now."

"You are a stubborn and prideful man."

Alex eyed his friend with a smile. "It's a wonder you put up with me."

Sam nodded solemnly. "It is." Then he broke into a grin. "When will I see you again?"

"I'm not sure. Since your people have moved north, it might be some time. I'll know more after I see whether my sister has written. If she hasn't, then I suppose my next letter will go to the officials in New Orleans."

"And what about Grace?"

"I'm still going to go talk to her."

"And ask her to wait for you?"

Alex fixed Sam with what he hoped was a look of annoyance. "I'll figure that out when I see her."

Sam laughed. "I suppose that's the white man's way."

"I'm going to miss you, my friend." He embraced Sam with a quick hug. "I hope it won't be too long before we meet again."

"I pray God will bring us together soon," Sam said. He mounted his horse.

"And I'll pray that God eases the tensions between our people."

Sam again gave him a solemn nod. "May it be so."

Fort Vancouver proved disappointing for Alex. There was no letter awaiting his return, and without it, he was hard-pressed to figure out what he should do first. He could send a letter out with the Hudson's Bay missives, or he could go see Grace first. The latter was far more appealing, so he made his way to Oregon City.

Upon arriving, he checked himself into the City Hotel. The town was growing by leaps and bounds. What had started as scarcely more than a good place to catch salmon had blossomed into a busy town. There were more stores and mills than had been there on his last visit. Great portions of land had been cleared, and the sawmills were working at full capacity. And with the late-summer news that the president had finally made Oregon a bona fide territory, Oregon City had been named its capital.

Of course, there had been other news as well. News about gold discoveries in California had sent many a man off to seek his fortune. Alex wondered if Grace's uncle had ever returned, and if so, whether or not he might have decided to return south and taken his nieces with him.

Alex knew the location of Edward Marsh's house, but before he went there, he intended to get cleaned up. At the hotel he managed a hot bath, although it cost him a pretty penny. Next he had a barber trim his hair and beard. Last of all, he put aside his buckskins for a pair of store-bought trousers as well as a new shirt and coat. He wasn't sure why he'd bought new clothes. It seemed silly, given he had no idea if he'd find Grace or if she'd still be free once he did.

He contemplated his choices as he crossed Main Street in search of a hot meal. He had plenty of credit and even some cash, so it wouldn't be hard to purchase supplies if he needed to go in search of Grace.

He was lost in these thoughts when the door of the Brick

Store opened and several people exited. The last one was Grace. For a moment all they did was stare at each other, and they probably would have remained fixed to the spot had someone not wanted to enter the store.

"I'm sorry," Grace said, shifting her basket from one arm to the other.

Alex quickly stepped forward. "I hoped I might find you."

Her eyes widened, and for a moment he lost his thoughts. She seemed unable to speak while he assessed her. She was dressed in a simple cotton dress of blue with her hair pinned atop her head. He thought she'd never been more beautiful.

"When did you arrive?" she finally managed to say.

"Just today. I wanted to clean up before I came looking for you." He grinned and swept his arm down his body. "What do you think?"

She smiled. "You look very . . . nice. Very different."

He decided to get right to the point. "I was hoping we could talk. It's important. Might we go somewhere more private?"

She opened her mouth to answer, but instead Alex heard a man calling her name. The tall, blond-headed stranger looked vaguely familiar as he approached.

He didn't even acknowledge Alex. "Grace, I asked the reverend about marrying us at the end of November, and he said he would."

Alex felt the wind go out of him. He saw Grace grimace. "This is Nigel Grierson," she said to Alex. "I don't know if you remember him or not, but he was at the mission for a short time."

Alex nodded. "I thought you looked familiar."

"Nigel, this is Alex Armistead."

Nigel extended his hand, but the look on his face was suspicious. "I'm Grace's fiancé."

Grace lowered her face and again shifted her basket. Alex

could see she was uncomfortable and hated that he was the cause of it. Uncertain what he could do, Alex forced a smile and tipped his hat.

"Congratulations." He forced the words out. "I'm glad to see you doing so well, Grace."

He turned and walked away, although it took every ounce of determination he had. She was going to marry Grierson, and Alex had no right to interfere with her happiness. Even at the cost of his own.

Chapter 25

Days after her encounter with Alex, Grace was still trying to figure out what had happened. Why had he come back, and why did he want to talk to her? He'd said it was important and yet walked away without another word. She'd thought he might try to come to her later that day, but when he didn't, she began to search for him. She went to the City Hotel and learned that he had already checked out. None of the other merchants had seen anything of him since that day.

Nigel had been unhappy at Alex's arrival and made no attempt to hide his feelings. He told Grace it wasn't appropriate that a woman engaged to marry one man should be traipsing all over town looking for another. Grace felt sorry for Nigel. She had a feeling he knew full well that she was in love with Alex.

"I have to find him."

"Did you say something?" Mercy asked, looking up from the bowl she'd been stirring.

"Nothing important." Grace pulled off her apron. "I think I'm going to change my clothes."

"Do you want me to keep making cookies?"

"Yes. That would be good." She left the kitchen, intending to head upstairs, but stopped when the front door opened.

"I've found something I think belongs to you—to us," Uncle Edward said, coming into the house with a large carpetbag under one arm. He stepped aside, and Hope entered.

Grace couldn't contain her joy or surprise. "I can hardly believe you're here. Just look at you!" Grace hugged Hope close, then stepped back. "You look somehow changed and yet the same."

Hope shrugged. "I suppose I am exactly that."

Mercy came running. "Hope! I've missed you so much, but now you're back and you'll be here for the wedding!"

"Wedding?" Hope looked at Grace.

Uncle Edward laughed and deposited Hope's bag on the floor. "Yes, indeed. Your sister is gettin' hitched."

"Uncle Edward is marrying also, but I don't believe they've set a date."

"Grace is marrying Mr. Grierson at the end of the month." Mercy frowned. "He's coming for supper tonight."

Hope's expression turned to one of disgust. "Nigel Grierson? You can't stand him."

Grace shrugged. "I find him better company than I did on the trail. Besides, that's not important just now. Tell me how you're doing. How did . . . well . . . how did everything go?" She hadn't told Mercy about the pregnancy and wasn't at all sure Hope would want her to know.

"Mr. and Mrs. Browning have a beautiful baby girl they've named Faith."

"Oh, that's a pretty name. I like that," Mercy declared. "No wonder you went to help. I didn't know they were going to have a baby. Beth said her mama is going to have a baby next year. I think it's so wonderful. I can't wait until I can be a mama."

"I hope that isn't true," Hope replied.

Mercy looked at her oddly. "What do you mean?"

"You said you can't wait, but I hope you will. You need to grow up first and then wait until you find a good man to marry."

"Both of you are certain to have your share of beaus. The town is full of single men," Uncle Edward said, shaking his head. "I suppose we'll have our hands full."

"Hopefully not for a long time," Grace countered.

Uncle Edward shrugged and smiled. "Well, my lovely nieces, I must bid you farewell and get myself back to town. I have a meeting with Dr. McLoughlin. He's feedin' me tonight, so don't wait supper for me." He headed for the door and turned. "It's good to have you girls all together again."

Grace agreed as Uncle Edward disappeared. Things hadn't seemed right without Hope. "I'm so glad you're back with us."

She studied Hope again. Her prettiness had developed into a more refined beauty. She seemed to have aged considerably during her absence. Gone was the flirtatious girl, and in her place had come a woman.

Hope nodded. "I'm glad to be here, but not so glad to hear you're marrying Nigel. Why are you doing that? I know you don't love him, and after the Right Reverend Martindale, I thought you'd given up the idea of loveless marriages."

Grace cringed. She couldn't very well lie. "It's a long story, and I don't have time for it now. Nigel is on his way to take me to see the house he's building us. It's big enough for all of us."

Hope shook her head. "Why can't we stay here?"

"Uncle Edward is getting married," Mercy said, looking displeased. "That means we can't stay here."

Grace felt Hope's look of disapproval before she saw it. She hurried to speak before Hope could voice her thoughts. "Don't say anything to him. We don't want him to worry about us. Uncle Edward is marrying a lovely widow with three little boys. I think they will be very happy together."

"I don't remember much about Uncle Edward," Hope replied. "I didn't know him when he came to me in town."

"I wish you had told us you were coming. We could have all been there to greet you."

Hope shrugged and ran her hand along the back of the wooden rocking chair. "I didn't want any fuss. When I arrived and explained who I was, someone pointed me out to Uncle Edward. I wasn't at all sure of him, but when he laughed, it reminded me of Mama."

"He has some wonderful stories of when he and Mama were young. I'm certain you'll enjoy them," Grace said. "Now, we're all three upstairs. Uncle Edward fashioned two more small beds, and they fit quite nicely. I'm sure they'll be perfect to accommodate his family after he marries." She grimaced and turned away. She hadn't wanted to turn the conversation back to the reason she was marrying Nigel. "Are you hungry? I can fix you something to eat."

"Hello!"

It was Nigel, with his customary call from the open doorway. Grace grimaced. There was no time to change her dress. She hurriedly gathered her sunbonnet and crossed the room to greet him.

"Nigel, look who's returned. You remember Hope, don't you?"

He smiled and gave a nod. "I do. I'm glad you made it back safely, Miss Hope. I suppose Grace has told you that we're to be married."

Grace looked at Hope and prayed she'd not say anything untoward. The last thing she wanted was further comments about their upcoming wedding.

"She did mention it," Hope replied.

"Good." Nigel seemed pleased. "I'm taking her to see our new house. It's not far from town, and I think you're all going to like it."

Hope said nothing more, and Grace was grateful. "I won't

be gone long. Mercy, don't forget you promised to finish baking those cookies." She dared a glance at Hope and saw the disapproval in her expression. "Hope, feel free to get settled in upstairs. If you need anything, just ask Mercy."

Alex wandered around Fort Vancouver, uncertain what he should do next. He'd left Oregon City like a man fleeing the law—barely remembering to collect his things from the hotel before riding out. He'd never been one to run away from a fight, but the news that Grace was engaged made him desperate to distance himself. The miles between them, however, had done nothing to ease his misery. He hadn't slept much since learning that Grace was to marry another. If only he could have talked to her first.

Once he'd calmed down and had a chance to think about it, he felt certain that she didn't love Nigel. No doubt she was marrying him out of necessity, and the more Alex thought about that being the reason, the more determined he was to return and stop her.

"Alex," one of the fort workers called, crossing the commons. "I have a letter for you."

His heart skipped a beat. Could it really be true?

The man approached, waving the missive. "It must have come a couple weeks ago, because I found it at the bottom of the mail pouch just as I was getting ready to fill it with letters to send out."

Alex took the letter and saw it was from his sister. He whispered a silent prayer of thanks. No matter what she'd written, at least she had been willing to write.

"Thank you." He made his way back to his room and opened the letter.

Alex had never made the trip to Oregon City faster than he made it that Friday. He could scarcely think straight since reading Adelina's letter. It was more than he could have hoped for, and now he could go to Grace and offer her his hand. He knew Grierson would be livid, but he didn't care. He loved Grace, and she needed to know it. Everything else could be sorted out another time.

He arrived at Edward Marsh's house and couldn't keep a silly smile from his face. Grace would be surprised to see him, but even more dumbfounded to hear him propose they marry. He dismounted and tied off his horse.

"Well, old boy," he said, patting the horse's neck, "this is it." He stepped up to the front door to knock.

When the door opened, Alex took off his hat to greet Grace's sister. "Good day, Hope."

She put her hands on her hips. "I suppose you've come to talk to Grace."

"I have."

"Better late than never." Her tone seemed reprimanding.

"What do you mean?"

"Grace is out with Nigel Grierson. He keeps taking her out to see the house he's building—for her." Her tone was full of disgust. "You do know he plans to marry her at the end of the month, don't you?"

"I do. I met up with her briefly last week. I heard Mr. Grierson say something to that effect."

"Then you're a fool."

Alex frowned. "Why?"

"Because she loves you, but you're going to let another man, whom she doesn't love, steal her away."

"Oh, am I?" He laughed, finally understanding Hope's hostile nature. "I don't think you have that right."

Her expression softened as she cocked her head to one side. "Really?"

"I'm here, aren't I?" He glanced around. "Point me in the direction of this new house."

Grace listened to Nigel as he proclaimed all the wonderful details of the house he and his brother Winston were building. She had to admit it was large—more than enough space for all of them. Just beyond the house stood a small cabin that she knew Nigel shared with his elder brother Winston while his brother Lionel was off with the militia.

"The windows won't arrive until next year, but we'll manage," Nigel told her with a smile.

Grace couldn't work up the same level of enthusiasm. "It looks very nice."

She couldn't stop thinking about Alex and felt certain Nigel knew this. There was no sense in pretending otherwise. She had considered backing out of their engagement at least a dozen times since she'd seen Alex but so far hadn't been able to muster the courage. Not that Nigel would listen to her. His confidence knew no limits when it came to the certainty he could win her.

"It won't be many years until this area is filled with people. I know this spot may seem far from town, but it's only a few miles. Once the city starts to build up even more . . . well, this will probably seem far too close for comfort."

Grace nodded. She couldn't help remembering Hope's plea that she rethink her plans. "It's very nice, Nigel, but I need to get back. I have a great deal of work to do. With the weather changing more every day, I need to collect some tree bark."

"I don't mind helping." He smiled, and his blue eyes seemed to twinkle. "I love being with you."

Grace sighed. "Be that as it may, I need to concentrate on what I'm doing, and you would be a distraction."

"A good distraction, though, right?" He chuckled.

She said nothing as she walked back to her horse and took up the reins.

"Wait, I'll help you mount."

"I'm not going to ride. It's hard to collect bark on horseback."

His expression turned sheepish. "Of course. I wasn't thinking."

Grace nodded and tugged the horse forward. She should say something in parting, but nothing came to mind. What she really wanted to say, she hadn't been able to find the right moment for.

But I must. I cannot deceive him anymore. I cannot marry him.

She heard Nigel bid her good-bye. Grace gave a little wave without looking back. There was no easy solution—no easy answer. She loved Alex, but Nigel knew that. She wanted to spend her life with Alex, but that didn't seem possible.

"And it isn't possible to make a living on my own that would support Hope and Mercy, much less myself."

She had tried to speak to Uncle Edward a few days earlier, but he was so distracted that Grace gave up trying to figure out his plans. He just kept saying how happy he was for her to marry. It seemed that the matter was settled.

Grace continued to walk, the gelding plodding along in step. She wove her way through the trees, looking for just the right samples. Her mind, however, was on the present circumstance.

If I break the engagement and refuse to marry Nigel, how will I take care of Hope and Mercy? Dr. McLoughlin might have some ideas. He'd been so kind to them since their arrival. Perhaps she could sell the sheep and return with her sisters to St. Louis. But there was no more there for them than there was here. In fact, there was less.

"Grace."

She looked up and found Alex standing only about ten feet away. She chided herself for not paying better attention to her surroundings.

"Alex." It took all her strength not to run to him.

He crossed the distance between them in a few long strides and took hold of her arms. "You can't marry Grierson."

She found it difficult to breathe at his nearness. Hadn't she prayed for this moment? Now he was here, and Grace wanted nothing more than to be in his arms.

"Did you hear me?"

Grace nodded. "I did, but I don't understand."

Alex's lips curled ever so slightly. "You can't marry Grierson. What's hard to understand?"

"Why can't I?" She couldn't tear her gaze away from his dark eyes.

"Because you don't love him."

The mist in her mind refused to clear. "How do you know that?" She shook her head. "How can you know?"

"Because you love me."

Chapter
26

"A nd I love you," Alex said after a very long pause.

Grace felt her mouth go dry. "But . . . you said . . ."

"I said a lot of stupid things, but I had my reasons. Grace, you must understand that I love you as I've never loved anyone else. I've known that for a while now, but my past held me back from saying it."

"Your past?" Her heart raced and she bit her lower lip to keep from blurting out additional questions.

He let go of her arms. "I was ashamed of my past."

Grace listened as he detailed all that had happened ten years ago in New Orleans. It was clear why he'd felt himself in bondage.

"Oh, Alex. I'm so sorry. What a terrible burden to bear alone."

"It was, but it was my own doing. I know that now. I should never have run away from my problems. I should never have run away from you."

"Me?"

He nodded. "I wanted to tell you how much I loved you, but

without having the past resolved, I knew I couldn't. I never intended to let myself fall in love, but with you, it just happened before I knew it." He chuckled and reached out to touch her cheek. "You've been all I could think about."

Tears came unbidden and Grace reached up to wipe them away, but Alex beat her to it.

"Don't cry. I've come back because the past is no longer a problem. When I came to you last week, I wanted to ask you to wait for me. I figured I'd have to go back to New Orleans and settle my affairs. I'd written to my sister earlier this year but had heard nothing. But when I returned to Fort Vancouver last week, I was given a letter from her."

"What did it say?"

He cupped her cheek. "Adelina told me how happy they were to finally hear from me. After ten years, they had thought me dead. She said there were no charges against me. Justice's father knew what his sons had done. Marshall, the one who burned down my parents' house, was forced to admit his guilt and went to prison, and their father said he wanted no more trouble. He demanded his other sons put the matter to rest and do nothing to further harm my family. Adelina said there have been no issues between the families for years." He grinned. "So you see, I'm finally free."

Grace didn't stop to think. She threw herself into Alex's arms and kissed him. But then she remembered when she'd done the same thing at the fort and he'd pushed her away. She stopped despite Alex's passionate response, and this time she was the one to step back.

"I'm sorry."

He shook his head and reached for her. "I'm not, and I was a fool to stop you the last time you kissed me like that." He pulled her back into his arms. "Grace, I love you, and I want you to be my wife."

She nodded, fighting back more tears. "I love you, Alex, and I want very much to be your wife. I never thought I'd hear you ask."

There was rustling in the brush behind her, and Grace turned to see Nigel walking away. He had most likely been listening for some time.

"I need to go talk to him," she said, pulling away from Alex. "Go to the house, and I'll meet you there."

"I won't leave you to face him alone."

"It's all right. He's a kind man and I never lied to him. He always knew there was someone else, that I didn't love him. I only agreed to marry him for the sake of my sisters. I had to have a way to provide for them."

"I figured as much. Why don't I wait here with your horse?"

Grace smiled and nodded. "Thank you."

She hurried after Nigel and caught up with him just as he cleared the forest and started across his recently cleared land.

"Wait, Nigel. Please."

He stopped and slowly turned. Great sadness filled his expression. "You don't need to say anything."

Grace went to him. "But I do. I never meant to hurt you."

"I know that. You were honest about everything." He released a heavy sigh. "I suppose down deep, I knew we'd never marry."

She smiled. "Nigel, you're a good man, and you deserve a wife who truly loves you. I want that for you, because I know what it is to marry without love."

"I was sure in time that I could make you love me."

Grace knew otherwise. "I'm sorry. Please know that I do care about you. You've been so kind to me—so helpful in caring for my animals."

"I'll keep on caring for them if you like." He shrugged. "It's no problem."

"Thank you. For now, that would be very helpful." She

touched his arm. "I'll pray that God sends you a woman worthy of your love."

She turned and walked away without saying anything further. She hadn't gone far into the woods when she spied Alex. He hadn't waited where they'd talked but had moved within range to help her should she need it. His protective nature made her smile.

"I believe I should go home and put Hope's and Mercy's minds at rest. They were very unhappy that I was going to marry Nigel."

He put his arm around her. "Not nearly as much as I was."

That night after Alex had left for his room at the hotel, Grace finished cleaning the kitchen and thought about how happy she was for the first time in such a very long time.

"I still can't believe you thought I'd throw you and your sisters out of the house," Uncle Edward said, bringing her his empty coffee cup.

"Well, there was no reason to believe you wouldn't need this house for your new family. How was I to know that the widow had a much better and bigger house in town?"

"Still, you should have known I would never have abandoned you."

"I didn't think you would abandon us. I just figured you'd need us out of the way. Now I know better." She took the cup from him and stretched up on tiptoes to kiss his cheek. "And I love you all the more."

His face reddened. "Well, don't let it happen again. You and your sisters and Alex too are welcome to stay here as long as you like. As far as I'm concerned, it's your home."

"Thank you. I haven't had a chance to ask Alex his preferences. I think he has to sort out a great deal before we can marry—especially where a job is concerned."

"I mentioned to him that I'm starting up my own lumber mill. I figured he might want to come in with me—maybe be a partner."

Grace couldn't hide her pleasure. "That might be a perfect solution. Alex loves working outdoors, but he's no farmer. I couldn't imagine him giving up trapping, but I think this might be something that would suit him."

"I hope so. It's a lot of work for just one old man."

Laughing, Grace went back to work. "You'll never be old, Uncle Edward. There's too much orneriness in you."

"That's a fact," he said, giving a hearty laugh. "Well, this ornery man is going to bed. I'll see you in the morning."

The house was quiet. Mercy and Hope had gone upstairs sometime earlier. Both were happy at the new turn of events. Grace had worried about how her announcement would affect Hope, but she seemed pleased.

Giving the kitchen one last look, Grace put away her dish-cloth. She blew out the lamp and made her way to the front of the house, where the fire in the hearth lit the room in a golden glow. It really was a comfortable little house, and it pleased her to think they might stay there.

She walked to the front door, thinking only to secure the latch, but instead she opened it and stepped outside to gaze up at the surprisingly clear sky. The stars seemed almost close enough to touch, and the full moon shone so bright that she could make out details along the river.

"Thank You, Lord. I know we've a long way to go, but I feel confident You will be with us every step of the way."

She hugged her arms to her body and just enjoyed the silence. She was half a world away from where she'd started, but somehow it felt like home.

"Grace."

She startled. Alex appeared from the shadows. "What are you doing here? I thought you'd gone back to the hotel."

He drew closer and took her in his arms. "I couldn't stand being so far away from you."

She laughed. "It's not even a mile to the hotel."

"Far enough that it's difficult to protect my treasure."

"Your treasure?"

"Yes, my treasured Grace." He kissed her gently, then turned her toward the house when she shivered.

"Since you're awake and obviously have nothing else to do, what say we plan our wedding?" He followed her inside, then drew her into his arms again. "I understand there's a preacher with an opening at the end of this month."

Grace had no chance to reply because his lips were once again upon hers. She sighed and lost herself in this most wonderful moment.

Tracie Peterson is the award-winning author of over one hundred novels, both historical and contemporary. Her avid research resonates in her stories, as seen in her bestselling HEIRS OF MONTANA and ALASKAN QUEST series. Tracie and her family make their home in Montana. Visit Tracie's website at www.traciepeterson.com.